Julia Latham

D1007936

Taken and Seduced

AVON

An Imprint of HarperCollins*Publishers*

AVON BOOKS
An Imprint of HarperCollins*Publishers*
10 East 53rd Street
New York, New York 10022-5299

Copyright © 2009 by Gayle Kloecker Callen
ISBN 978-0-06-143300-9
www.avonromance.com

First Avon Books paperback printing: April 2009

Avon Trademark Reg. U.S. Pat. Off. and in Other Countries, Marca Registrada, Hecho en U.S.A.
HarperCollins® is a registered trademark of HarperCollins Publishers.

Printed in the U.S.A.

10 9 8 7 6 5 4 3 2 1

She looked up at the man standing before her.

She noticed his eyes first, deep and brilliant as blue sapphires. They watched her solemnly, with no emotion. His lean face was composed of sharp lines, angling down until they met at a square chin with a cleft in the middle. He had generous lips. She wanted to think they were made for smiling, but everyone always told her she had too much foolish optimism.

His black hair hung neatly to just below his ears. He wore a tunic over wool breeches, with a cloak falling from his shoulders. Though she could hear the sound of water nearby, she did not look anywhere else, for she guessed that this man was the one who controlled her fate.

He pushed the sack lower, until it puddled around her waist. Lifting her bound hands free, he calmly said, "I will remove the gag if you promise not to scream."

She hesitated, but at last gave a stiff nod. His long arms reached around her to untie the gag behind her head, leaving her to stare helplessly at the center of his broad chest . . .

Romances by Julia Latham

TAKEN AND SEDUCED
SECRETS OF THE KNIGHT
ONE KNIGHT ONLY
THRILL OF THE KNIGHT

*To my fifth-grade teacher, Marilyn Reiser: even when
I was a child, I knew you and I would be lifelong
friends. You helped nurture my love of books and
taught me how to write. You know you have my
gratitude.*

TAKEN AND SEDUCED

Chapter 1

Lady Florence Becket stood in the lady's garden of her father's castle, enjoying the oasis of privacy in the middle of the bustling center of the marquess of Martindale's small empire. She hugged herself and rubbed her arms, staring out at the mountains beyond the walls, wondering if she'd ever again be permitted to ride those paths. On a horse she became one with the animal, flying on the wind, as if she weren't deformed, as if she could walk without a limp like other people.

Her future home was out there, too. Was the convent nestled near woods and streams? Would she be able to walk as she communed with God, or would they keep her locked up, as if praying required four stone walls?

Florrie had watched as her three older sisters married, had known for many long years that there would be no husband for her. Her father had been brutally honest when he'd told her there would be dowry money for her sisters, but only a little saved for her entrance into the convent—when her sisters no longer needed her.

She took a deep breath, and her usual optimism prevailed. There was education to be had for nuns. She would serve a purpose—and not just as her sisters' servant. Perhaps someday if she worked hard, she could even become the prioress.

Her view of the mountains was suddenly disturbed; a horse-drawn cart was riding beside the half wall of the lady's garden. Straw had been mounded high in the back. As the cart pulled to a stop, blocking the garden from the rest of the ward, she frowned up at the driver. He was hunched within a cloak and didn't glance her way.

She only managed to call "I think—" when suddenly two large men emerged from the side of the cart, barely disturbing the straw. They vaulted over the wall, and before she could even take a step backward, they were upon her, stifling her scream with a gag. Terror stunned her, melting her bones, washing through her with a sick feeling of futility. Though she struggled, they tied her hands with ease, and when she tried to kick, one lifted her off the ground while the other bound her ankles. As she wriggled futilely, she saw that they didn't hide their faces from her, and that frightened her more than anything else. They were two grim men, both black-haired and tall, and they maneuvered her as if she weighed nothing at all.

To her horror, they suddenly dropped her feet-first into a sack and pulled it up over her head. Her world narrowed to shadows that smelled of grain and must, and she felt as if she soon wouldn't be able to breathe. They lifted her again, and her lungs emptied in a rush as she was flung across a broad shoulder. Everything around her jostled and upended as they shoved her onto the cart. The man holding her didn't ease his grip, so she was unable to roll away. Instead she was shockingly aware that he wrapped himself around her to hold her still. His muscular arms were as strong as the ropes that bound her hands and feet. The light dimmed even further as another gradual weight pressed her down, and she realized that the other men were covering them both with straw.

God above, they were going to succeed with this audacious plan!

She used every bit of her strength to squirm and push, even butting her head, but the man held her too firmly.

"Be still, my lady," he said at last in a low, gravelly voice. "Cease struggling and 'twill be easier to breathe."

He was right—her panicked struggles were only making her more and more aware that she couldn't take enough air into her lungs. She moaned, but went still just the same.

He said nothing more, and the cart began to move, jostling her in an uneven rhythm. She kept waiting for someone to notice the strange man driving the cart and stop him, but no one did. She heard the blacksmith's hammer meeting his anvil and the call of a goose girl herding her flock. The crash of metal and the grunts of men practicing their weaponry in the tiltyard strengthened as they drove into the outer ward, then faded as they reached the main gatehouse.

No one was going to stop a man hauling straw, she thought with despair, and her prediction came true as they left behind the sounds of the soldiers in the gatehouse. At last she sagged in her captor's arms. She would have to see what fate had in store for her, or perhaps even rescue herself—unless these foolish men planned to demand a ransom for her return. She almost gave a tired laugh. As if her father would part with a large sum of money on her behalf. But she could never let her captors know that, of course. She would have to stall until . . . until what? Did she think she would somehow escape their notice and limp away through the unfamiliar countryside alone? If they only wanted a woman for base needs, surely for a penny or two they could have had someone willing.

Nay, the kidnapping had happened because she was the daughter of the marquess of Martindale, the only one unmarried, the easiest target.

In that terrible moment, tears of futility and fear stung her eyes, but didn't fall, because Florrie was not a woman who let circumstances dictate her emotions.

"Not long now, my lady," murmured the man's voice.

He did not sound angry or triumphant; she did not understand what he was feeling. The only way to discover the weaknesses of her captors was to study them, look at their faces, and judge them by their actions.

And so far, their cowardice at kidnapping a helpless woman showed them in the vilest light.

"Not long now" seemed to go on forever. Florrie took shallow breaths, for the air was growing too hot and stifling. The sack rubbed roughly against her face. When the man relaxed his hold, she tried to move away from the heat of him, but wasn't successful. Perspiration broke out on her skin. The cart seemed to angle ever higher, and she almost wanted to grunt a sarcastic laugh. Hadn't she just been dreaming about roaming the mountains?

At last, the cart came to a jerking stop, and she groaned her relief. The man pulled her across the wooden bottom, then set her upright on the edge, legs dangling. Someone loosened the sack and slid it down her face. With relief, she breathed in fresh, cool air through her nose—

And looked up at the large man standing before her.

She noticed his eyes first, deep and brilliant as blue sapphires. Narrowed, they watched her solemnly, with no show of emotion, as if his response would only be dictated by her behavior. His lean face was composed of sharp lines, angling down until they met at a square chin with a cleft in the middle. Though his mouth was a flat line, he had generous lips. She wanted to think they were made for smiling, but everyone always told her she had too much foolish optimism.

His black hair, which hung neatly to just below his ears, was held in place by a peasant's cloth cap. His clothing was just as nondescript, a tunic belted over wool breeches, with a cloak falling from his shoulders. The two other men, dressed nearly the same, stood behind him in a clearing that was shaded by immense oak trees. Though she could hear the sound of water nearby, she did not look anywhere else, for she guessed that this man was the one who controlled her fate.

He pushed the sack lower, until it puddled around her waist. Lifting her bound hands free, he calmly said, "I will remove the gag if you promise not to scream. As you can guess, we have taken you far enough away that no one will hear you regardless."

She hesitated, wishing desperately she could somehow thwart him, but at last she gave a stiff nod. His long arms reached around her to untie the gag behind her head, leaving her to stare helplessly at the center of his broad chest. He smelled of warm man and wool garments, hay and horses.

Uneasy, she was glad when he stepped back and carefully pulled the gag from her mouth. She gasped as the dry cloth tugged free of her skin. Before she could even ask, another man stepped forward and held up a wineskin. He was just as tall and dark as the first man, but the blue of his eyes was as bright as cornflowers. His face was a little softer, broader, and younger—but with the same cleft in his chin. Surely they were brothers.

"My lady?" Brother Number Two said, offering the wineskin.

She nodded gladly, taking several deep sips. The respectful way they spoke to her showed that at least they knew whom they'd kidnapped. Perhaps they would not injure her—unless she proved uncooperative. As he stepped back, she could not stop her shudder.

"You are cold?" asked Brother Number One, with some incredulity in his voice.

His body brushed her knees as he stood before her. She understood his disbelief—after all, they'd been plastered together beneath straw, building even more heat on a summer's day.

She swallowed again and spoke. "Can I not simply be a frightened maiden, sir? Who are you and why did you so cruelly take me from my home? When my father discovers—"

His blue eyes seemed to go dark with winter's ice. "Your father, the marquess, is in London, my lady. It will be some time before he discovers what has happened, and by then, we shall be far from here."

"Then what is your purpose?" she demanded, trying not to tremble with her fear of the future. "Why so brazenly risk yourselves to kidnap me in broad daylight?"

She gasped as Brother Number One lifted her against him with one arm. She tried to rear back, but realized a moment later he was pulling the sack down her hips. As it collapsed to the ground, he set her back on the edge of the cart.

He put both hands on either side of her hips and looked into her eyes. She held her breath, staring up at him, feeling as if no man had ever really looked at her like this, with such intense focus.

"Lady Florence, my name is Sir Adam. Your capture was necessary, because I had to find a method to convince your father of my sincerity."

Bewildered, she said, "But you just said it didn't matter if he knew about this insane plan of yours."

"Nay, you should listen more intently. I said it wouldn't matter if he knew, because he couldn't stop me. Nothing will stop me from issuing him a challenge of combat to the death. And if he needs more of a reason than an honorable challenge to face me, your captivity will provide it."

She gaped at him. "You want to kill my father." She could not be surprised at that. Her father had made many enemies, and acted however he wished, with no care about God's laws, or man's.

"I want to *fight* your father. If it leads to his death, then that is God's judgment."

"But . . . why?"

Sir Adam finally looked away from her, his mouth set in grim lines. "That is not your concern. Only know that a grievous wrong has been done by him, and I demand justice."

"So you counter one grievous wrong with another?"

He glanced at her, and if she thought she saw a flash of regret in his eyes, she had to discount it, for he spoke coldly.

"Trust me, my lady, the wrong done to you in no way compares. And if you are obedient, nothing worse will happen, and this adventure will soon be over."

She stiffened at his too casual words. "But if you have your way, my father will be dead."

"You so easily discount his famed skills?" Sir Adam asked, arching a dark brow. "Even though he is a generation older than I, he yet enters tournaments and fights for his king. A battle between us might be legendary."

Florrie looked away, afraid he might be able to read the truth in her eyes. Martindale *was* once a famed warrior, but his youth and strength were long gone, lost to age and illness. But he was so vain, so worried about showing weakness, that he made certain the world still thought him a knight of great renown. He had sworn his family and servants to secrecy, and no one dared cross him. She would never go back on her oath to her father—nor did she want to give such information to a man who wanted him dead, a man who could use such a secret to his advantage, in whatever feud he pursued.

She lifted her chin and stared at him coolly. "So who does your bidding?"

He stepped aside, so that she could see the other two men. Already they'd been bringing saddlebags out of hiding in the trees, where she could hear the occasional neighing of horses out of sight. The men gathered wood against the encroaching twilight. Only then did she realize with dismay that night would fall soon, and she would be alone with her kidnappers.

"This is Sir Robert," said Sir Adam, gesturing to the dark-haired man who looked like him.

But instead of wearing Sir Adam's cold expression, Sir Robert grinned at her and doffed his cap to reveal hair that fell into waves. "My Lady Florence, 'tis a pleasure to meet you."

She was taken aback by his easy charm, as if he'd come to court her instead of kidnap her. "And you agree with your brother's methods that led to this introduction?"

Sir Robert met Sir Adam's gaze, his grin fading into simple amusement. "You are observant, my lady. Aye, he is my brother, the head of our family. I follow him obediently."

She thought she heard Sir Adam give a choked cough, but when she turned to him, he was still regarding her impassively. Then she looked at the third man, redheaded, with freckles scattered across his tanned face. He was shorter than the two brothers, and as he squatted to put flint to steel to spark a fire, he only gave her a brief look of disinterest.

"And this is Sir Michael," Sir Adam said.

"Another relation?" she asked.

"Nay, a loyal knight and companion. Do not think to turn him against us, for it shall not work."

Sir Michael gave a faint smile and continued to prepare for the night.

All around her was wilderness and strangers. Though she'd always longed to leave home and travel, this was not how she'd anticipated seeing the world, bound and watched, taken hostage to persuade her father to do something she knew he never would.

What would happen if Sir Adam discovered her presence was useless? She'd seen his face and could identify his features—would he have to rid himself of her?

A sick feeling of nausea sank into her stomach, and she realized it had been many hours since she'd used a privy for her private needs.

She looked between the three men, feeling a little desperate and frightened. Surely they could not deny her something so basic.

"I—I have need to . . . I—I need a woman's privacy."

Sir Adam only studied her as embarrassment flamed through her cheeks. She desperately wanted to look away, but somehow didn't.

"And I am supposed to allow you to walk into the trees alone," he said.

Panic rose in her throat at the thought of his accompanying her. "What else do you expect me to do?" she cried.

She looked to the other two men for support, but they busied themselves with their backs turned, as if leaving her to Sir Adam's care—to Sir Adam's decisions.

To her surprise, he began to untie the knot that bound her ankles. As her feet were released, she felt a rush of blood and pinpricks through them, and she moved them in circles in relief.

"Do you give me your oath that you will remain nearby?" he asked.

She nodded, afraid to say the words she didn't mean. He took her waist in his big hands and set her on the ground, making her feel like the most fragile of women, though she'd never felt like that before. Her legs were too weak to support her after the hours of confinement, and she swayed against him, ashamed that he had to support her. Better that, than to fall on her face in front of him. He caught her bound arms, held her still, looking down on her from his great height.

"You did not speak the words, my lady."

She sighed. "I promise." But she was lying. Why

should a man who'd kidnapped her expect her to tell the truth? She held out her hands to him, and when he only cocked his head, she said, "It might be easier for a man to . . . with hands bound, but I have a skirt to hold up." Was he going to make her explain every detail?

Saying nothing, he freed her hands. Moving her wrists with a relieved sigh, she looked about the clearing and decided to head downhill, hoping that if she could escape, she could head for the valley.

She took several limping steps.

"Are you injured?" he suddenly demanded, coming up behind her.

It would serve him right if he'd wounded the daughter of a marquess. Without thinking, she said, "I guess I am."

He caught her arm to stop her, turned her about to face him, then dropped to his knees. As she gave an incredulous stare, he reached for the hem of her skirt and lifted it, tossing it across his shoulder and reaching to touch her.

"Show me where," he said gruffly. "You need healing."

No man had ever presumed to touch her ankles—or anything else. She could feel the cool competence of his hands even through her stockings. She gaped at him, then at last slapped down her skirt and pushed at his immovable shoulders.

"I am not injured! Well . . . not recently. When

I was a girl I broke my left leg and it never healed correctly. 'Tis shorter than the other."

Very slowly he rose to his feet, towering high over her head. Her gaze followed his ascent helplessly.

"I did not mean to lie!" she insisted with breathless fear. "Tying me up made my legs lose all feeling."

He took a deep breath but said nothing, only turned her about and gave her a push—a gentle push, to her surprise. She took several steps, realizing he still followed her. Though she wanted to cower, she sent him an arch look over her shoulder.

He halted. "Leave just a few trees between us, my lady."

Her heart raced at the thought of eluding him. "Sir, do not come charging after me if I take what you think is too long. Women are not like men."

For a moment, a puzzled look came over his face, as if he were trying to make sense of her words. She frowned at him, feeling confused, then turned away and stepped into the brush at the base of the trees. She deliberately made a lot of noise, cracking sticks, rustling bushes.

"Far enough, my lady," he called.

She quickly did what she had to, then began to move more cautiously downhill, watching where she placed each foot.

She gasped and stumbled to a halt as she heard

a man clear his throat. Sir Adam was in her path, leaning against a tree, arms crossed over his broad chest. He watched her coldly. How had he—she hadn't even heard movement! He would have had to *rush* to get past her.

Regardless, he had found her out. She waited for his reprisal, chin lifted. How could he blame her? But would he punish her?

To her surprise, he grasped her arm above the elbow and pulled her with him as he slipped through the thinning line of trees, away from the encampment. She wanted to dig in her heels, panicked that he meant to punish her in private.

"I am not going to harm you," he said stiffly. "I want to show you where you were headed. Go before me."

He thrust her forward, keeping his grip on her arm. She had no choice but to stumble before him, her limp even more pronounced on the uneven hillside. She went through the last of the trees, then cried out as she suddenly leaned out over a cliff. Sir Adam caught her against him and held her there, her back to his front, while the entire valley spread out before her. They were on the edge of the mountain, sheep dotting the valley below in pastures separated by rough stone walls, and the narrow Hawes Water glimmering in the distance.

She shuddered, her every sense reeling at the thought that she would have rushed right over the edge in her flight from him. Now she couldn't stop shaking, even as he held both of her arms and kept her tight against him. She could feel his thighs at her backside, as well as the hard muscles of his chest.

It was as if they were alone in the world.

Chapter 2

A dam Hilliard, earl of Keswick, stood on the edge of the mountain, Lady Florence's slight body held firmly against him—and he felt as if the recent events of his life were like a plummet from this cliff. He had spent many years formulating his plans, examining every possible result and action, accounting for everything.

Except for Lady Florence herself, small and fragile, yet full of a trembling courage as she asked for answers that he couldn't give. She'd even tried to escape him, the silly fool, and could have killed herself. He wanted to shudder with guilt at the thought, but he could not betray his emotions to her. And what emotions could they be? She was the daughter of his enemy. He'd expected her to be bold and arrogant, a product of everything he'd heard about the marquess of Martindale.

But she seemed nothing like he'd imagined, nothing like he was prepared for, and it unsettled him. Then again, he was unused to spending any time at all with women; he hadn't even been raised near them.

How could he have anticipated . . . her?

He deliberately allowed her to stand too close to the cliff, holding her securely, yet wanting her to feel terrified by what her haste had almost cost her. And she *must* have been terrified, because she quivered wherever they touched.

He had promised himself he would be firm, even ruthless where she was concerned.

But her soft trembling did things to the inside of him that he'd never felt before. He wanted to press deeper into her, wrap his arms around her, lean down and smell her hair. She was so very . . . different from him.

His confusion finally made him step away from the edge, bringing her with him. As he let go of one of her arms, she reached for a tree and held herself against it, giving another shudder.

Though Adam wanted to ask if she was all right, to promise he wouldn't let her be so near to danger again, he only said in a harsh voice, "Now you see why you need to remain with me at all times. Our journey will be perilous."

She glanced up at him, her face pale, heart-shaped, with eyes a brilliant emerald green. They looked up at him now with accusation, which he understood. Her nose was pert, her mouth small like the rest of her, a pink bud of curves that could easily pout, but didn't. She was very obviously afraid of him and trying not show it. He couldn't help but admire her courage. Her brown hair was braided straight down her back, swinging almost to her waist. He had not realized that women wore their hair so long. It made him feel . . . strange, and he couldn't stop the image that flashed in his mind, of that hair unbraided, sliding about her shoulders, covering the front of her.

What was wrong with him? He was five and twenty years old, no longer a boy.

Women had been made for men to take care of; surely it was only those instincts he was fighting. And fight them he would, for she had to be afraid of him, so that she would not attempt to escape.

He roughly pushed her ahead of him back up the slope, into the thickening stand of trees. When they came out into the clearing, Robert and Michael looked at them both, Michael with his ever-present concern—such adulation was hard to get used to—and Robert wearing only an amused smirk.

Michael had set out cheese and apples and twice-baked bread. They'd had no time to hunt for their supper. Lady Florence stood beside him, looking down at the meager fare. Adam couldn't read her expression. He hoped he would not have to force her to eat. But she sank gracefully to her knees, as if her damaged leg didn't bother her, and hesitantly took a wedge of cheese. He frowned, wondering how such a permanent affliction had affected her life. From what he'd seen during the several days he'd spent spying within her castle, she'd been as any other maiden, as far as he could tell. She'd overseen the servants in the great hall, assisted her married sister, and dealt daily with the outside servants in the dairy and the laundry.

But always she'd taken several solitary walks in the little garden next to the castle. It was a useless garden—nothing planted that was edible, only flowers that were pretty to look at, but served no purpose.

He remembered thinking she limped a little, but he'd dismissed it. And then he'd had to handle her roughly. When he'd thought he'd injured her, the earlier memory of her limp fled his mind. He felt like an idiot. What good was all his vaunted intellectual and military training when one young woman could scramble his brain?

Michael looked up at him, his face colored by the setting sun. Adam tensed, hoping he would not say "my lord," and reveal what Adam needed kept secret.

"Sir, will you eat with us?"

Adam tried to relax—until he leaned past Lady Florence for an apple and noticed her cringing away from him. He gritted his teeth. He was an honorable man, and to have done something to frighten a lady did not set well with him.

But it would be worth it in the end, he thought. The marquess of Martindale would suffer at Adam's hands for his terrible deeds.

Robert stood up. "Sir Adam, may I speak with you in private?"

Adam glanced at Michael, who nodded to accept responsibility for Lady Florence. Then Adam went to the edge of the clearing with his brother.

"Robert, what is it?"

Robert took a sip from his wineskin. "'Tis all happening as you planned, big brother."

"Of course, it is."

"Thanks to Michael and me."

Adam rolled his eyes. "I could have done it without you."

"I see not how," Robert answered, wearing a grin. "I still cannot believe you were just going to leave me behind. I'm three and twenty, and you cannot keep me sheltered forever."

"'Tis a brother's duty to protect his family."

"This is my fight, too," Robert said, his usual smile fading. "I did not appreciate having to follow you without permission to be a part of restoring our family honor."

"You are right."

"And another thing—" Robert stopped and gave him a surprised glance. "Did I just hear you admit that I was right?"

"You did. I can see that your services, and those of Michael, are of valuable assistance."

"Very well, then." Robert cleared his throat. "I know we go to London and the marquess, but what about the League of the Blade? Those noble knights"—he chuckled—"have known our every move our entire lives."

Adam sighed. "They do not know our intentions, which means they would not be following us. They are more concerned with their good deeds. Our revenge is nothing they have considered."

"They had nineteen years to help our family," Robert said, shrugging, "but they never did."

"The League helps the innocent and oppressed, Robert," Adam said patiently. "We are neither of those. So we can help ourselves."

"You always defend them. I think that is one of the reasons Paul left."

Adam inhaled and then let it out with a sigh. Paul was his youngest brother by three years, who had left them before Adam had announced his plans for Martindale. Paul was angry about the way they'd grown up, and needed to escape, to make his own way in the world. Though Adam grieved, praying that Paul would be well, he had understood his brother.

But Paul hadn't understood Adam, and it was one of Adam's greatest regrets.

"Paul's reasons for leaving are his own," Adam said quietly. "But as for us, now we travel toward London, letting enough time pass so that Martindale will hear that his daughter is missing. Then we send him the challenge. He will be forced to face me in combat, before the London court."

"And then you defeat the great warrior."

Adam arched a brow. "As if there's any doubt."

Robert shook his head as he smiled. "Such confidence, big brother."

" 'Twas bred into me."

Robert only nodded. Without discussing it, they both turned to look back at their little campfire, and the young woman who knelt beside it, a half-eaten apple in her hands.

"I can take a turn watching her tonight," Robert said casually.

"We all need our sleep."

"She won't mind sleeping with me."

Adam gave a small smile. "She is not the kind of woman you've been with before, little brother."

"And that's why she'll help me learn about ladies at court."

"I think not."

Robert gave an exaggerated sigh. "So she is your prisoner, instead of ours?"

"She is my responsibility, just as you are. And I take such things very seriously."

"When you finally need help, you *can* call on me."

Adam put a hand on his brother's shoulder. "My thanks, but I will not need help with her. She is simply a sheltered young woman who I've succeeded in making afraid of me. She will be biddable."

Robert smirked again. "And you think *I* haven't had enough experience with women."

Before Adam could reply, Robert sauntered back toward the fire, leaving Adam to trail him.

They passed the rest of the meal in strained silence as darkness descended and a wind rose up from the valley to rustle through the trees. Adam did not disguise his focus on Lady Florence. She met his gaze once or twice, always looking quickly away. She turned over and over the dried bread in her hands as if distracted, crumbling it without seeming to realize it.

At last Adam decided to get on with what she must already be fearing: the sleeping arrangements. "'Tis time to rest, for we'll arise early in the morn."

Lady Florence seemed frozen in place, her eyes darting nervously from Robert, who packed away their supper, to Michael, who began to remove blankets from the saddlebags.

"Lady Florence, do you need to relieve yourself once more?" Adam asked.

She blushed and didn't meet his eyes as she quickly shook her head.

"I do," he said. "I will return in a moment."

When he came back, Lady Florence was as frozen as when he'd left her, as if her refusal to accept it would stop the coming night. The other two men took their turns for a moment in the trees, and Robert settled down on his blanket, his cloak closed about him. Though it was summer, this part of the lake country had chilly nights. Michael walked to the edge of the clearing, taking the first watch.

Adam spread his own blanket, then knelt on it. "Come here, Lady Florence."

He saw the shiver that passed through her, and with regret, he knew it wasn't from the cold. He hadn't imagined how terrible it would feel to keep a young woman afraid of him. He kept reminding himself that the end result would be worth it, that even *she* might understand his motives once she knew everything.

He was lying to himself—she would understand nothing when her father lay dead on the ground.

She rose unsteadily to her feet at last. "I will sleep in the cart."

"Since you'll be sleeping tied to me, I think proximity to the fire will keep us warmer. We won't be sleeping in the cart." He deliberately deepened his voice. "Come here, Lady Florence." When she didn't move, he said, "Now."

She took the two steps to his blanket and knelt down. Adam tied a rope to his wrist, then looped it tightly about hers, leaving enough loose rope for comfort.

He said, "This wouldn't have been necessary if you hadn't lied to me."

She didn't answer, only narrowed her eyes. She obviously had much to say to him—if she weren't afraid.

He couldn't look at her anymore. Lying down on his side, he held open his cloak. "Join me, Lady Florence. I will keep you warm."

Feeling shocked and disoriented, Florrie knelt on the wool blanket, her back to the fire, and gaped at Sir Adam. His long body took up most of the blanket; his boots rested in the sparse grass. He waited, his cloak held open, as if he fully expected her to lie against him! He was a kidnapper, a man out to kill her father. She didn't even want to touch him.

"Is there another blanket?" she asked.

"No."

Of course not. She didn't believe him, but what could she do? He was punishing her for her disobedience, which she so little deserved. She was a prisoner—she was *supposed* to try to escape. He would do the same thing!

Feeling foolishly brave, she ignored his offer of warmth and lay down with her back to him, leaving a foot of space between them. She thought she heard an evil chuckle behind her, which only made her clench her jaw with determination. She was close to the fire; it would keep her warm. But soon enough the wind seemed to infiltrate that small space behind her. Her front was almost too hot, her back freezing cold. But every time she glanced at the rope binding her wrist, and thought of all it represented, she swore to herself that she would bear the cold. Soon she couldn't control her shivers.

Suddenly he was right behind her, not quite touching, and she hadn't even felt the blanket shift. She gave a little start, but he did nothing else. How did he move so silently?

"Ready to give up?" he asked in a soft voice from above and behind her.

His breath puffed gently against her ear, and she had the strangest urge to shudder. 'Twas the cold.

He didn't wait for her response. She gasped as he tucked his body behind hers, knees in the bend of her knees, hips pressed to hers. After he pulled the cloak over and around them both, his arm came to rest over her waist, his big hand near her stomach. She forgot how to breathe, even as she heard his even breathing behind her.

Though warmth seeped into her bones, she couldn't relax. What did he mean to do to her under cover of darkness? His companions would see nothing—would say nothing. She was only a pawn to them. Though she tried to hide her fear, she couldn't stop the occasional quiver.

"Are you still cold?" he asked.

She could feel the rumble of his voice where his chest met her back. She shook her head, not trusting her own voice. His hand at her stomach frightened her. He could move it . . . anywhere.

But after several long moments, she realized he didn't plan to do anything. He'd fallen asleep. She stifled a groan and closed her eyes at last. She'd never been the kind of woman men made fools of themselves over. Even her close proximity didn't affect Sir Adam.

But he affected her, and she didn't like it.

It was a long time before she could sleep, and even then her sleep was fitful. She awoke every time Sir Adam moved, as if she expected him to pounce. At one point, someone was rebuilding the fire, and when she opened her eyes, she saw Sir Robert glance at her. To her astonishment, he winked, as if this were all a game to him. She gave him the most intense glare she could manage and slammed her eyes shut.

Some time before dawn, she must have finally fallen into a deep sleep, for she only awoke groggily when Sir Adam shook her arm. She blinked, feeling stiff and exhausted, and opened her eyes to the gray light. Sir Robert and Sir Michael were already up, only flattened grass the proof that they'd slept.

But Sir Adam was still behind her, she thought uneasily, wondering why he, too, hadn't left her alone. And then she remembered the rope at her wrist.

She could feel him coming up on his elbow behind her, the way his chest slid up her back. Though she didn't want to, she looked over her shoulder to see his face above hers. For a moment, he wasn't looking at her, and she was able to study him. His black hair was rumpled from sleep, and there was a crease along his cheek where he'd rested against his arm.

And then he met her gaze. For a frozen moment, neither of them said anything. His blue eyes, the color of frigid lake water, seemed to bore into hers, and she wondered what he was looking for, what he saw. His hand rested on her hip. She realized she could feel the length of each of his fingers, holding her as if she were his possession.

And then he slid away from her and rose to his feet all in one smooth motion. The rope binding them together gave a tug, lifting her arm.

"Arise, Lady Florence," he said, looking down on her from his great height. "We must depart."

"Where are we going?"

"You will see."

She grumbled as she arose stiffly from the ground, cold now without his warmth. "Why is it a secret? Whom will I tell?"

"Whom *might* you tell?" he countered. "After all, I will not give you such a chance. Now, shall we refresh ourselves this morn? Robert says there is a stream nearby."

She held out her wrist, but he ignored her, only turning away and tugging her along with him. Frantically, she looked behind her for help, but Sir Michael was only folding up their blanket, and Sir Robert was wearing that same silly smile. How could he find amusement in this terrible situation?

She heard the stream before she saw it, and she came up short when Sir Adam stopped right in front of her. She was forced to catch his elbow or fall. She cursed the uneven ground. But her captor didn't berate her.

"Shall I have a moment of privacy first," he said, "or will you?"

She held up her bound wrist, but again he ignored her.

"Very well, I will."

To her horror, he stepped behind a tree, and the rope gave gentle tugs as he unfastened the necessary clothing. Florrie was so embarrassed that even the tops of her ears burned.

When he emerged a moment later, he didn't even seem bothered by such intimacy.

"We'll find you another tree," he said.

She was so upset, so beside herself with mortification, that she only groaned and gave him a push. He didn't budge, only looked down at her with puzzlement.

"Was there some purpose in that?" he asked coldly. "After your foolish escape last night, I could very well stand over you while you—"

"Enough!" She covered her ears. "I have never been treated so horribly in my life!"

He gripped her wrists, pulled her hands away from her ears, then bent down so that he was speaking directly into her face. "This situation will not change, Lady Florence. The sooner you accept and submit, the easier this will be on all of us."

"I am supposed to make this easier on *you*?" she cried, aghast.

"Then easier on yourself. Your behavior this morn will determine whether I gag you for the day. I cannot have you screaming for help."

Her mouth sagged open. "*Gag* me? Will that not look suspicious?"

" 'Tis amazing what the hood of a cloak will hide," he said, folding his arms over his chest.

"Ooh, you—" But she broke off when he only arched one of his devilish eyebrows.

Marching around him, she found her own tree and did what she had to, grumbling and cursing at her awkward skirts. When she emerged, she marched right past him, knowing she was spoiling the effect of her outrage by limping. He could have remained still, yanking her to a halt, but he followed her silently. At the stream, which bubbled over rocks on its way downhill, she dropped to her knees, plunged her hands into its icy coldness, then splashed her face, hoping to scrub away her exhaustion. She would need all her wits about her this day.

Sir Adam knelt beside her and did the same, then took several deep gulps from his cupped hands. She could not help staring at him with bemusement. How was he connected to her father? She'd never seen him before. He seemed to have the manners and speech of a wellborn man, but there was something . . . different about him. Besides being a kidnapper, of course. Though he was gruff, and she was embarrassed at how close they had to remain, he was treating her with a modicum of civility. He could have terrorized her, attacked her—anything, since she was at his mercy. Little did he know, her father probably wouldn't care.

But Sir Adam's entire focus seemed to be to challenge her father—not kill him, just challenging him as a noble knight would. But there was something in Sir Adam's past that made him think he needed a reason for her father to accept the challenge—and that reason was her.

She needed to discover what was going on, and to do that, she had to stop being too afraid to even think. Sir Adam and his men were trying not to hurt her; she had to forget her circumstances and evaluate the situation.

Though her family had little use for her brain, she did have one. It was not as educated as she would have liked, but it did work. She had to use it now, to prove her worth by figuring out the puzzle of her captors.

Sir Adam turned to look at her, water dripping from his lips. Not breaking their shared gaze, he ran the back of his sleeve over his mouth.

She wouldn't have any problem studying him—he was far too compelling.

Then he tugged on her arm. "Are you finished, my lady?"

What kind of kidnapper would address her so

properly? She suddenly realized it was a mistake on his part. It gave his intentions away. He wasn't going to hurt her.

"I am ready, Sir Adam."

It was time to be bold, to see just how far he could be pushed. It was a risk that already made fear war with determination inside her, but she would not spend this journey cowering in fear.

Chapter 3

Back at their encampment, when Adam lengthened the rope at Lady Florence's wrist, but didn't remove it, he was surprised at her lack of protest. She only gave him a glare with those cool green eyes and looked away.

"Can you ride, my lady?" he asked, remembering to keep his voice gruff.

"Of course." She glanced at the four saddled horses being brought out of the trees by Michael. "You are not bringing the cart?"

"It will slow us down," Adam said.

"I should tell you that forcing me to ride on your horse with you will only make us look suspicious and draw unwanted attention."

He held up the rope that connected them, tamping down a smile. "You may ride alone. Unless you need my assistance."

He had a sudden thought that he might enjoy the day more if she was across his lap.

He shook such foolishness away. This wasn't about enjoying the company of a woman. He would have to participate in such a novel experience another time.

"I shall ride alone," she said, tilting her small nose into the air.

He'd chosen a smaller gelding for her, and now Michael led it forward.

"I hope you are used to riding astride," Adam said.

" 'Tis how I ride best," she answered primly.

Robert and Michael exchanged a glance, and then Robert choked on his laughter. Lady Florence looked between them, betraying only a hint of uncertainty, before she focused on Adam. He wasn't going to enlighten her about their amusement. As was his long-trained habit, he turned away to examine each horse and its equipment, so that he knew its condition for the start of the day. Due to the rope between them, she begrudgingly followed him about.

At last Lady Florence stood beside her horse, ignoring Adam, looking around as if for something to stand on to help her mount. He took her by the waist to set her in the saddle. She caught the pommel, gaping down at him, then pressed her lips together without speaking. He removed the rope from his wrist and carried it with him as he mounted his own horse at her side.

She frowned at him. "So I am to be leashed to you like an animal."

He shrugged, noticing that she no longer seemed as afraid of him. He didn't know if that was good or bad. "You have proven that it is necessary. If your behavior improves, things might change."

She said nothing more, only took hold of the reins and guided her horse in a circle to follow Robert and Michael, forcing Adam to stay with her or let go of the rope.

At last they began the day's journey, moving out of the trees and climbing steadily to the top of the moorland summit. All around them the county looked as barren as wasteland, all heather-covered moors with little evidence of trees. But below them spread the next valley, where there would be more game to hunt for a hot evening meal.

Adam, riding beside Lady Florence, took the lead. She said nothing for several hours, and when she wasn't skillfully guiding her horse around rocks and holes in the path, she looked everywhere with interest, as if she'd never seen any of it before. Had she not traveled between her father's many properties? He had prepared himself for tantrums and pleas, sadness or sullenness. Instead, she seemed . . . aware and curious. Perhaps she was looking for something—or someone—to help her?

She continued to dominate his thoughts that morn. His memories of the night spent pressed against her were uncomfortable for him. Though he'd feigned sleep to lull her into relaxation, he hadn't been able to find much rest. He'd never spent an entire night with a woman. None had ever made him want to. But with Lady Florence, his body had been too aware of how soft she was, how her curves fit perfectly to his. Even the smell of her hair had proved too distracting. And her soft skin where he'd touched her wrist—

He adjusted his seat in the saddle and tried to think of something else. She was his prisoner, after all, and would never be more than that.

Once or twice, Robert tried to start a conversation with her while Adam played his part as the cold, remote leader. But she only hunched her shoulders and shook her head, as a cowed prisoner should. But something was . . . wrong about her behavior. Her eyes seemed to dart everywhere, studying, searching. Whenever an occasional shepherd appeared in the distance, Adam was always tense, wondering if she'd shout for help. He formulated plans to excuse her behavior, but he hadn't had to use them—yet.

Florrie was relieved when at last they stopped for their midday meal on the lower slopes of the mountain. They used a stone wall separating pastureland to lean against, breaking the effect of the wind, and letting her feel the warmth of the sun. Adam sat beside her, as usual, although to her surprise, he removed the rope from her wrist so she could eat in peace.

"Thank you," she said coolly.

He said nothing, did not even look at her.

But he'd been looking at her enough that morn. She'd felt it. He was a mass of contradictions: polite but cold. He was a leader who kept himself separate even from his men, both of whom had spent the morn chatting behind her as they rode.

Sir Robert handed her a slice of dried apple. "So why is your family castle here in Westmorland, such a barren land?"

Though she wanted to answer immediately, she deliberately hesitated and looked at Sir Adam, letting him think he cowed her. He only looked away.

" 'Tis not barren," she said, her voice full of hesitation. "Sheep are a great livelihood, and what our people cannot grow, they can trade for our cloth goods."

"But why build here?" Sir Robert persisted.

"The castle was built several centuries ago, to gather men to be used to counter Scottish raids. 'Tis not my father's only land, of course. He has many properties in different counties."

"Where?" Sir Adam asked impassively.

She glanced at him, surprised he'd entered the conversation. "I—I do not know."

"So you have never been to these properties? Your father does not travel to each of them?"

"Of course he does," she said without thinking, then realized what he'd uncovered.

"But he never took you."

" 'Tis most likely because she was fostered," Sir Robert said.

Was he trying to help her? She nodded quickly, although that was a falsehood. She knew Sir Adam was watching her closely. She did not want to give him any more information about her father.

"You are lying," Sir Adam said abruptly. "So your father forbid his family from accompanying him, keeping them all secluded."

"Hardly secluded," she shot back. "You did see the prosperous castle, did you not? And besides, they all went with him whenever they wanted to."

"But not you."

How had this become about her? She sighed. "My leg made it hard to travel."

"Then he must not have seen you ride."

"Complimenting your prisoner now? How unusual."

" 'Tis not a compliment, but a fact."

Sir Adam went back to his bread, and she thought he was done.

"So you didn't foster with another family?" he asked. "Or was your castle too distant from another to make such sharing easy?"

She saw even Sir Robert and Sir Michael glance at each other again, as if they didn't understand their leader. But she understood. He was trying to discover everything about her father and her family. It wouldn't do him any good.

"I was fostered," she said.

Those cold blue eyes pinned her.

"Briefly," she amended at last.

"Is that where you broke your leg?"

Was her life so very easy to read? Of course it was, she thought, sighing. "Aye. They sent me home to recover and never asked me back. I did not mind. Being the youngest, I was a comfort to my mother, who was often bedridden." She could have groaned. Why did these things keep tumbling from her lips? She wasn't ready to talk about herself—she wanted to understand Sir Adam.

"So did *you* foster?" she asked.

He only arched a brow at her and looked away. She gritted her teeth, but told herself to be patient. He would become used to her, would eventually slip up and reveal something useful. She noticed that he narrowed his eyes as he gazed into the distance, and she turned to follow his line of sight.

A shepherd strode toward them down the hill-side, making a path through his large herd of sheep with his every step. Florrie stiffened as Sir Adam's hand rested on his dagger.

"Oh, do not hurt him!" she said softly, putting her hand on his forearm.

He looked at her hand, then back up at her. She didn't move it, only felt the steely hardness of his muscles and the tension of a man who focused on only one thing.

"His fate rests in your hands." His voice was a low rumble that made her shiver. "You know what you must do."

She nodded. "I shall say nothing. I give you my word."

"But is your word good?"

She stiffened. She'd spent her life ignored, discounted, and lonely, all of which she'd tolerated and even understood. But just a suggestion that she might be dishonest offended her. Why was it so easy for her to react to Sir Adam's every word? The only pride she'd ever felt had been in her ability to remain calm no matter the situation. Though other people had wondered how she could remain content and happy, she'd had no choice.

But all of her hard-won equanimity was fleeing beneath Sir Adam's cool regard.

"My word is good," she said simply, refusing to rise to his provocation.

The shepherd was almost upon them now, and to her surprise, Sir Robert and Sir Michael gave the young man open, easy smiles. The shepherd was dressed in a simple tunic and rough breeches, and he doffed his cap.

"Good day," the shepherd said. "I be Arthur. We get few travelers here."

He wouldn't want these particular travelers, Florrie thought, once he saw Sir Adam's forbidding face. She turned—and then had to cover her mouth rather than betray her surprise. Sir Adam's entire posture had changed. He lounged easily against the wall, his arm resting on his bent knee, his open face a study in pleasant ease.

"Good day to you, Arthur," Sir Adam said.

He even smiled as he spoke, and that smile brightened his face and lightened those cold eyes. She realized suddenly that he was a truly handsome man. In some ways that made her feel easier—she knew where she stood with hand-some men.

"Would ye share a meal with us?" Sir Adam continued.

Arthur's face shone with happiness. "I will, sir, if ye do not mind."

The shepherd happily sat beside them. If he realized no one introduced themselves, he didn't seem to care once he saw the cheese, fruit, and twice-baked bread. As he ate, he talked happily about the lost lamb he'd found yesterday and the wolf he'd driven off last week. Florrie's three cap-tors answered sparingly but with feigned interest, biding their time.

As the pace of his eating slowed, Arthur began to glance shyly at Florrie. She smiled at him, and when she would have spoken, Sir Adam sud-denly took her hand. She blinked at him. He smiled at her, giving her all his attention. His thumb ran lightly over her knuckles, back and forth, so slowly it somehow made her want to squirm. She couldn't stop looking at his face, at his even white teeth and the day's growth of dark whiskers that almost disguised the dimple in his chin.

"Do ye travel far today, sir?" Arthur asked.

His voice startled Florrie, and she looked away from Sir Adam.

"It will depend on milady's pleasure," Sir Adam answered.

Florrie felt herself blushing at his low and intimate tone. And though he held her hand lightly, it was almost all she could think about.

Wide-eyed, Arthur stared between the two of them, then shook his head.

"Fools in love," she thought she heard him murmur as he rose to his feet. "I thank ye for sharin' your meal," Arthur continued. "This be a lonely place at times."

Sir Robert and Sir Michael gathered together the remains of the food, and Florrie found herself assisted to her feet by Sir Adam. He tucked her hand in his arm with all the grace of a lover. She waved good-bye to the young shepherd, and when he was far enough away, she yanked her hand free.

"And what was the point of that performance?" she demanded in a low voice.

Sir Adam's face had returned to its usual impassivity. "The boy needed to understand that there was no point in showing interest toward you."

"You do not think my being surrounded by three men would have brought home that point?"

He ignored her. "And by showing him that we were relaxed enough to be playful around him should ease his suspicions. You did not seem like a captive."

"So you also did that for the benefit of whomever might be looking for me."

"Of course."

And then he slipped the rope back around her wrist and helped her to mount. Florrie wasn't going to be distracted.

As the midday sun slid behind clouds, and their small traveling party resumed the journey, she said gravely, "This performance will fool no one. Word will spread as more and more people see us. My father's men will come to rescue me. It would go well for you if you release me now."

"And abandon a plan I've been anticipating for four years? I think not."

"What happened four years ago to set this plan in motion?" she asked, too curious to resist.

Not looking at her, he said, " 'Tis none of your concern."

"If it's about my father, it *is* my concern. Did he oppose you at court or best you in a contest of wills?" Sir Adam could very well have met her father—it wasn't readily apparent that her father's health had faded, because he was good at projecting vitality and strength.

Sir Adam didn't answer.

She slapped her hand on her thigh. "How can you speak of fighting my father, but not tell me why?"

"Because 'tis none of your concern."

"He's my father!"

"And for that I pity you."

She opened her mouth in shock, but could think of no response. He obviously blamed her father for something terrible, and she could not gainsay him. The marquess of Martindale was not a nice man; he had no friends, only allies or enemies. He'd put two wives into the grave with his obsessive need for a son, but all for naught.

Florrie sighed and let their conversation die. The only interesting thing that happened during the afternoon was that they passed three beggars going in the opposite direction. After giving her a warning look, Sir Adam dropped her leash, so that it dangled near her thigh. Florrie was uninterested in escaping at the moment, but *he* wasn't to know that.

The beggars were dressed in a combination of animal skins and poorly sewn cloth. At their waists hung metal clapdishes, which they opened and closed noisily as they begged for attention.

"Please, sirs," one had called, his face hidden behind a hood, "can ye spare a bit for poor folk?"

Florrie expected Sir Adam to give them great leeway; instead he rode right up to them and fished in a pouch at his waist for three coins, which he tossed into each clapdish. Then he continued riding at her side, as if he hadn't just done a good deed.

Was he simply a kind man caught up in a desperate situation that he felt honor bound to resolve? She couldn't even be afraid of a man like this—but he wasn't to know that.

This journey—though she'd been forced into it—was proving the most interesting experience of her sheltered life. No one usually paid any attention to her, and yet now she was the focus of a secret mission. These men didn't know that her father wouldn't care that she'd been kidnapped—if they knew the truth, they'd probably take her home, and the adventure would be over.

She suddenly realized the direction of her thoughts. How had this become an adventure, rather than a frightening kidnapping?

And was she being a fool to even entertain such a thought?

Chapter 4

They avoided a small village late in the day and made camp in a stone cattle shed in the center of a grazing pasture, where four stone walls met. A wide stream followed the path of one wall, and Adam saw Lady Florence eyeing it with longing. And he didn't think she was simply thirsty. He waited for her request.

Not long after their supper—a rabbit Michael had snared and roasted—she approached Adam where he was grooming the horses. Adam saw that Robert, who'd been assigned to watch her, was standing nearby.

"Sir Adam, I need to wash," she said hurriedly, "and I need more privacy this time."

"So you don't want me bound to you."

"I do not."

She took a deep, fortifying breath, and he could not help watching the way her small breasts rose.

"If I don't wash after a day riding a horse," she continued, "then I will not be able to stand myself."

He felt the need to rile her, to keep her afraid of his intentions. Leaning closer to her, he murmured, "I don't mind a little perspiration."

For a moment he could have sworn that she looked curious rather than afraid, but she turned away from him and shuddered. Nay, he must have been wrong. She was his prisoner—she was afraid of him.

"If you are not bound to me," he continued, when she remained silent, "my men and I will have to stay near."

She whirled back to him, mouth open, and he held up a hand.

"We will keep our backs turned. But we cannot risk you escaping again."

She gave a dramatic sigh and flung her arms wide. "Where will I go on foot?"

"Mayhap the village we just passed."

"I know no one there, and I have no money!"

He shrugged. "You make the choice."

She put her hands on her hips and said between her teeth, "Do you have soap?"

"I do."

"Oh." She looked taken aback. "And a drying cloth."

"I do."

"Do not men simply . . . shake the water from themselves?"

He squelched a smile. "Like a dog?"

"Well . . . I cannot imagine you would normally bring such luxuries on a journey."

"They are not just for you." He turned back to the horse. "I like comforts when I travel."

He heard her sigh. "I do not suppose you have a change of clothing for me in this magic saddlebag of yours."

"I do not. But I could give you a clean shirt to wear beneath your dress."

"Instead of my smock?"

He glanced over his shoulder. She looked horrified—and then intrigued. It was going to take him some time to understand how her mind worked.

They waited until dusk for her bathing rituals. Adam knew the other two men had already washed themselves, for their wet shirts lay strewn over a stone wall to dry. They'd positioned themselves a stone's throw away, one up and the other down the stream, their backs to Lady Florence's chosen bathing spot. Adam left her with the ball of soap in its leather pouch, a cloth, and a clean shirt, should she choose to use it. Then he went several paces out into the pasture, away from the wall, and stopped.

"You're not far enough," she said immediately.

"I will not turn. Now wash quickly, and remember, if I cannot hear you, it will be my angry face you see rather than my back."

Suddenly he heard the rustling of garments, then the splashing of water.

And his mind began to torture him.

The stream wasn't deep enough for her to immerse herself . . . so, was she kneeling and washing at the water's edge, naked? He imagined her hands lathering the soap, then those hands rubbing over herself—over him.

He was only with her a day and a half, and already he was aroused by her most of the time.

Was this what it would have been like if he'd grown up near women? Or would his body have finally become used to their presence? He couldn't imagine so. It was almost painful to think of her fair form, nude, glowing softly in the dying light.

He fisted his hands at his sides, staring out into the growing darkness. He had a mission, he reminded himself. He would calculate again how many days it would take before Martindale heard that his youngest daughter was missing. Martindale would think he was after a ransom, of course, that he wouldn't have taken her very far as he waited to send a missive threatening her life.

But Adam's mind, usually so logical, seemed to repeat the same figures and suppositions over and over again.

He heard water splashing softly, and imagined it sliding in little trickles down between her breasts. He groaned.

At last, after what seemed like an eternity, she called softly, "I am done."

He strode back toward her. He was aware of both men disappearing into the growing darkness, released from guard duty. He almost didn't want to be alone with her. What kind of cowardly thought was that?

Adam saw that she hadn't made use of his shirt, but her hair was damp, and her skin seemed to glow with moisture.

"Down on your knees," he said harshly, staying on his side of the stream.

"But—"

He pointed to the ground, and she dropped down.

"I need to wash, and my men cannot guard you."

She looked up and down the stream. "Where did they go?"

Was there a note of panic in her voice? That should have pleased him, because a frightened captive would behave. But it was more difficult than he'd imagined having a *woman* afraid of him. He didn't like how it made him feel.

"They've gone to scout our surroundings, to judge if we've been followed, and to see if the way ahead is clear." He loosened the laces of his tunic at the back of his neck and pulled it over his head.

She gave an actual squeak of surprise.

Wearing a forbidding frown, he continued disrobing.

Florrie knew she should turn away or close her eyes. Her heart banged with panic, her mouth felt dry, yet still she watched Sir Adam as he lifted his shirt up his body and over his head. In the last light of day, his torso seemed to glow, each hill of muscle etched vibrant with shadows. She was not ignorant; she'd seen more than one man without his shirt on, performing the same chore Sir Adam now did.

But . . . something was different. Looking at his chest incited a new response inside her that was confusing and even—exciting. Surely it was because this was an adventure; she was taking each new experience inside and trying to understand.

Then he leaped over the stream, and she gasped, sinking back onto her heels. He ignored her as he knelt down, giving her that impenetrable stare. She waited, barely breathing.

"Soap?" he said without emotion.

Heat flooded her face as she passed it to him. He washed himself quickly with his hands, dunking his head briefly. And she didn't even try to pretend that she didn't watch him.

He saw the cloth she'd used to dry her body, then thrown across the wall. "No sense in wetting another one."

And he used it on his body! Then he took the clean shirt he'd originally offered her and donned it. She almost expected him to hand her his soiled shirt to wash. Since she was still pretending to be afraid of him, she was going to meekly agree to the task. Instead, he efficiently washed his own shirt and spread it to dry beside the others.

He rose at last and pointed to the cattle shed, now dark and gloomy in the twilight. "Come."

And she did, without a protest, her mind still

examining everything that she'd just felt. Once inside, they were free of the breeze. There was plenty of fresh hay stored, so the smell was tolerable, and the horses would be happy. She could barely see, except for the beams of moonlight coming in through the shuttered window.

When he began to bring out food, she could not help asking, "Are you going to start a fire?"

"Nay, I do not want a nearby farmer to wonder who uses his shed. The hay will keep my men warm. And I shall keep you warm."

He looked at her, as if preparing her for the inevitable. She bit her lip and said nothing.

While they were eating, the other two men returned. Both reported seeing nothing, and Sir Adam only grunted a response. While they ate quietly, she wondered if eating in the dark made conversation seem foolish.

At last, Sir Adam looked at her. "Find a spot in the hay to spread a blanket. I will join you in a moment."

Once again, she did as he wanted, almost biting her tongue to keep from protesting. But she had to lull him into thinking he frightened her. The three men stood at the door and spoke in low tones, their forms as dark as shadows. What could not be said in front of her? Were they planning something else to capture her father's attention? Instead of feeling afraid, she felt impatient. Sir Robert left the shed, Sir Michael wrapped himself in a cloak near the door, and Sir Adam approached her, a big, dark outline in the stone building. He stepped over her body, then sat down beside her.

She lay on her back and frowned. "What if I don't wish to lie on my side?"

"I do."

He stretched out along her body, his chest pressed to her arm, his head propped on his hand. His knee rode over her thighs, startling her. It was heavy and hot, and she felt as if he were about to climb on top of her. She was shocked by how curious she was about how it felt to have a man in such an intimate position.

"My long legs have to go somewhere," he said.

She quickly rolled to her side, and barely heard his chuckle as the sensation of him once again pressed against her. She'd had fleeting memories of sleeping together all day, had told herself she would become used to it by now. But she'd just seen his sculpted chest nude, and now it was pressed against her back, lifting with each breath. His hips were tight against hers, and to her surprise, she felt . . . something long and hard. Did he hide something within his clothing? She didn't know what it was, but she wasn't going to ask. He had even forgotten to tie her wrist to his, for which she was grateful.

Wide-eyed, she waited for him to fall asleep, but gradually realized that he hadn't. And that kept her awake. She thought hours might have passed, while her wide eyes burned with fatigue and she concentrated on slowing her breathing and emptying her mind. Nothing worked. At last she turned her head to speak, and he abruptly covered her mouth with his hand.

"Say nothing," he murmured against her ear.

She froze, sensing tension in his voice, and suddenly fearing it. What was happening? She heard the unusual sound of birdsong at night, only a moment before the window shutters near her feet burst open. A man's body blocked the moonlight. At her back was nothing but the rush of air as Sir Adam leaped to his feet. With a punch, he knocked the man back out the window, then turned to face the strangers coming through the door.

Florrie scrambled backward through the hay until she was up against the wall. Digging frantically, she at last found a tool handle. She ran her fingers along it until she knew it was a pitchfork. Holding it in front of her, she prayed she wouldn't have to use it.

She couldn't see much unless the men staggered through the faint beams of moonlight. She heard muffled curses and groans, and she panicked. Were these her father's men, come to rescue her? How could she shout that they weren't to kill anyone on her behalf?

Another man slid through the window and crept toward her. She didn't know how to feel— until he passed through moonlight, and she saw his ragged beard, narrowed eyes, and triumphant, gap-toothed grin.

He wasn't her father's knight, not a knight at all.

She screamed and waved the pitchfork. Then he was plucked away from her by Sir Adam, who dealt him a hard blow. As Sir Adam tossed the thief out the window, another came up behind him. Florrie swung the pitchfork with all of her might and hit the stranger in the back of the head, staggering him into Sir Adam, who caught him roughly. Sir Adam stared at her in obvious surprise. She lifted her chin, feeling proud of herself.

After that, it all seemed to be over quickly. She saw the glitter of sparks only a second before Sir Michael brought a small fire to life. So much for not caring if a farmer saw the light. Had they been lying to her, perhaps anticipating this very attack? She didn't understand anything, but was going to demand answers.

After they were done with the attackers, of course. She watched mutely as they tied up the three men. They dragged them outside, and she went to the door to see Sir Robert binding another two out by the wall. They left the gagged men in a heap, where only an occasional groan could be heard.

When they returned to the shed, she backed away to let them through the door. "What will you do with them?" she asked breathlessly. "They are thieves, are they not?"

Sir Adam squatted down beside the fire, motioning Florrie to join him.

He wiped a trickle of blood from his chin. "You realized quickly that they weren't here to rescue you."

She remembered the triumphant gleam in her attacker's eyes. "They were not knights."

"They were thieves, the same thieves we passed on the road today."

She went still, her mind racing. "But the only men we passed . . ." And then it came to her. "The beggars?"

He nodded and took a drink from a wineskin.

"But you were nice to them. You gave them money."

"The money allowed me to get close enough to examine them," he said. "They didn't have the gaunt, desperate look of beggars."

"You knew they were coming for us!" she said, aghast. "That's why you didn't allow a fire, why you wanted us protected in this shed."

"I always want you protected, my lady," he said dryly.

She slapped at his arm. "You could have warned me!"

He looked down at where she'd touched him, and she held her breath.

Mildly, he said, "And what if I'd been wrong? You would have lain awake all night for no reason."

"As if I could sleep with you stiff with waiting behind me."

Sir Robert, who'd taken Sir Michael's place indoors, gave a soft laugh. Sir Adam frowned at him.

Florrie was already thinking ahead. "You were waiting outside for them, Sir Robert?"

He nodded.

"And somehow you alerted your brother—the birdcall!"

He only grinned.

"That was very well done."

"My thanks, Lady Florence."

"But we weren't alerted early enough," Sir Adam said.

Sir Robert sighed. "Aye, they were wily. I missed them at first, since they crept along the low wall."

Sir Michael lifted his head. "Lady Florence did not miss her opportunity. She handled herself well."

She felt foolish blushing at praise—from a man who was one of her kidnappers.

Sir Robert grinned at his brother. "Michael tells me she saved your hide."

"And I returned the favor," Sir Adam said, arching a brow.

Florrie watched him turn back to stare almost broodingly into the small fire. She was not about to thank him for saving her. He didn't need to know just yet about her enjoyment of this strange journey.

They sat about the fire in companionable silence for a while longer, until at last the excitement began to fade from her body, leaving exhaustion in its wake. She yawned, and her head nodded.

She found herself scooped up by Sir Adam. As she stiffened, he immediately set her on the blanket and came down behind her. She thought again of how he'd behaved when the thief had come in through the window.

Turning to look over her shoulder at him, she said, "You protected me."

He blinked sleepy eyes at her. "I protected my prize." He lifted her wrist and tied the rope that bound her to him.

She gave him a glare. "And I thought you simply forgot to tie me up earlier tonight."

"Nay, I did not. I needed my hands free."

She turned away and curled up with her hands beneath her cheek, the rope easily forgotten. Regardless of the danger, she at last admitted that she was almost . . . enjoying herself. She had a strong man to protect her along the way, she was riding and seeing sights she'd never seen before—and she *wasn't* taking care of her oldest sister, Matilda, who was pregnant with her second child.

Wherever this journey ended, Sir Adam would eventually realize that he could not challenge her father. No one was going to die. She could feel free to watch the adventure unfold. It would have to be an adventure that she could cherish for the rest of her life, for it would be her last.

She fell asleep wearing a smile, not even realizing that in her drowsy state, she snuggled back against Sir Adam.

The next morning, as rain drizzled across a gray landscape, Florrie stood in the doorway of the cattle shed and watched as Sir Adam checked the bindings on his prisoners. Feeling hesitant, she wondered what he would do, how he would take his revenge on men who'd dared attack him. Sir Robert and Sir Michael watched with impassive expressions. She wanted to demand their intercession, their compassion, but knew they gave their leader their complete loyalty.

So she waited, out of the rain, biting her fingernail, tense as she fought the urge to speak.

Sir Adam turned his back on the bound men and moved toward his horse. He removed something from his saddlebag and tossed it to Florrie, who almost dropped it in surprise. It was a woman's wool cloak. He'd had one all along. Saying nothing, she only glared at him as she drew it on and fastened it at her throat. He motioned to her horse, and she couldn't help glancing at their prisoners, who'd begun to squirm as they fought the ropes.

"But . . ." she began, motioning to the thieves.

"A shepherd or farmer will find them soon enough," Sir Adam said blandly. "Or they can take turns biting at the knots in each others' bindings."

As the five thieves heard that, muffled oaths exploded from behind their gags. Florrie's face eased into a smile. Sir Adam wasn't going to kill men who'd tried their best to kill him. Some ruthless knight was he. Her last fear of his supposed cruelty faded away. Happily, she mounted her horse, and when they were out of sight of the thieves, almost held out her wrist for his rope. At the last moment, she remembered to wait, and he reached across the space between their horses and grabbed her hand. She tried to pull away, even after he looped the rope tight. All it got her was a wince of pain at the abrasion—and the satisfaction of knowing he still believed she wanted to escape.

The rain continued to fall all morning, and though Florrie was damp, at least she wasn't cold. They kept to the side roads, more paths than highways, as they wound through the hills and across the moorlands. She could not miss that it was Sir Michael with whom Sir Adam discussed their choice of direction. Sir Adam, obviously raised to be a knight, perhaps knew the main highways better than the ones that would keep them—and their kidnapping of her—better hidden.

At last the road led down the steep hillsides of a dale, then followed the path of a river. Sir Adam wouldn't tell her its name—as if such a thing would matter to her, she who'd lived so sheltered a life. Knowledge of names wouldn't help her escape, but he obviously wasn't taking chances.

They saw a traveler or two every hour now, and she knew they were nearing a town rather than a village. Sir Adam could no longer keep her by his side with the rope leash, but she gave him no cause to doubt her intentions—yet. A plan was bubbling to life inside her, and the excitement of it almost made her giddy. He would have no cause to doubt that she was his "unwilling" captive—even though she wasn't. She was learning about him in bits and pieces; she could be patient.

They took a turn in the road, and the town spread out before them, with a castle high on the cliff and immense arches of stone spanning the river.

Sir Adam lifted a hand, calling the party to a halt beneath the spread of an ancient oak tree, its branches giving them shelter from the rain. "We need provisions. Robert and Michael, you will both go into town—"

"What town is it?" she interrupted innocently.

He only gave her a look, then turned back to his men. "While I remain here with our companion."

"Your *captive*," she said, giving him a smile. "Do not make me stay here. Let me go, too. I have never seen . . . whatever town it is. Maybe we can even sleep in real beds tonight! I promise to remain silent for such a wondrous reward."

Sir Adam waited to answer her as a farmer driving a covered cart went by, glancing at them with little interest. "My lady, you cannot be trusted."

"I know you'll hurt people if I disobey you."

He blinked.

"I would not risk that," she continued with wide-eyed innocence.

He ignored her and nodded to their two companions, who avoided Florrie as they rode away. She had expected no less, but she deliberately pouted anyway, hoping to deceive Sir Adam while she waited for her moment.

She didn't have long to wait. A larger party appeared within the hour, several women and men, including children, all with close enough looks to be a family. As Sir Adam watched them, studying them as he did everyone, she tapped her horse's flanks and rode into the lane beside the family, nodding pleasantly. She didn't look at Sir Adam, but felt his presence come up beside her before she could see him.

"What do you think you're doing?" he demanded in a low voice.

"What does it look like I'm doing?" she said through smiling lips. "What a lovely child you have!" she cried to one of the younger women. Then she scowled at Sir Adam, who watched her warily. "I had to leave my own little boy at home. My husband believed the journey too arduous. Separating a mother and child is far worse, or so I think!"

She was drawn into a conversation about children that lasted until they reached the open gates of the town. From the family, she learned it was Richmond, in Yorkshire's North Riding.

She glanced at Sir Adam with an intimate smile, hoping he realized he could no longer keep such information from her. His face was impassive, a husband tolerant of his silly wife, but those blue eyes were as dark as mountain lakes in the winter.

In the process of slowing to go through the gates, she maneuvered herself to the far side of the family, keeping them between her and her frustrated captor. Then she eased into a cantor, and took off down a side lane. Before he'd even worked his way through the family, she turned up another lane and he was out of sight.

Chapter 5

Adam was not surprised in the least when Lady Florence galloped away. He had to admire her horsemanship, even as he maneuvered carefully through the jostling crowd of adults and children. When he was free, he saw her down several streets as they rode parallel to each other.

Why did she continue riding instead of asking for directions to the local constable? A smart woman would do so if she were far from home and needed to return. Instead, she continued riding with purpose, but not out of town.

He came around the edge of a stone house, and she was suddenly there, at the end of the street. But . . . it shouldn't have happened so easily. She gave a large gasp when she saw him and tried to escape, but the street was far narrower, and there were children herding several pigs in front of her.

With her horsemanship, she could have escaped when she'd first entered the town . . . but she hadn't. Instead she looked crestfallen as he rode up beside her, and even slumped in the saddle. But he could have sworn those green eyes were alight with mischief. What was she up to?

He went along with her performance, acting stern and disappointed, promising with his eyes he'd reveal his anger when they were alone. She gave every impression of meekness as she rode at his side.

Was this behavior something about women he didn't understand? God knew, there were so many things about the fair sex that eluded him. But for now he would hold his questions until they were able to speak in private.

He led her back the way they'd come, but met up with Robert and Michael before arriving at their original meeting place. The two men looked at her, then him, but he only shook his head. They passed by the town on a path near the river's edge, below the cliff. It was many hours later before he finally allowed them to stop for supper and make camp in a stand of trees several paces in from the road. He didn't permit her to wash herself, knowing punishment was necessary.

But punishment for deliberately allowing herself to get caught?

As the sun set, he sent Michael and Robert to scout the roads before and behind them. They both glanced at the crestfallen Lady Florence, Robert looking like he wanted to speak, but they did as they were told. When they had gone, Adam saw her grow tense, waiting.

He squatted down beside her. Where once it would have bothered him that she cringed away, now it didn't. It was all a game to her.

"Come lie beside me, Lady Florence," he commanded, taking her wrist.

She gave a shaky sigh and crawled onto the nearby blanket with him. Then she glanced up at him with luminous eyes. "So you're not going to punish me?"

"Sleeping in the filth from the road is not punishment enough?"

She nodded, dropping her gaze. "Of course it is. I was foolish to think I could elude you."

He only growled and pulled her down before him. He enfolded himself around her, driven even more to distraction by her compact curves, and the softness of her hair. Without thinking, he released the leather tie holding her braid together and spread her hair across her shoulders.

She tensed but didn't look back at him. "What are you doing?"

"Punishing you." He combed his fingers through her hair slowly, felt the way she tried to pull away. He caught her hip and held her more firmly against him. "Do you dare resist me?"

He was trying to push her past her limits, wanting the truth, but he was losing the battle to ignore the temptation of her. She would fight him soon, or cry, or finally tell him everything. But could he last that long? Holding back a groan, he rolled his groin even harder against the sweet curve of her ass.

"What is that?" she suddenly asked in a clear voice.

He froze. "Did you hear something?"

She pushed her hips back against him, and he couldn't help inhaling swiftly at the pleasure of it.

"Nay, *that*," she said. "I have felt it every time you lie with me. Do you carry a hidden weapon within your clothing?"

He was so taken aback by her naïve forthrightness that he actually snorted. He took her shoulder and pressed her onto her back, grimacing against the sensation of her sliding against him. Somehow he had to be the one in control of this situation.

Bending his elbow and propping his head on his hand, he looked down at her, seeing open curiosity. "I know you are an innocent, Lady Florence, but do you know absolutely nothing of the male form?"

She blinked at him in puzzlement, until at last something connected in her mind. Her pale skin blushed a fiery red, and he could barely stop himself from grinning down at her. She was so very complicated—confusing him one moment, frustrating him the next, and now amusing him.

When she tried to move her hips away from him, something dark came over him, and he kept her body tight against his. He leaned over her until their faces were but inches apart.

"My lady, this part of a man's body isn't always

so noticeable. But it comes to attention when a lovely woman is nearby."

The play of expressions on her face was fascinating. She was obviously embarrassed and confused—and then, to his surprise, indignant.

"Now you are lying to me, Sir Adam!"

He blinked. "Lying? The evidence is obvious."

"You are not feeling emotions for me."

"Not romantic emotions, that is true," he said dryly. "But a man doesn't have to feel any emotion if his body is lusting."

She gave his shoulder a little push, scoffing, "You are teasing me again. Is this some kind of punishment?"

She didn't think he told the truth? Or she didn't think she could inspire a man to passion. Who had led her to believe such a thing?

And why wasn't she frightened of him?

He'd lost all control of this kidnapping, and suddenly, with her body against his, her lips pouting, he wanted to kiss her. Her eyes went wide as he leaned even closer, and her face paled.

Kiss his captive, a woman at his mercy?

But, ah, even with the dust of the road, she smelled so wonderful, a sweet, musky woman. Her softly parted lips beckoned to him, the warmth of her breath lured him, and before he knew it, his lips touched hers in the briefest of kisses, as tantalizing as a deeper kiss, because it was so forbidden.

He reared back, inhaling and closing his eyes.

Their relationship had altered; her behavior had changed everything. At last he dropped his forbidding-captor mask and spoke plainly. "Why are you not afraid of me?"

She licked her lips as she slowly pulled her gaze from his mouth. Adam almost lost his breath, his will to resist her hanging on by the briefest thread.

She shrugged, then looked down at her fingers, which were twisted together as if she didn't know what to do with them.

As if she wanted to touch him.

And he so wanted to touch and explore her.

"I know you won't hurt me," she said in a small voice.

"That still doesn't explain why you did not finish your escape today. I saw the whole thing."

Her gaze flew back to his. "You did?"

"Aye! You were not even riding fast, and you deliberately waited for me to catch you. Tell me why."

She sighed. "I had to make you think I wanted to escape. Otherwise you'd think I was against my own father—and that is not true! You've told me nothing about your connection with him, after all."

"So you do not want to escape?" he demanded with exasperation. He wondered if her upbringing was as stilted as his, but that couldn't be—she was the daughter of a marquess. "Why would a woman want to be dragged from her comfortable home and used against her father?"

"Well, I do not want to be *used*. But I am bound for the convent, and this is the first adventure I've ever had . . ."

Her voice trailed off, and she looked up at him wearing a hesitant smile.

Now it was his turn to gape. "The *convent*? I kidnapped a *nun*?" He put several inches between their bodies.

"I am not a nun yet, not even a novice," she quickly said. "I shall take the veil when my sister, Matilda, no longer needs me."

And here he'd been telling her about how he lusted after her. A nun. "And you *want* this cloistered life?" he said weakly.

"Nay, I do not, but my wishes are unimportant. I will do as my father commands, because it is my duty to him."

"So 'twas your father's idea."

She nodded, not even looking sad or angry. He didn't know what to think.

"So I'm not kidnapping you, I'm rescuing you."

"Nay, I do not think that."

"But you want to be with us instead of at home."

She nodded, smiling. "Although 'tis dangerous, I am rather enjoying myself. But I couldn't let you know that too soon, or you might return me home immediately. I know my future duty, but I don't have to live it right now. Please tell me you won't take me home."

"So that's why you faked an escape attempt today."

She gave another nod. "You are not too angry?"

He hesitated before shaking his head. "But I still do not understand you. I am going to challenge your father, and I'm making you part of it."

"I cannot control what you do," she said softly. "My father will understand that. Are you going to return me home now that you know the truth?"

She stared up at him, all soft woman, pleading with emerald eyes.

"Adam, can you not answer me?" she whispered, reaching up to touch his chest. "Will you still take me with you? I would like to have memories to dream of when I leave the regular world."

He looked down at her hand, which seemed to burn his flesh through his clothing. And he wanted her more than ever, this woman he didn't understand, who thought a kidnapping and dangerous journey were part of an innocent adventure.

He should think her a fool; instead he found himself pitying her. How had a cruel bastard fathered such a woman?

He rolled on to his back and flung his arm over his eyes with a sigh. "My plan has not changed. You will ride with us."

She actually gave a joyful laugh. He looked at her dubiously and found her staring up in contentment at the stars glittering through the branches of the trees. There was silence hanging in the night, and darkness all around them but for the glow of their small fire.

"I like sleeping out of doors," she said softly. "Have you done it often?"

He couldn't stop looking at her happy expression in disbelief. "When necessary." Now that she was not "pretending" to be frightened, her worried expression was gone, and her pink mouth was curved into a natural smile. How could she smile so easily, after what her life had been like? Condemned to the nunnery because of a limp? Or was there more to it?

He wouldn't care; he didn't want to feel anything for her but a lust that he would control.

"You do not like to talk about yourself." She said it in a playfully accusing manner.

"And you talk too much. I cannot imagine you taking a vow of silence."

She actually giggled. He sighed and closed his eyes, trying to think only of sleep.

"I'm cold," she whispered.

He stiffened in more ways than one. "Where is your cloak?"

"Wet. I laid it across a shrub to dry."

Gritting his teeth, he rolled back onto his side, and she did the same. He didn't want to touch her, but she literally took his arm and pulled it across her body, snuggling closer, tucking her hips right up against his groin. She sighed with contentment, as if she didn't care that she aroused him. Or didn't understand the very real danger of him losing control.

But he never lost control.

And he was never going to be able to sleep.

Florrie awoke before Adam did. She lay unmoving, wickedly enjoying how warm and safe she felt snuggled in his arms. She'd known him less than four days, but already he inspired trust in her, as well as a need to understand him that was almost a physical ache.

She knew what was wrong with her. As a young girl, she used to dream too much about bold adventures. It had taken her away from the dreary uneasiness of her home, where her mother grew weaker with every miscarriage, and the entire household tiptoed around in fear of the marquess's reaction to his continued lack of a son. In Florrie's dreams, bold knights always rescued her—and instead, in real life, one had kidnapped her.

Her secret amusement turned to confusion. Before she'd confessed her future vocation, he'd actually told her that he lusted after her—or his body did. She'd often heard her father telling her sisters to be wary of being alone with a man, that men wanted what wasn't theirs, endangering her father's plans for their marriages.

Did Adam actually . . . want her in that way? She'd been shameless in her quest for warmth before they'd fallen asleep last night, and he'd been most reluctant. Surely, now that he knew she was to be a nun, he would not let himself think that way about her.

But he'd kissed her. The soft press of his lips had been most tender, the closeness they'd shared far too attractive. She wished she'd kissed him back more, explored what she might never have again.

But as she lay there in the warmth of his embrace, she felt him stir and press into her with a slow roll of his hips. And to her amazement, she could actually feel that part of him growing. She was embarrassed and intrigued and overcome with a languid sensation of pleasure that she shouldn't be feeling. He lowered his head to hers, then rubbed against her hair. Did he want to kiss her again? How would she resist him? He wasn't even truly awake.

But she realized the moment he was, because his entire body grew tense against hers before he quickly sat up. She pressed up on her elbow and looked over her shoulder at him, forgetting until this moment that he'd unbound her hair the previous night. It slid about her shoulders, and he watched it, his eyes a dark blue smolder.

Biting her lip, she looked away from him. Though she wanted to experiment with his kisses, she knew he would be upset at her behavior.

The sun was shining through the trees, Robert was already gone, and Michael was frying something in a skillet over the fire. That got her attention, and she sniffed in appreciation.

Michael glanced at her, betraying no emotion. "I caught fish while you two slept."

He looked past her at Adam, who gruffly said, "Good work."

Was Adam embarrassed to be sleeping while his two men completed their assignments? But he was their leader, and had taken charge of her. That was an important duty—except now he knew she would prove no trouble to him.

She decided to ignore him and concentrate on fingering the snarls from her hair, which was a difficult task. She looked up in surprise as a comb was tossed into her lap, but Adam turned away before she could thank him. Gratefully, she used it until she was able to braid her hair, which would definitely have to be washed soon. But she could hardly ask for a bath. Perhaps the stream they'd camped near might be deep enough for her to do as Adam had done the previous morning, dunk her head.

She rose to her feet and approached Adam, who'd returned from the trees and was beginning to saddle his horse while they all waited to break their fast.

"Might I go unaccompanied into the woods this morn?" she asked cautiously.

He looked down at her, and she realized that his habitual cold and aloof expression was gone, as if it were something he'd put on to frighten her.

He did not smile at her, but he nodded. She felt . . . lighter, happier.

As Lady Florence walked away, Adam frowned and forced himself to stop watching her, only to find that Robert had returned, and was regarding him with wary confusion. Sighing, Adam approached the fire and both men.

"You let her go alone, big brother," Robert said.

"I will watch over her in a moment. I do not think she can go anywhere." Then he told them about her confession that she was bound for the convent and wanted an adventure.

"Should we believe her?" Michael asked, since Robert was too busy chuckling.

Adam hesitated before answering. He'd believed her words as she said them, so convincing had she been.

Or perhaps so blinded by lust had *he* been.

But she *could* be lying, all to lull him into relaxing his watch over her. Then she could escape, or bring the nearest constable down on his head.

"We cannot afford to believe her," Adam said at last, "not without proof. We have to remember whose daughter she is."

"One proof will be if she returns this morn," Michael said.

"Too easy," Robert answered. "She would be foolish to leave until there were people to help her."

"Then the next town," Adam said firmly. "We can test her there."

After they finished debating their plan, Lady Florence returned from her grooming. Her braid was now wet, as if she'd washed her hair.

She smiled at Michael. "Is the fish ready? I am famished!"

Her merry voice was so lilting and pleasant, like a forest stream burbling over rocks. And then Adam caught himself thinking such foolery, and he knew she could lure him into danger if he allowed it.

Chapter 6

For the first time, Florrie rode among the three men with no rope marking her as a prisoner. They knew her motives now, and they still accepted her—well, of course, they accepted her. They were still hoping to use her against her father.

And it didn't bother her in the least. Nothing would come of it, she insisted to herself. She had plenty of time now to discover what they held against her father. She would be patient.

She tried talking to Robert and Michael through the morning, and although they were pleasant, they did not reveal anything personal to her.

And then there was Adam, who studied her as if she were a creature he'd never seen before. He didn't watch with interest so much as with intensity. Why didn't he simply question her instead of staring? She'd tell him almost anything. But why should he believe her? So she forced herself to relax and enjoy the countryside, where the moors had begun to steadily shrink into small hills.

After such an awkward morning, she was relieved when the road they took merged with another, and there were more people traveling—and more muddy holes to carefully navigate. They were obviously approaching another village or town, and when Adam said nothing about his intentions, she could no longer control her curiosity.

"Do we need more supplies?" she hinted.

He glanced at her, and her breath caught as his expression eased into a faint smile. My, did he not realize how handsome he was when he relaxed?

She smiled in return. "I promise this time I will do whatever you say, even if it means waiting outside the village."

He shook his head. "We go in together. We cannot have you missing the wonder of another quaint village."

She laughed aloud with excitement. How glad she was that she'd told him the truth!

"But I cannot call you Lady Florence, for obvious reasons."

"I'm called Florrie," she said.

He cocked his head and seemed to look her over. Even that simple gaze made her pulse flutter.

"Florrie suits you. 'Tis much less proper than Florence."

"And I am not proper?" she teased, then blushed as she remembered her sinful pleasure at sleeping beside him. Surely *that* was not proper.

He rolled his eyes. "We cannot call you Florrie,

either, for fear your name should reach the wrong ears. I will call you Katherine today."

And now she had a secret identity on her grand adventure!

Unlike Richmond, with its castle and many inhabited streets, this truly was a village, with a small green surrounded by thatch-roofed stone houses at the junction of two roads. A two-story inn made of gray stone dominated the crossroads, and there were many horses enclosed within the yard.

"A popular place," Florrie said. "Where will I wait?"

"If they have a public room, we shall eat our dinner here today," Adam said.

Ah, it was good to no longer be treated as a captive, she thought with anticipation.

Michael nodded. "Robert and I will keep watch over the horses and purchase our supplies."

"But do you not want to eat with us?" Florrie asked, feeling sorry for them.

Adam gave her an impassive glance, and she realized that this was not a pleasant jaunt for them; they'd probably been hired for this task.

"Never mind," she said ruefully, giving the two men an apologetic look.

Robert only laughed and shook his head, while Michael appeared uninterested. Perhaps a public inn in a nondescript village was nothing to them, but to Florrie, it was another chance to see—and do—something new.

Adam helped her dismount, then took her arm to lead the way inside. She did her best to appear simply tired and subdued, but she could not help looking everywhere as they passed through an entry room where a man—the innkeeper?—stood behind a counter. The public room was off to the right, and at midday, the tables were mostly occupied with men. A huge fireplace dominated one end of the room, and although it was stacked with logs, it was not lit on this fine summer's day.

"If we were here tonight," Adam said quietly near her ear, "this would be a much more boisterous room."

"This is a tavern where men come to drink?" she asked.

"'Tis the best place to gather. A man can learn much here, as drunken tongues wag foolishly."

A man in a leather apron and cap came to lead them to a table, and soon they were eating steaming lamb pie. Florrie chewed slowly, enjoying the rare treat after so many days traveling. She watched Adam, whose his eyes were constantly scanning the nearby tables, the windows, the door. She knew he was concerned about being confronted.

"So you come to such places often?" she asked.

His eyes met hers again. "Nay."

"Oh, but I thought . . ." Her words died.

"I have come on occasion, but that is all. I, too, did not travel in my youth."

Then he put a spoonful in his mouth, as if he regretted those words.

"So that is why 'tis Michael who guides our journey."

He nodded.

"Why did you not travel?"

He seemed to chew his food even more slowly, before saying at last, "I was not permitted to. My brothers and I were well guarded."

"Why?"

"I cannot speak of it."

She resisted the urge to sigh loudly. "How many more brothers do you have?"

"One. He is my youngest brother by three years, named Paul."

"Why is he not serving at your side?"

"He left us before we undertook this mission."

' "Undertook this mission'? You sound like this was an assignment from your lord."

He frowned. "You mistake me."

"Then why say it in such a way?"

" 'Tis the only way I know."

He was such a mystery! What young man was not permitted to travel in his youth? Boys were usually given much more freedom than girls. But she sensed a direct approach with questions would not work.

"Where did Paul go?"

At last this seemed to reach him, for pain flared briefly in his eyes. "I know not. He wanted to make his own way in the world, and I could not gainsay him."

"Do you miss him?" she asked softly.

"I spent my life taking care of him, and without him at my side, nothing seems right. But surely you understand that. Two of your sisters are married with their own homes."

"You know much of me," she said dryly. "And the third, Matilda, is married to Father's heir, but they live with us," she added with a sigh.

"You do not sound pleased."

She used her spoon to break open more of her pie. "I must confess, I am not as close to my sisters as you are with your brothers."

"But . . . I thought women were naturally bound together with love and support. We were taught—"

He broke off and quickly took another bite of his pie, but Florrie wasn't fooled. He'd revealed something he hadn't meant to say. He'd been *taught* about women? What kind of a curious education had he been exposed to as a child? She decided not to press him yet. The more familiar he became with her, the more he would speak.

"Women are often very close to one another," she said slowly. "But my sisters have always been encouraged by my father to count on my assistance whenever they needed it."

"But not the other way around."

She smiled at him. "I did not ask for much. I was more content with my life than they could ever be. They were far too concerned with finding the proper husband, and what they had to do to prepare themselves for such a hunt."

He blinked. "Looking for a husband is like a hunt?"

She lifted her nose in the air. "There are only so many noblemen to be had, after all," she said primly, then smiled. "My father was determined to be allied with the best families in England."

"But not through you."

She shrugged. "I understood. The dowry money was better spent on attracting a viscount for Agnes and an earl for Christina. Matilda, married to Father's heir, Claudius Drake, will be a marchioness someday. For me, Father has set aside money for the convent, of course, but 'tis hardly the same amount necessary for a marriage."

"But with that money, you could have attracted a mere knight, could you not?"

Those blue eyes she'd once thought of as perpetually cold now studied her. Was he teasing?

She found herself blushing again. "Nay, my infirmity made such a thing difficult, so Father determined it best that I represent the family in the church. I understood, and I accept it. It will be a better life in many ways."

"How?" he asked, straightening on his stool as if in surprise.

"I am looking forward to the education afforded a woman in a convent. And I will be doing God's work—not my sisters'."

Though he smiled and seemed to mean it, she thought his face almost seemed . . . stiff, as if he wasn't used to expressing emotions. How curious.

Suddenly someone came to a stop in the rushes next to their table. Florrie looked up to see Michael nodding to them, his red hair falling forward over his brow.

"Sir, there is a problem with the horses. May I have a moment of your time?"

Adam nodded. "Katherine, please remain here and finish your meal. I will only be absent a short time."

And then the two of them were gone, leaving her alone in the public room. It was a novel experience, since she'd never been totally alone with strangers—unless you counted her kidnapping. She continued eating, thanked the server for refilling her cider, and looked at all the people and the way they were dressed. Fascinating.

Several men began to openly stare at her. She should feel uncomfortable, but she didn't. She knew Adam would protect her. It was an unusual feeling to have a man's protection, and she relished it, however temporary it was.

A plump woman wearing an apron to cover her simple gown stopped near the table. "Excuse me, mistress, but I be Mistress Lingard, the innkeeper's wife. Your husband had to step away, did he? Do ye want company?"

Florrie was flustered by the fact that Adam hadn't assigned her a last name. But of course, she didn't *need* to introduce herself. "Mistress Lingard, how kind of you to offer, but I would not want to keep you from your duties. My husband will return in a moment."

And indeed, she saw Adam entering the public room. More than one person watched him approach, and she could understand why. He looked imposing and dangerous, a man used to command. Florrie felt a thrill at being with him.

He gave Mistress Lingard a nod and looked at Florrie. "I regret the delay. Have you finished eating?"

She nodded and rose to her feet, taking his arm as if she always did. "Mistress Lingard, the meal was delicious. My husband could not stop complimenting your establishment."

Adam gave Florrie an impassive look, but she wouldn't feel guilty for her boldness in naming him husband. Why else would "Katherine" be traveling with three men? Mistress Lingard blushed as she saw them to the front entrance.

Adam had not been able to ignore the feeling of relief he'd felt that Florrie had not tried to leave them. Robert had stood guard near the public room to watch over her, but still, she'd passed their little test quite well.

He watched the way she waved a greeting to

Mistress Lingard, the liveliness in her step as she strolled with her hand in his arm. She was so . . . happy, so content with the meagerness she'd been handed in life. He didn't understand her.

He saw Michael and Robert waiting with the horses. "Katherine, remain with the men. I will return in a moment." He went back inside the inn.

When he returned to her, carrying a wrapped parcel under his arm, he saw her look of curiosity, but she did not question him.

Not until they had left the village did she give a pleased sigh and smile at him. "How did I do?"

"You passed," Robert said.

Adam shot him a frown, then winced when Florrie's smile faded.

"Passed?" she repeated.

"I needed to be certain you could be trusted not to betray us," Adam said.

She nodded solemnly. "I understand. Of course you could not simply take my word. That is why you left me alone?"

"It is."

Taking a deep breath, she donned a small smile. "Then I passed."

She was hiding her disappointment, and something deep within Adam ached, confusing him. Had she spent her life hiding her feelings?

Though he'd meant to wait until later that evening, he removed the parcel from his saddlebag and leaned toward her horse to hand it to her.

As she held it, she raised wide eyes to his. "What is this?"

"Open it."

He thought he heard Robert snicker behind him, but he ignored his little brother. This was a necessary purchase.

Florrie untied the string holding the cloth together, then lifted up the plain green gown, with a linen smock beneath it. He suddenly realized it matched her eyes, and he hoped his brother didn't notice that.

She gasped, wearing a delighted smile. "Adam, thank you so much! Where did you purchase something ready-made?"

"The innkeeper's wife said she kept garments on hand for travelers in need."

"And I am in need," she said fervently.

She met his gaze, and there was a softness in her eyes that made him uneasy. But she said nothing else, only folded away the clothing and slid it into her saddlebag, all while controlling her horse with her knees. Adam was reluctantly impressed.

Traveling was much easier now that they'd left the moorlands for the plains of Yorkshire. Farm fields spread as far as the eye could see, dotted with the occasional castle, manor house, or monastery. Adam couldn't stop himself from glancing at Florrie frequently. Each new building in the distance was a cause for her to experience wonder, whereas Adam had to be wary for the hue and cry of being discovered. It had been three days since he'd taken Martindale's daughter—more than enough time for the villain to hear about it. Adam was ready to reveal the next move in his plan.

As they rode along, Robert came up beside Florrie. "Adam says you mean to become a nun."

Adam winced, but Florrie only smiled.

"I do," she said. "It has not yet been decided when I shall enter the convent."

Robert stared at her as if she were something he'd never seen before. "And you do not mind?"

She laughed. "You men seem to think women are used to the freedom to decide our own path. We are seldom allowed to choose our futures. If not marriage to a man I hardly know, then service to God. There is not much difference, when one is given no choice."

"But you give up the possibility of happiness and children," he said, his face full of disbelief. Adam glared at him, and Robert quickly amended, "I mean no disrespect, I just thought all women wanted to be mothers, and would be sad not to have the opportunity."

Her expression smoothed into bemusement. "No man has ever asked such forthright questions of me. 'Tis refreshing. But aye, I would have liked a child of my own. For now, I help my sister, Matilda, care for her babe. It eases me in its own way. But why should I mourn for the life I know I will not have? All that will do is make me—and everyone around me—miserable. I will not live like that. One can choose to be happy and content."

Such a thing was foreign to Adam's very nature. Choose to be content? When there had been wrongs done to his family? He would not be able to live with himself if he did nothing.

Robert seemed to be mulling the same thoughts, because Florrie had to say his name twice to capture his attention.

"Aye, my lady?"

"You are a younger brother, Robert. Do you not have to be content with your lot?"

"But I cannot change that."

She only cocked her head as she smiled at him.

"Oh, well, your point is that you cannot change what your family insists you do," he said.

"Exactly. And I am content."

"I am more than content to be the younger brother." Robert jerked his thumb at Adam. "He is not content."

"I have noticed that," Florrie said.

Adam ignored them.

She continued, "He feels the need to protect you in some way."

"Aye, that's true," Robert said agreeably.

Adam's shoulders were stiff with tension. He didn't like the discussion leading to things he didn't want raised in front of Florrie. Although he may trust her not to leave, he did not trust her with the truth of his family legacy.

"He tells me that your brother Paul has gone off to find his fortune."

"Aye, that's true."

Robert's usually glib smile was a shadow of itself, and Adam understood why. Robert and Paul, only a year apart by birth, had always been close. But Paul was a driven man, and Robert went along with whatever happened.

"You did not want to go with him?"

Robert shot her a grin. "I was *content* where I was."

They shared a laugh.

"And where was that?" she asked, her inflection staying as melodious as always.

Adam glanced sharply at Robert, but his brother had been well trained.

"You do not need to know such things, my lady," Robert chided her.

She heaved a sigh. "I can try. The mystery of your family calls to me. I shall keep asking questions, and you stop me when you need to."

"'Tis not a game, Florrie," Adam said, keeping his tone serious. "Much as we might trust you to remain with us, you are Martindale's daughter. You will not be permitted to know everything about us."

"Not even why you're so determined to challenge my father?"

Robert's usually cheerful face grew solemn. "'Tis too sad to speak of on such a beautiful day."

Florrie's open face showed every emotion. Adam could see worry and sympathy in her changeable eyes. She would show him pity if she knew everything, and he wouldn't stand for that.

Chapter 7

That evening, it was far easier to find a grove of trees to shelter them near a river. As they rode along the embankment, looking for the perfect place to conceal them, Adam could not miss Florrie's excited glances at the water. He guessed she wanted to bathe before she donned her new garments, but never once did she ask him for such a boon. She was *content* to wait for his word.

She made no sense to him. They ate their meal while the sun still hung low in the sky, savoring the duck Michael had snared by the river and then roasted. Florrie had plucked the feathers while Michael had prepared the fire and the roasting spit. Adam had watched their camaraderie with amusement. Michael did not give his loyalty easily, and even now he withheld his true attention. But Florrie was growing even on him.

After the meal, Adam was helpless to stop watching as Florrie licked her fingers to taste every last bit of juicy goodness. The sated expression on her face made his groin tight with desire. But he was used to ignoring his own discomforts, and he had more than enough reason to this time. Florrie was the daughter of his enemy—and she was to be a nun. That was enough reason for him to remain as distant from her as possible.

But then all his good intentions went up in smoke.

"Adam?" Florrie called from across the fire.

"Aye?"

"Might I bathe in the river tonight?" Before he could answer, she added quickly, "without a guard?"

"You may," he said. By the light of gratitude in her eyes, one would have thought he'd bestowed the greatest jewels of the kingdom upon her. When he should have been relieved to grant her something pleasant, he felt . . . guilty for doing so little. But she was his prisoner, and she was glad to be so. Why should he feel guilty that he could not offer her more?

Without asking any other favors, she found the soap and cloth in his saddlebag, took her new garments, and disappeared through the stand of low-hanging willow trees. Adam had deliberately chosen the place for the way the trees would offer her privacy for her bath.

And he hoped his brother never found out such a truth, or Adam would never hear the end of it.

The three men finished their meals in companionable silence. Bees buzzed through the humid evening air, and the setting sun gave the land a mellow orange glow. Adam felt . . . content.

Michael cleared his throat. "My lord, do you still plan to enter York on the morrow?"

"At dawn. I'll try not to wake Florrie, and I'll return before midmorning."

Suddenly, her scream rent the peaceful air, and all three men jumped to their feet. Robert and Michael moved north and south of her position to come in from above and below her on the river. Adam headed straight through the willow trees, his feet making no sound as he sought out each perfect footfall. It was second nature to him now. His ears were alert for the sounds of men or battle, but all he heard was Florrie's desperate breathing. He unsheathed both his sword and dagger.

When he came out on the embankment beside the river, she was laboring to run through thigh-deep water, awkwardly limping, sending terrified looks over her shoulder. Except for trees lining both sides of the river, he saw nothing else but her—and she was naked.

Her long brown hair streamed down her body, hiding one breast and curling around the other as if to frame it. It hung all the way to her hips, yet revealed the dark hair at the juncture of her thighs.

He'd never seen a woman entirely nude before. And it was probably a good thing, because he was having trouble remembering even how to speak. However would he have concentrated on anything else?

His voice sounded unused as he croaked, "Florrie?"

"Snake!" she screamed again, letting all within a hundred paces of them know what she feared.

He prayed that Robert and Michael heard her explanation and did not emerge to embarrass her further. But if she was embarrassed, her fear was worse, because when she finally reached land, she kept up her limping run straight at him. He dropped his weapons just as she flung herself into his arms as if she'd crawl up his body to flee the beast that terrorized her.

His hands were full of wet Florrie: a small, plump breast, the curve of her hip, then her smoothly muscled legs as she wrapped herself around him. He caught both of her thighs, felt the heated warmth of her womanhood pressed against his groin. Her breasts seared his chest as she flung her arms around his neck and held on. He put one arm beneath her hips and the other around her back. Damn, but his hands were shaking where they touched her wet flesh.

"Snake," she whispered against his neck, shaking.

Even her warm breath made him shudder.

Holding her against him, he stepped closer to the water and tried to focus on her fear rather than her nudity. "I see nothing except a stick floating in the current."

She stiffened. "What?"

He turned sideways, so that she could view the river without twisting her body.

Tentatively, she raised her head. He gently traced his finger down her cheek, pushing her hair aside so that she could see. He felt her sag when she saw the long black stick.

"It does look like a snake at a quick glance," he offered, trying to keep his breathing from betraying his desire.

"I only *gave* it a glance," she whispered, sagging against him in relief.

Her lips were so close to his bare throat that he stopped breathing altogether. They stood frozen as even more of the sun's rays disappeared beneath the horizon at his back.

Then she slowly looked up at him, and things became worse. Her breathing was still ragged; he could now see her breasts rise and fall, pink nipples hard little buds where they rubbed against his tunic. He wanted to taste them. Her eyes were wide and uncertain, even as they dropped to his mouth, just above hers.

"Oh my," she whispered.

Daughter of his enemy—future nun.

None of that mattered when she was warm and wet and naked in his arms, her ankles linked behind his back. He slid both trembling hands down to the round globes of her buttocks, and pressed her even tighter against him, his erection cradled against the depth of her. Her eyes half closed, and she shuddered.

Daughter of his enemy—future nun.

Adam was not a man to forget what really mattered. Disappointed in his behavior, he took a deep, fortifying breath, then lifted her away from his hips. She released her legs and slid to the ground to stand.

She kept herself pressed against him, and he knew that it was due to embarrassment, not passion. But such knowledge didn't seem to matter to his body. With his hands on her bare back, he enjoyed the feel of her wet hair tangled in his fingers. He wanted to pull her harder against him, revel in her breasts pillowed against his chest.

"Can anyone else . . . see me?" she whispered.

He bent and spoke softly, wanting to smell her hair. "Nay, 'tis only I."

She trembled, and he finally, reluctantly, removed his arms altogether.

"Turn around, please," she whispered.

He did. "Do you want me to stay?"

"I do not think it a good idea. Please accept my apology. I promise not to overreact again."

"There is nothing to apologize for." He cleared his throat as he picked up his weapons. "I will see you back at the fire."

Florrie could not stop staring at his broad back until he disappeared through the trees. And then she ran into the water and dove beneath, hoping to cool her heated flesh. Oh God, what had just happened? She understood nothing of what her body was feeling. She only knew that she seemed not to be able to think around Adam.

Coming to the surface, she rinsed her hair once more. She scrubbed at her body as if it would erase the feel of him—but nothing would. She'd shamelessly wrapped herself about him. What must he be thinking of her?

She already knew, she thought. He'd pushed himself between her thighs, and the sensation of that was something she'd never experienced before. She'd barely stopped herself from moaning over it. Was this . . . desire?

Thank God he'd been honorable enough to stop when she'd been unable to. She groaned and covered her face with wet hands. The situation was truly desperate when she thought her *kidnapper* more honorable than herself. How was she going to face him? And what if the other two men had seen her?

She took a long time dressing, donning her necklace with its family pendant, putting on her new smock and gown even though she would have to sleep in them. She washed her previous garments with a ferocity that did nothing to settle her uneasy mind, then spread them across shrubbery to dry.

At last, when she could barely see any longer, she made her way back through the willow trees to the fire—and Adam. She glanced at him, only to see that he was paying particular attention to stoking the fire. Was this just as awkward for him? Someone had spread out a blanket, and she sat on it as far away from him as she could.

But her hair was still wet, and she could not go to sleep like that. She still had Adam's comb, so she leaned closer to the fire and began to comb through the wet strands of her hair, spreading them so they could dry. She eventually faltered, for no one was speaking. She looked up to find Robert grinning at her.

"So how was the snake?" he asked, before dissolving into laughter as he exchanged a glance with Michael.

Florrie couldn't help but smile. "Very well, I was a fool many times over. Adam pointed out that it was a stick. Remember, I have never bathed in a river before."

"Regardless, you were wise to be aware of your surroundings," Michael said.

Though she was still embarrassed, she was glad they could tease her, happy with the camaraderie. Robert began to talk to Michael about a tournament he'd competed in, and she listened with interest.

Adam didn't join in. Through the veil of her hair, she studied him. His face, flickering with the firelight, was as impassive as ever, coldly beautiful in its severe way. His beard had still only grown in lightly, but it shadowed his face, making him look dangerous. What was he thinking? She realized that if he wanted to punish her father, he could easily abuse her, as many men would. But he was an honorable man.

How could she learn the truth about him?

At last, her hair was dry enough. Michael and Robert had already retired to their cloaks and blankets. When she stretched out on her side, Adam stiffened.

"Nay, 'tis warm enough tonight," she said quickly. "My cloak will give me enough comfort. Surely you would sleep better without me." She saw the lump that was Robert shake.

Adam gave his brother a frown before saying, "If you are certain . . ."

Relieved, she nodded. "I am. Good night, Adam."

Long minutes passed, and she found herself trying to get comfortable. There was a lump beneath her hip. Although the air was warm, the cold from the ground seemed to seep slowly into her. Several shudders escaped her. And then she felt footsteps behind her, knew immediately who it was even before her cloak was lifted.

Adam slipped in behind her. "I was cold," he said shortly.

She bit her lip to keep from chuckling, then sighed as the hot length of his body pressed up against her from behind. He felt so good. She barely kept herself from snuggling deeper into the cradle of his hips. She heard his voice rumble in her ear and she shivered, but not with the cold.

"Please accept my apologies for my behavior earlier," he said. "I have a man's weaknesses, and they are worse where you're concerned."

She turned her head to look back at him. "You must know I do not believe you were at fault. I provoked you shamelessly."

"You were frightened, and I took advantage of you."

She tried to smile. "Maybe we are . . . uneasy with each other because we are together all the time. I am not used to such a thing, and . . . I think you are not either."

"Though that may be true, 'tis a shameful thing to be unable to control oneself. I have never . . . had that problem before."

"And I am not helping you by being cold every night."

"Then we are in agreement that 'tis the constant togetherness that is bothering us."

She winced, wondering why that explanation made her feel bad. "Agreed. And we will stop apologizing for the past—and stop blaming ourselves," she added for his benefit.

"Very well." He lowered his voice until it was only a rumble against her back. "Sleep well."

With a sigh, she forced herself to relax, one muscle at a time, until at last the day's journey caught up with her, and she fell asleep.

* * *

Adam had long ago been trained to awaken at whatever hour he needed to. He opened his eyes well before dawn, surprised to find that instead of Florrie's back against him, she had turned in her sleep. She now snuggled against him, face first, one arm over his waist, one knee slid between his thighs. She breathed softly against his neck.

His body surged to life with a primitiveness that astounded him. He clenched every muscle and bit off a groan. Was this going to get worse each night? One morn he might wake up and find himself between her thighs!

But nay, he could not believe that. He was in control of his own body—even if she wasn't in control of her own. There was sensuality buried beneath her prim nun's surface, and he wondered if she even realized it. Very carefully, he slid his legs away from hers. She stirred and frowned, and as he looked down at her sweet face, he wanted to kiss her.

Suddenly, he felt eyes on him, and glanced up to see his brother sitting up, watching them. Adam froze for a moment, but Robert only grinned and shook his head.

Adam eased out from under the cloak and rolled to his feet. Ignoring his brother, he went through the trees to the stream to wash himself, using the first gray light of day to guide him. There were birds singing in the distance, and he tried to let the peace of the morn wash over him. It was difficult. He heard the crack of a twig and whirled, then relaxed.

Robert had followed him. "She is growing comfortable with you, big brother."

Adam knelt on the bank of the river and only gave Robert a frown before scrubbing his face. He shook the water away and said, " 'Tis natural. She is an innocent woman, who thinks this journey is nothing but an adventure."

"And what does she think of you?" Robert said, wearing a grin.

Adam couldn't quite meet his eyes. "She sees me as a protector, something she's obviously never had."

"And you've never had anyone to protect."

Adam's gaze shot to him, and for some strange reason, he felt angry. He didn't know why. "Did I not have you and Paul?"

Robert sat down on a log, hands dangling loosely between his knees. "Peace, brother. Since you were six you have protected us, to the detriment of any kind of normal life. I should have clarified what I meant: you have not had a woman to protect. It think it is different than you imagined it to be."

Adam wanted to stay on the defensive, but he found his shoulders sagging. He went to sit beside his brother.

"Different is not the right word," he said tiredly. " 'Tis far more challenging than I had ever imagined. She is . . . she is . . ."

"A woman. Now you see why I had to occasionally escape just to be with them."

"I have been with women," Adam said stiffly.

Robert chuckled. "I have to admit, I wondered about that. You were always so focused on our training, and on your work training others. Once I was *permitted* to hear about Martindale's role in the crime against our family, at least I understood your obsession."

" 'Tis not an obsession." This was a long-running argument, so his response was mild. "And you were given the information when you were old enough to understand it, just as I was."

Robert sighed. "That is in the past."

"And our future." Adam seldom allowed himself to think of the end of the journey, how he would feel, what he would do when at last he faced Martindale across their two swords. But now, in his mind's eye, he imagined Florrie there watching them, perhaps standing between them. He angrily shook that thought away. This was none of her concern. She could not understand his need for justice; she was a woman.

But wasn't that his current problem?

"But Florrie is in our *present*," Robert continued. "What will you do if she grows too attached to you?"

Though Robert didn't speak the words, Adam understood the rest of his concern—what if *Adam* grew too attached to *her*?

"I will not let it happen," Adam said coldly. "She is Martindale's daughter."

"I hope you remember that in the night."

Robert playfully hopped off the log, as if he expected Adam to reach for him. But Adam just stared at the mist that hung low over the dark water.

"I shall return from my errand before midmorning," Adam said. "Let her sleep as long as she wants."

Back at the campsite, Michael had already saddled his horse. After instructing the knight to hunt more game while he waited, Adam rode away, and within the hour he'd reached York. He had timed it well, for after riding past the homes lining the lane, he could see the gatehouse ahead, and the portcullis lifting up to admit people to the town. It was easy enough to find the one haberdashery, situated in the same vicinity as all the craftsmen and merchants.

Dismounting from his horse, he left it tied to the rail outside and went in. His message was already written, ready to be sent to London. In it, he revealed his identity to Martindale, his capture of Florrie, and his challenge to meet the man in combat. He didn't even consider that Martindale might betray his actions to the Crown. Nay, the man had too many of his own secrets to keep hidden.

Since he knew that the League of the Blade was

probably not looking for him, he decided to take a chance and use their messengers. It couldn't be helped—he needed Martindale's response as quickly as possible, and only the League had messengers waiting every fifteen miles between York and London.

Adam would have an answer by the end of the next day, when they reached Nottingham.

When Florrie awoke, she was surprised that the sun was already above the horizon. She was alone on the blanket, which *didn't* surprise her. But although she could see Robert, who seemed to be mending a leather strap, there was no one else in their encampment.

Robert's eyes met hers, and he gave her his usual cheerful grin. "A good morning to you, my lady."

"Florrie," she said without thinking. "Otherwise you'll speak too formally in front of strangers."

His grin widened. "You are learning the rules for disguising oneself quickly."

She shrugged, and looked about again.

"Michael is washing down at the river," he said. "He'll keep an eye out for snakes."

She blushed, even as she remembered that her screams had brought Adam to her. She found herself reliving the hard feeling of him within her arms, between her thighs. It was difficult to focus on Robert. "Oh, do not tease me any more. You cannot imagine how embarrassed I feel."

"Do not feel so. You're defenseless. I should teach you how to use a dagger."

"I cannot imagine Adam would approve. None of you would be foolish enough to trust me with a weapon."

"And speaking of my big brother, he should be returning soon."

Hesitantly, she asked, "Where did he go?"

"Into the nearest town. He had a message to send."

"To my father?"

Robert only shrugged. "He'll tell you what he thinks you should know."

"You obey him well."

"Have we not already discussed how we younger siblings treat the elder ones?"

She found herself giggling. "You are silly, Robert."

"When I want to be."

"All the time," said Michael from beyond the fire, as he approached.

Florrie stood up. "I will be back."

When she returned, Adam still hadn't arrived, and she found herself feeling uneasy. It wasn't that she feared being alone with Robert and Michael. It seemed to her that it was far more dangerous to be alone with Adam.

But he was always so careful about being followed on this journey. What if someone had captured him?

But by the time she finished the meal Michael

had prepared, Adam was riding toward them, looking as impassive as ever.

Florrie's overwhelming relief worried her. She didn't like feeling so concerned about him, so drawn to him. She was a woman who'd always relied on herself for the contentment that marked her life. She could not let a man who would only briefly be with her become so important. She had never given her family any power over her happiness; it must be the same way with Adam.

But her body didn't want to heed her mind, for it reacted to his presence with an awareness that was far too needy.

She stood with her hands on her hips as he approached. "So you sent a message to my father?" Adam glanced at his companions, but she quickly added, "They did not need to tell me. What else would I assume?"

Adam dismounted, and Michael led away his horse. It was interesting how much Michael took care of Adam, almost like a servant rather than an equal partner. Yet she knew Michael was also a knight, just as Adam was. Since Adam would call this journey a "mission," every mission needed a leader, she guessed.

Adam lifted a wineskin and drank, still watching her.

"Are you going to tell me?" she prodded.

"When there is something I think you should know, I will inform you."

He was reminding her of her place within this traveling party; she would do well to remember it. She nodded, letting him have his secrets. Slowly but surely, he was beginning to talk to her. She would discover the truth soon enough.

Chapter 8

After two days journey through drizzling rain, they made camp on the outskirts of Sherwood Forest long before the sun began to set. Adam saw Florrie give him a confused look, but he ignored it. She would find out soon enough why they were stopping early.

He thought he was getting better at ignoring other things where she was concerned. Since they spent so much of the day huddled in cloaks against the rain, he'd been able to avoid looking at her. When they stopped for meals and rests for the horses, she'd avoided his gaze as much as he'd avoided hers. They were both trying to be sensible about their attraction.

With the rain, no one had slept well the previous night. They'd had a hard time finding dry ground, and ended up sneaking into an abandoned barn at dark, too near a village for comfort. They hadn't been able to light a fire, and had been miserably damp all night.

But at last the rain had stopped, and the sun

was peaking out from beneath low gray clouds. Sherwood Forest provided welcome shelter. The trees were plentiful, oaks with twisting branches, birches with their pale white bark. They made a bold campfire, and spread all of their damp clothing about it to dry.

Adam watched Florrie sigh as she settled near the fire. He felt a twinge of conscience, knowing it was his fault she was on this journey, sharing their discomfort. But it could not be helped. He looked at his men. "I will return before nightfall."

She glanced up at him. "You are buying supplies?"

"Aye." And retrieving other things as well.

"Good luck," Robert said, watching him without smiling. "Are you certain one of us shouldn't accompany you?"

"I would rather you stay with Florrie."

She propped her head on her fist and sighed.

Adam knew that, now that he'd alerted Martindale, there was more of a chance that he could be in danger. But the League's message system was much more organized—and quicker—than any regular messenger Martindale could hire. Even if the man decided to respond to Adam's challenge by rescuing his daughter instead of meeting him in honorable combat, it would be at least another day before Martindale could have men nearby.

Adam reached Nottingham within an hour. He kept his cloak about him, his hat low over his brow, and took his time exploring the environment around the haberdashery. He didn't see anyone lurking about waiting. At last he entered the building to retrieve his message, only to be told that there *was* no message.

Adam questioned the man behind the counter quietly, as there were still customers purchasing hats in the store. But the man was adamant—Martindale's steward told the London messenger that there would be no reply to Adam's missive.

Did the man not care about his daughter? Or did he think Adam wouldn't dare harm her?

Or perhaps he assumed that Adam would do exactly what he was going to do: travel to London and issue the challenge in person. Martindale would have several days to prepare, but what did that matter? One was either prepared for combat, or not.

Of course, Martindale could be planning to rescue Florrie. Adam would take precautions, starting with his journey back to their encampment using a different path. It was almost completely dark by the time he returned, but the forest hid them well. He dismounted and led his horse inside.

Robert melted out of the trees before Adam reached the fire, then accompanied him the last several yards.

"Good trip?"

"Interesting."

Michael stood up as they approached. "Interesting?" he echoed.

Then all three men glanced at Florrie. She was seated on a log, holding her skirts wide. Her hair must have dried, for she'd pulled it back away from her face. She was watching Adam carefully, waiting. And then he decided that her reaction to the news would tell him more than keeping it a secret.

"Yesterday morn," Adam began, "I sent a message to your father, revealing that I had you, and wished to challenge him."

She slowly stood up. She didn't look worried, as he thought she might have.

"And you hoped to hear from him today?" she asked. "Surely 'tis much farther to London."

"The messengers I used are organized and swift. They reached London yesterday evening, delivered their message, and returned to your father this morn for a reply." He hesitated, not wanting to hurt her, but not seeing how he could avoid it. "Martindale chose not to send one."

Instead of revealing confusion or tears, her expression remained strangely impassive. She wasn't surprised at all by this news.

It was true that Martindale had never treated her well, kept her in service to her sisters, planned to send her away when he had no more need of her. But Adam didn't believe that she was inconsequential to her father; Adam had done his research. He knew Martindale was arrogantly protective of his possessions, including his daughters. And Florrie was his.

Could she know something of her father's past, the secrets he held? Then Adam would have to discover them. It was time to begin using his persuasive talents on her. He could talk to her more, reveal a bit about himself to induce her to do the same.

But he wouldn't resort to seduction—he could not imagine using her in such a way. There were other methods of persuasion. Florrie was friendly and talkative. She would eventually slip and say what he needed to hear.

At last, Florrie seemed uneasy with the silence. She clasped her hands together and looked at the fire. "I wonder what my father is thinking. After all, you could be . . . hurting me."

Robert exchanged a troubled glance with Michael, who only looked away and kicked at the ground, as if it wasn't his place to be involved. Then he silently led Adam's horse away.

Adam approached the fire and sat down, reaching for a wineskin. "Or he could assume I would be too intelligent to do so. I am using you against him, which means I would take care of you. But he could have any number of plans against us, which is why we must be even more careful from now on. He now knows the general vicinity we're traveling. How does he react when he's threatened?"

She sank down beside him, wrapping her arms about her knees. "If you're speaking militarily, of course I do not know. But 'tis no secret that my father has a terrible temper. He could be waiting to attack you when you reach the city."

"But if I have *you*, 'twould be foolish of him to risk your life."

She said nothing.

"You cannot think your own father wants you dead," he said softly.

She gave him a swift glance. "Nay, not that. I am still . . . valuable in many ways. But protecting himself comes first in his mind."

"Why? What does he feel so strongly about protecting?"

She hesitated for only a moment, and he thought she might be about to reveal something he could use. But at last, she shook her head. "Protecting his life, his position. His power is all important to him. And you're threatening it. Perhaps he's taking this to King Henry."

"Nay, he would not do that," Adam said with conviction. "He doesn't want made public what exists between my family and his—yours."

Florrie noticeably flinched as he tied her to her family, and against him. She looked at him with imploring eyes. "Tell me what it is, Adam."

And for a moment, he considered it. Blood had been spilled, his family destroyed. She might be so outraged by the truth that she would no longer speak so easily to him. Nay, it was best to wait for the right time.

He looked away from her, back to the fire, and reached for the meat kept hot on a spit for him. "I cannot speak of it now," he said softly. And because she might take his silence better, he added, " 'Tis too painful."

Compassion flooded her eyes, obviously driving away her doubts. She put a hand on his arm, and it took everything in him not to flinch. But not because of the problems between their families; nay, when she touched him, he didn't care who she was, only that he desired her.

Michael silently returned from the horses and looked evenly at Adam. "You've made your presence known in Nottingham," he said.

Adam nodded. "Now that the marquess has not responded, I sense possible problems. We cannot remain here." He stood up, relieved when Florrie's hand dropped away from him. "If anyone is now pursuing me, I want them mislead. Michael, I bought dry blankets in town. Let us leave the wet ones behind."

Michael and Robert exchanged slow smiles.

Florrie looked at all three of them with a bewildered expression. "Why would we leave blankets?"

"While you're packing away your belongings," Adam said, "we'll show you."

Only a brief time later, they stood near the horses, ready to journey in the night. The moon was shining, and if they kept to the edges of the forest, they'd be able to see well enough to travel for several hours yet.

Florrie watched in surprise as Michael and Robert arranged the four blankets in mounds around the dying fire. By the low light, it almost seemed as if someone slept there. She met Adam's gaze and gave him a slow, impressed smile.

"Robert, remain behind for several hours," Adam said. "Your report will prove interesting."

Florrie felt like the night would never end. They'd been journeying for several hours after dark, and the horses had to pick their way slowly over tree roots and rocks and around mud holes. But they seemed well trained for such work, never once giving any of the riders a problem.

She had plenty of time to think. Had she made a mistake not showing more emotion at her father's apparent rejection? Part of her had thought he'd send a blustering letter of threats since Adam had one of his "possessions."

She'd been taken aback by the absolute silence. Adam was so certain that a response could have come had her father chosen to send it, that she had no choice but to believe him. Though Adam challenged her father, she already knew that he was the more honorable of the two men.

And she was used to being ignored; she would not let it bother her. Most of the time, it freed her to do what she wanted, within limits. And right now, it allowed her to be traveling the English countryside, on an adventure that she'd never have again. Because when her father had her back, he might finally have had enough of her, and she would be hastened off to the convent.

But as she rode in the moonlit darkness, listening to ancient trees rustle on one side of her, seeing farmland stretch away endlessly on the other side, she couldn't imagine being confined inside four high walls.

She glanced at Adam who rode straight in the saddle, his eyes seeing everything. At the convent, she would never see men again—would never see him.

Would this adventure turn against her, make her remember for the rest of her life what she'd be missing? Nay, she had always known what she'd miss; she wanted good memories to cherish.

At last he called a halt, and they made camp in silence. Were they thinking about Robert, she thought, glancing to the north every so often? Was Adam worried about his little brother? Or did men think differently?

She and Adam slept side by side again, the wet ground from the night before an unpleasant memory. The shared warmth between them always made her relax.

She wasn't sure how long she slept before she heard their voices. Robert had returned, and Adam was no longer beside her. She guessed that they would speak more freely if they thought she slept, so she didn't open her eyes.

"You were right, Adam," Robert said, sounding tired. "You were followed."

Florrie tensed, but Adam's tone was just as calm as ever.

"I saw no one as I left Nottingham," he said, "and if they'd followed me immediately, they would have attacked us."

"Then they tracked us," Robert continued. "But I do not actually know who they were. There were only two of them, and they didn't attack. I watched from up in a tree, and heard their curses when they discovered our ruse."

"Two men?" Adam said, his voice contemplative. "Surely Martindale would have sent more."

Michael said, "But perhaps they had to spread out to find you?"

"So Martindale's men could be all over the countryside," Robert said, not sounding too bothered by that.

Awfully confident, wasn't he? Florrie thought.

"I still have a hard time believing he could send men north so quickly," Adam mused.

"Unless they were already here," Robert said, "at a nearby castle or manor house. He has property all over England. Only a swift messenger would have to be sent to alert his soldiers."

"A good thought, Robert."

Robert sounded exasperated. "Adam, 'tis not necessary to compliment me as if you're still training me. I know I'm your little brother, but I am also a—"

He broke off, and Florrie almost groaned. Also a what? Knight? Perhaps they'd misled her about their titles, and Adam really was still training him. She lay still, listening intently.

"It bothers me that we were found," Adam said.

"But they didn't trail us farther," Michael added. "We are not even going directly south anymore, as we would be expected to do to reach London."

"Do you think Martindale has Bladesmen working for him?" Robert asked.

In the somber silence that followed, Florrie found herself feeling an old excitement she'd thought buried. Were they actually discussing the League of the Blade? She'd always been told they were nothing but legend, tales to make a fire-lit evening exciting. But these men spoke of Bladesmen as if they'd actually met some of them.

When she was eight, confined to her bedchamber for many long weeks because her leg was broken, her nurse had lifted her spirits with tales of the League. As an adult, Florrie had made herself leave such fantasy behind, because no one was going to rescue her. Yet still, it was wonderful to hear that legends could be the truth.

"If Bladesmen are working for Martindale," Adam said impassively, "there is nothing we can do about it. And Martindale would not even realize it himself, due to their vows of secrecy. Right now we must concentrate on the fact that we are being followed. We should try to spend more evenings under shelter, giving us more defensible positions. I will have the two of you circle back occasionally during the day, to look for people following us. But that will exhaust the horses, so we'll have to take the most remote paths available, and not always in a direct line to London."

There seemed to be nothing else to say, and they fell silent as they returned to their various blankets. Michael must be taking first watch, because she already heard Robert's deep, steady breathing. Adam finally slid in behind her. Florrie stretched and blinked, turning to look at him drowsily over her shoulder.

"Go back to sleep," he murmured.

She smiled and thought to relax back on her blanket, but suddenly, misleading him that she'd been asleep bothered her. "I heard what the three of you were discussing. So you think that my father sent men."

He sighed and shook his head. " 'Twould appear so. Are you pleased?"

She gave that thought. "I should be, I know. But if they capture me, they'll return me home. I do not want to leave just yet."

"But now is when our journey is becoming truly dangerous," he warned.

"And I find that I don't care." She smiled at him with relish.

His dark eyes seemed to lighten as his gaze took in her face, then centered on her mouth. Would he kiss her? Did she want him to? For a suspended moment, as her shoulder leaned into his chest, they stared at each other. Her breathing felt too fast, her heart seemed to find a new rhythm. She felt his hand on her hip, and then it slowly slid up her waist. Bending over her, he put his face against her neck, inhaling deeply. She gave a quiet moan and rubbed her cheek against his soft hair.

But when she felt his fingers brush the underside of her breast, she stiffened without thinking, so shocked by the pleasurable tension that was building inside her.

He froze, and suddenly she was desperate for him to continue. She brought her hand up to his head and held him against her, threading her fingers through his hair, while her body arched as if she could make him caress her.

"Florrie." He spoke against her neck, her name a whisper on his lips.

She shuddered and turned her head. Her cheek slid along his short beard and then his breath was on her lips. She waited, wanting his kiss, ready to pull him to her.

And then his mouth pressed to hers, several gentle, sweet kisses that made her forget everything but him. Pleasure shot through her, and only intensified when his hand at last captured her breast. She trembled and quaked, feeling him knead her through her garments, as sensation flooded her body and centered between her restless thighs. This was glorious and unexpected, and at last she knew why men and women craved each other.

She realized that he was watching her, and felt no embarrassment. Slowly his kisses deepened, parting her lips. And then she felt his tongue seeking entrance. She hadn't imagined such a bold kiss. His mouth captured her moan even as she yielded to his persistence. He took her open mouth in a kiss that was hot and deep and wildly exciting, so unexpected.

His hand moved between her breasts, caressing, tweaking her nipples through the bodice of garments that she desperately wished were gone. To her surprise, his other hand slid beneath her body, then across her belly. She shuddered as he cupped between her thighs, pressing through her skirt. His touch was like a spark igniting a flame through her body. She wanted more. His other hand tugged at her neckline as if testing what clothing could be pulled down. She felt him touch the pendant she always wore—

And then he froze, his body so stiff it was as if they'd never enjoyed a single caress. His warm, pleasurable hands left her. He slowly lifted his head, looking past her face, his expression one of shock and growing darkness as he came up on his elbow.

"What is it?" she whispered, the first blush of shame overtaking her. Did he think her sinful now? Was she supposed to resist and prove herself a true lady?

And then she realized he hadn't let go of her pendant. He was lifting it into the firelight, which made the Martindale crest, a rearing dragon on a shield, glitter.

And then he met her gaze, and for a moment, she saw pain in those dark blue depths. She rolled onto her back, touching his chest, desperate to find out why he was looking at her that way.

"'Tis my family crest," she said softly, not hiding her confusion. "You know who I am, who my father is—why should this bother you?"

He sat up and she did the same, facing him. He reached beneath his own shirt and drew out a leather pouch that hung around his neck. He loosened the lacings and spilled into his hand another Martindale pendant on a chain.

Chapter 9

Florrie stared at the mark of her family in confusion. This was a bigger, heavier pendant, the sort a man would wear. And Adam's hand briefly trembled beneath it, which was almost frightening.

"Where did you get this?" she demanded.

From across the fire, Robert groaned as he sat up. "Adam, just tell her the truth. I am going to sleep with the horses, where I can have true peace."

Florrie didn't watch him leave; she couldn't take her gaze from Adam, whose face had gone so cold. What had happened to the man who'd kissed her so tenderly, touched her as if she were the most delicate of creatures?

He stared at her.

"Tell me," she said firmly. "I need to know."

"When I had but six years of age," he said slowly, "I enjoyed hiding from my parents."

She didn't know how this connected to their matching pendants, but she was willing to hear anything about him, anything that would help her understand what drove him to risk his life.

"There was a coffer in their room that was my favorite hiding place." He was looking at the fire now, but seeing the past, for his gaze was unfocused. "One day, I hid there, waiting to be discovered, and ended up falling asleep. When I awoke hours later, I heard an argument between my father and another man. My mother was crying."

Florrie's stomach was tense with a terrible premonition. She didn't want to hear the rest—but she needed to.

"So . . . I lifted the lid the tiniest bit. My father and a stranger were struggling before the fire." His eyes narrowed in concentration, staring at another fire many years later. "I remember so vividly the flash of firelight between them, the shadows of their bodies, then the glitter of a dagger."

She couldn't help the gasp that escaped her, and she covered her mouth with a trembling hand. In her mind, she chanted like a prayer, *Oh God, Oh God*.

"He killed my father right before my eyes." Adam's voice was dispassionate, almost as if he spoke about a stranger's death. "I dropped the lid in terror, and then I heard my mother scream. I was too afraid to look, too afraid to reveal myself. I never heard the man leave. When I finally lifted the lid again, they were both dead. I climbed out, looking at the blood that was seeping through the woven mat on the floor." His voice hardened. "And then I saw this."

Stunned, sickened, Florrie stared again at the heavy pendant he suddenly held before her face.

"Recognize it?" he demanded with sarcasm.

He lifted her own chain again, and she had to move closer or have it break in his grip.

He leaned toward her. "Your father murdered my parents."

She was trapped by the pendant in his fist, by the passion and determination in his cold eyes. Tears stung her.

"I—I cannot believe my father a murderer," she whispered. But was she protesting too quickly? She knew he was a ruthless man.

Adam suddenly let the pendant go, and she sank back on her hands.

"The man had brown hair like yours," he said. "Solid and stocky, not tall."

She bit her lip.

"Martindale was seen secretly leaving the castle. He was an open enemy of my parents because of old political issues." He lifted the pendant in his grip. "Does he give these out like trinkets, that just anyone would wear it? Or are they only for family?"

Nausea suddenly rose within her as she remembered the solemn occasion when her father had granted her the pendant on her sixteenth birthday.

And she thought about a frightened little boy, watching his parents killed, finding this same pendant.

"I put it in the purse on my belt," he said, "not even realizing what I'd done. I never told anyone I had it, and years later, as an adult, I realized that if I'd have shown it to someone that night, it might have been enough proof to take to the king the accusation of murder against Martindale. So 'tis *my* fault he wasn't punished then."

Oh God, Adam even blamed himself for his parents' murder going unsolved. She suddenly crawled away from the fire as her stomach heaved.

She returned weaker, tired, full of sorrow. She raised watery eyes to Adam, who watched her without expression. He was a man who'd spent his life waiting for vengeance. Did he even realize that?

"I—" Her throat seemed to close up. "I know not what you want from me."

"Anything in your father's behavior that might seem suspicious!" he commanded.

She gaped at him.

In a painful flash, she remembered caring for her ill father, his raving during the fever, the terrible secret he wanted no one to know. Had Adam's parents discovered it? Would her father actually kill someone to protect an ancient family scandal?

But whatever had happened long ago, she had seen what guilt and bitterness did to a man. Would Adam become the same way?

She couldn't let that happen! More than ever, she had to make sure Adam and her father never met at all, let alone attempted combat. Because if Adam realized he could not have justice, what would he do? Florrie felt as if fate had put her there, trapped between two men. She would save Adam's soul—perhaps his life—by whatever means she could contrive.

But going against a man, even for his own best interests, was so very foreign to her. She had always been forced to go along with others, to be content whenever her life was altered on someone's whim.

But now, looking at Adam, she felt a sense of power and purpose like she had never known before. She would save him.

Adam stared at Florrie, at her pale face and tear-filled eyes. She believed the evidence implicating Martindale, that much was evident. And it obviously hurt her to know such a thing about her father, regardless of how he had treated her.

And Adam hated to be the one to reveal it all to her. There was a sympathetic pain inside him that he hadn't imagined feeling for her.

She rubbed her wet eyes. "I cannot imagine a reason that . . . someone would kill . . . your father, and especially not . . . your mother."

"Someone?" he echoed. He heard his own bitterness, saw the way she flinched. But he had a right to be bitter; his parents were wiped away, his childhood destroyed by one man.

"Can you not say who it was, Florrie?" he asked softly.

"My f-father."

And then she started crying, hiding her face as if embarrassed.

He suddenly felt like a monster. It wasn't her fault, and it wasn't his. They were only the innocents who had to suffer. He put Martindale's pendant back in the pouch at his neck. And still she cried, her body so forlorn as it shook.

He reached for her then, and though she stiffened, he pulled her across his lap and put his arms around her. She collapsed against his chest and wept even more. He held her slight, trembling body and found himself kissing the top of her head, caressing her arms and back as if somehow he could make everything right between them.

But that could never be. A terrible murder stood between them.

She quieted at last, and he realized she'd fallen into an uneven sleep. He laid her back on the blanket, brushed a curl from her cheek, and regretted the wet tearstains he'd caused. Then he looked up and saw Robert at the edge of the clearing. His brother watched solemnly, which was so very unlike him.

Adam motioned for him, then pointed to the

blanket across the fire. Saying nothing, Robert came over and lay down, still giving Adam occasional searching glances. Robert must have heard much of it, and Adam felt bad about that, because Adam didn't often speak so emotionally about what he'd seen when he was a child, what had given him nightmares for so many years. He hadn't wanted to burden his brothers.

Paul had left before Adam could tell him the identity of their parents' killer. Adam had been told Martindale's name on his twenty-first birthday, but Robert had been nineteen, Paul eighteen. He'd thought them too young to know, too young to feel this desire for justice. In some ways he was glad he'd held it inside, for Paul wasn't tainted with the knowledge. And Adam had tried to spare Robert, had wanted to do this alone, but Robert wouldn't hear of it. And neither would Michael, who came from a long line of knights loyal to the Keswick earldom.

At last, he lay down behind Florrie and pulled her close against him. He thought *he* was comforting *her*, but he wasn't even certain about that.

Deep inside him was a tight little feeling of dread. Could Florrie know something important—yet not realize it? Adam was not about to angrily confront her; that would solve nothing.

Talking would. He'd already begun to coerce her with words, with the exchange of the stories of their lives. Such persuasion would work on a softhearted woman like Florrie.

Because any other form of persuasion would cost him too much. He'd almost seduced her tonight, little caring that he had to remain alert for the men who followed them, that his brother was nearby, that Michael could return at any moment.

Florrie was like a fever in his blood, an obsession he was trying desperately to fight. And kissing her, tasting her mouth and her sweet response, touching her body—all of that had only made everything worse.

Yet he wanted to experience it all again, regardless of the terrible tragedy between them. He was so disappointed in himself. He was glad she knew the truth of her father's crimes, for surely she would want to avoid any kind of intimacy with him.

If only he could link her with her father in his mind, but he couldn't. She must be nothing like the man he'd grown up hating, the man he'd spent the last few years learning everything about. Florrie was kind to a fault, innocent, and Adam himself was the one trying to take her innocence away. Somehow, he had to stop himself.

He fell asleep leaving several inches between their bodies, praying that Florrie would know it was for the best.

Adam awoke before dawn to the sounds of Michael moving about camp, preparing for their departure. Robert was slowly rising, giving Adam a strange look—

And then Adam looked down at Florrie, who was once again curled up in his arms, facing him, her arms about his waist.

"The truth doesn't seem to have changed her feelings for you," Robert said softly.

"When she awakens, she will think differently," Adam answered.

He shook her gently, and she moaned and burrowed closer.

"Florrie."

Her eyes fluttered and opened, staring up at him. She searched his face, her expression confused, until her memories returned. The pain was there, but not as great. Now she looked sad, but as if she'd come to terms with it.

"Good morning," she said, blushing a little as she sat up and disentangled herself from him. "I—I guess I have no control of myself when I sleep."

He almost said he didn't mind—but that would be encouraging her, and it wouldn't be right to do that. He let her rise to her feet without his help.

"Is there a stream nearby?" she asked.

He shook his head. "We have enough wine and water in our skins until we reach another." He glanced at Michael. "By midday?"

Michael nodded. "We shall travel west of Nottingham, almost into Derbyshire, rather than toward London. We'll confuse anyone following us—and replenish our water supplies."

Florrie nodded, then excused herself to go several paces into the forest. Adam remained nearby, and as she returned, she was startled to see him.

Understanding flooded her face. "Surely if the men following us had found us, they would have attacked?"

Adam shrugged. "We do not know their mission. We must remain cautious. You should keep your hood up from now on."

She sighed. "I hope the weather does not become too hot."

She lowered her gaze from him and went to her horse to open one of the saddlebags. She hadn't been able to wash, so he wasn't certain what she—

And then her chain and pendant dropped into the bag and disappeared. So she'd decided not to wear the crest of her family. It was not as if he could forget about it; perhaps she didn't want to be reminded.

They began the day's journey very cautiously, taking roads that seemed more like deer paths. They were constantly wary of being followed, and when they came upon another traveler, they spoke little.

It wasn't until they stopped for a midday meal, in a field hidden from the road, that Florrie fixed Adam with an intent stare.

"Would you mind continuing the story of your childhood?"

He looked up from the dried apple pieces that he was eating. "I am surprised you want to talk about what Martindale's crime led to."

"I have always faced the worst things that happened," she said simply. "I cannot exist by pretending everything is sunny. But even when bad things happen, I have to keep going on with my life, to make it the best it can be."

Adam hid his amazement. Many other women would be denying the facts or too upset to talk about them. But Florrie was not like most other women. She made it so easy to admire her, reluctant though he may feel.

Michael glanced between them, shook his head, and went off to care for the horses. Robert lay on his side, propped his head on his hand, and listened with open curiosity.

Florrie felt hot with embarrassment, ill with sorrow—but she was also determined to understand the path Adam had taken because of the past. "So what happened to three orphaned little boys? Did other family members take you in?"

He shook his head. "We had no other family."

She had been hoping for some happiness in his life. But he wouldn't want her pity, though it burned in her chest. She waited.

When he looked into the fire, she had her first inkling of unease. He didn't want to talk about this part of his life. Was it so very terrible? Or something else?

"If not family . . ." she prodded.

"My father's friend, Sir Timothy, took us away to protect us. At that time, though some suspected your father, there was no proof, no motive."

He gave her a meaningful glance, and she pretended she didn't understand his subtle query about her father.

"And, of course, I did not know any of this," he continued. "Sir Timothy became our foster father, and he treated us well."

A great breath of relief left her lungs.

"But we had to remain in hiding, in case there were plans to eliminate the whole family."

"In hiding? Did you leave the country?"

"Nay, we lived with Sir Timothy in a very remote castle, away from contact with the rest of the world. We spent our days in military training, our evenings on more formal studies."

"But . . . you were so young. You did not play?"

"Our toys were wooden swords and daggers. Is it not often so with boys?"

He said it almost smiling, but she thought she sensed curiosity, as if he was actually asking her. But of course he was—he was raised in a very sheltered manner. Now she knew why he had traveled so little. His guardian had been waiting for the boys to be old enough to protect themselves.

She knew that most people never traveled far in their lives. But the family of a nobleman had to move from home to home, overseeing the bailiff in charge, using up the foodstuffs so they could be replenished. And just being with Adam, she knew he had not been raised by peasants. His speech and manner betrayed his well-educated background. He would have traveled—but the death of his parents loomed over his whole life. It still controlled him even now.

But it was good that he was talking about it, trying to release its bitter hold. Bitterness was already inside him, like a disease that held a person and never let go, only sank deeper until one couldn't get rid of it.

"Aye," she said at last, "boys like to mimic the heroic knights in their lives. And you had Sir Timothy to follow."

He nodded, a small smile curling one corner of his mouth. "He is a good man, and he cared for us even though it put him in danger."

"Did his wife act as your foster mother?"

"He had no wife."

Robert rolled on his back and muttered, "No women at all."

Florrie stiffened and focused on Adam's brother. "Pardon me?"

Adam shrugged. "He chose not to marry. He said it was because he never found the right woman. As I grew older, I always worried that having to care for us made him too fearful to bring a woman into such danger."

Although that made Florrie's heart ache for this wonderful man she'd never met, she could not help glancing at Robert. He'd said "no women at all" with long-suffering disappointment, as if it was about more than Sir Timothy's lack of a bride. Was it only bitterness about not having a foster mother? But Adam had skillfully deflected her from questioning his brother, and she let it go—for now.

"You have already told me you did not travel," she said slowly. "Now I understand why. So you only knew that castle, and the people within it."

He nodded.

"But surely such restriction began to chafe when you grew older."

Robert harrumphed and folded his arms over his chest. When Adam rolled his eyes, she felt amused, but the effort to smile was still too difficult. Her father's sins were weighing heavily on her soul.

"We understood the need for caution," Adam said firmly.

"Not me," Robert said. "I escaped."

Adam shot him a warning frown.

Robert came up on his elbow. "'Tis no secret that I have never understood your absolute dedication to . . . how we were raised. You know I admire Sir Timothy, but he was often swayed by others."

Swayed by others? What others? Florrie wondered with fascination. She hoped in their argument, they would forget her presence.

"I did not allow you to escape for long," Adam said dryly.

"So you were sent after him?" Florrie asked in surprise. "Sir Timothy allowed that?"

"I had seventeen years by then. Sir Timothy felt it best that I begin to prove my readiness. I was humbled that I'd earned his trust."

This time Robert snorted and fell back on his blanket. "You always had their trust. You were the good boy."

Their trust. Again, he'd referred to more than one person, not just Sir Timothy. It almost sounded as if they were raised by a group of men.

"So was it dangerous chasing after your brother?" she asked almost playfully.

"Oh, dangerous," Robert said sarcastically. "There were women everywhere."

She covered her mouth, surprised that she'd almost laughed aloud. She liked Robert's sense of humor.

"It could have been dangerous," Adam said with a sigh.

He wasn't offended by his brother, which Florrie liked to see.

"You were fifteen, Robert, and we look like our father," Adam continued. "Who knows what trouble you could have found yourself in if you'd been recognized? Or if you'd been challenged by other boys? Thankfully, I got you away before any of that happened."

"You got me away before the dairymaid could—" Robert broke off and glanced at Florrie.

Was that a blush staining his cheeks?

"I may have only had sisters," she said, "but there were many boys living in our castle or in the village. Boys are definitely preoccupied with girls. My sisters sometimes could not escape them."

"But not you?" Adam asked.

She smiled. "I was the good friend, the one boys confided in. I did not mind. Life was much more peaceful that way."

"They wanted your help with your sisters," he said, shaking his head.

"Aye, but they were good companions, too."

"Like us?" Robert said, suddenly smiling again.

His moods were so mercurial, Florrie thought with exasperation. "I am not so certain good companions begin with a kidnapping, but I might be willing to overlook your flaws."

Chapter 10

For the rest of the afternoon, Adam made sure their small party wound through the Bardon Hills of Leicestershire, hoping to confuse anyone who might have picked up their trail. The Charnwood Forest flowed through hills, and he led them west for several miles through the trees, then backtracked to the south dragging branches behind them to disguise their trail.

That evening, he decided to make good on his promise to give them more protection while they slept. After dusk, they crept into a farmer's barn, overly warmed by an ox, a mule, and several goats. Though the animals gazed at them with interest, they seemed to take no other notice. Moonlight streamed in several small windows, giving them enough light. He sent Michael and Robert out to scout their surroundings, and then they would each take turns keeping watch through the night.

Adam looked around at the small barn, with its

piles of straw below, and a loft above filled with hay. Florrie hugged herself and looked up at the loft uncertainly.

"You and I will sleep up there," he said.

Before she could answer, they heard the sudden deep barking of a dog somewhere outside.

"Damn, the men must have strayed too close to the cottage," Adam said in a low voice. "We have to leave at once." He grabbed the reins of her horse and led the two animals toward the door.

But it swung open before they reached it, and Florrie caught his arm. A man carrying a torch and an ax stood there. He brandished them both menacingly. Florrie gave an exaggerated cry and flung herself against Adam, surprising him.

"Oh, I knew we could find no rest!" she cried forlornly, then began to weep with great sobs.

Though he already had a dagger hidden in his hand, Adam held her instead of defending her.

The farmer's broad, creased face was gradually changing from fury and fear to wary curiosity. But he didn't lower the ax.

"Who are ye and what are ye doin' in me barn?" he demanded.

"Sir," Adam said with hesitation, "me wife and me could afford to stop no place else for the night. I could not make her sleep outdoors again, sir, not in her condition."

He felt her stiffen in his arms, but her weeping only lessened as if she were too exhausted to do more.

The farmer looked beyond them to their horses. "There be only . . . two of you?"

Just as Adam nodded, Florrie suddenly swooned, giving him enough warning to scoop her into his arms. She gave the perfect approximation of being dazed.

She looked around with incomprehension, then saw the farmer. She cringed against Adam without speaking, as if the stranger frightened her.

The farmer lowered his ax and moved from foot to foot. "I never have hurt a woman," he grumbled. "No cause to look at me like that."

"She means it not, sir," Adam said. "We've just been travelin' so long, tryin' to start a new life where there's more work."

But that was a mistake. "A big man like ye should have no trouble," he said, suspicious again.

Adam nodded. "Me wife cannot take the cold, sir. I hear 'tis pleasant down by the Channel, and I'm a good soldier."

"Young fools always think the livin' is better somewhere else," the farmer mumbled as if to himself. He shook his head. "Well, ye better come inside and be fed, or me wife will have me head for leavin' a girl out here."

"Nay, sir, we could not be imposin'," Adam said quickly. "With your kind permission, the barn will be fine on a summer's night."

"Get in the cottage. She's cookin' stew, and she's known for the dish clear to Bosworth."

Adam gently set Florrie on her feet. "Let me remove the saddles, sir, to ease the horses. I'll return to see to them after your kind offer of a meal."

Helpless to do anything else, Adam finally strode before the farmer toward the cottage. It couldn't be much more than a single room, made of wood with clay mixed with straw in the cracks to keep out the drafts. Florrie hung on his arm.

Whispering, she said, "You forgot one thing."

"What is that?"

"You are speaking with a common accent," she said, "but I was never good at mimicry. I will give my origins away if I speak too much."

"Then play shy and let your husband do the talking."

She groaned.

"Is the mistress all right?" the farmer asked.

"Simply tired, sir," Adam called back respectfully.

Florrie felt like the biggest fool, because people who had so little wanted to help them. The cottage was only one room with a loft above, and she could see two little faces peering down on them. The farmer's wife stood near the fireplace, stirring a small caldron that was hung over a fire. There was a scarred table with two benches, a simple bed along one wall, and a cupboard with her cooking spread across the top. Drying herbs and vegetables hung from the ceiling beams, and Adam had to duck to miss them.

He pulled his cap from his head, still gripping Florrie's arm. She leaned her head against his shoulder and peered at the curious woman.

"This is me wife, Mistress Ascham," said the farmer.

Mistress Ascham was dressed in a plain, clean gown with an apron pinned to her waist and a linen cap covering her hair. She bobbed her head. "Guests," she said, smiling. "I *thought* the dog's bark was more excited than scared."

Florrie couldn't help glancing up at Adam. The dog had sounded ferocious to her. They had passed it tied up next to the front door. Though it growled, at a word from its master, it hadn't moved.

"They're travelers movin' to a new town," Master Ascham said, putting his ax on pegs in the wall and thrusting the torch into the fire. "No money for an inn."

"Then sit at our table and share our food." Mistress Ascham motioned to the table. "James and Jasper, come set out the bowls."

Florrie saw that Adam didn't try to hide his amazement as this family accepted them without suspicion. His expression came across as a man who couldn't believe goodness might be shown them. He'd lived a guarded, protected life, where he'd obviously been taught that one should never trust strangers.

Florrie prided herself that her abilities had helped their situation. She'd always been able to think and react quickly. What honest man could resist a frightened woman? And Adam's idea to make her with child had been the final thing Master Ascham had needed to hear.

After she and Adam sat down side by side on a bench, she gratefully washed her hands when Mistress Ascham passed her a basin, soap, and a drying cloth. James and Jasper, two little boys of near the same age and the same sandy hair scurried back and forth from the cupboard to the table, bringing wooden bowls, spoons, two plain cups, and two tankards. She noticed that the farmer and his wife had no drinking vessels before them. Florrie realized that the Ascham boys had given their parents' only tankards to the guests. She was feeling terrible about taking advantage of such a sweet family, and wished they could leave money, but then the Aschams would know they'd been lying. All she could do was accept the hospitality.

And watch the show that was Adam. He was a totally different person, and she guessed even less like his real self. The noble, reserved man was the one she'd been traveling with, not this jovial, overly cheerful stranger. Once again, he introduced her as Katherine, and this time he was Edmund. "Edmund" was wonderful with children, and had the little boys giggling with his stories of mistakes he'd made training his horse. The family clearly had never been able to afford the ownership of a horse, and the fact that Adam had two reduced the boys to awe.

Florrie would have loved to join in the conversation, but her "shyness" prevented it. So she kept close to Adam, eating her hot stew—such a treat!—and smiling at the Aschams.

At first, Mistress Ascham wouldn't allow Florrie to help clean the dishes from the table, so Florrie was able to watch Adam take a broad piece of wood from near the hearth, and using his knife, carve it into the form of a horse. Though it was crude, there was an elegance to the way the neck arched that made Florrie think that with more time, the carving would be quite lifelike. Another skill she never would have suspected in her kidnapper. But perhaps, being isolated as a child, he'd had to develop his own interests.

As he carved a second horse, Adam and Master Ascham discussed Adam's training as a soldier. Florrie was listening avidly, hoping for more of a glimpse into Adam's world, when she saw Mistress Ascham gesture to her.

Florrie gladly came over to the cupboard, and without being asked, picked up a cloth to dry the dishes Mistress Ascham had just washed in a basin of soapy water. The farmer's wife couldn't be much older than Florrie. Though her husband had more years than she did, they seemed very happy together.

Mistress Ascham handed her one of the wooden cups. "So ye're movin' south for yer health?" she said softly.

"Aye, mistress," Florrie said, then could have bitten her tongue. She'd already had to answer questions several times at dinner, and her speech was stilted from concentrating so hard at sounding common.

"Ye're sure ye did not run away because of the babe?" the woman asked kindly.

Florrie tried to speak with hesitation, even as her blush betrayed her unease. "Nay, mistress, Edmund says there's more soldierin' near London. He could become a knight with his skill and hard work."

"Me thinks he was once beneath you—milady?" Mistress Ascham still spoke kindly. "Ye cannot quite hide yer upbringin'."

Florrie bit her lip. If anyone following them questioned these people, they'd know exactly who she and Adam were. She had to trust in the Aschams. "Mistress, please, say nothing. I love him so, and we want to be happy together."

"I know, I know," the woman said on a sigh, passing over a wooden platter to be dried. " 'Tis very obvious ye care for each other."

It was? Florrie thought with a mixture of surprise and unease. Surely it was all because of Adam's skill at pretending.

Before they could speak more, Master Ascham sent the boys with their new toys up to the loft and offered his own bed to the guests.

Florrie stared wide-eyed up at Adam, who put his arm around her even as he spoke. "That will not do, sir. I cannot drive ye from your bed. The loft in the barn will do us fine on a summer's night." When the farmer tried to protest, Adam held up a hand. "Ye cannot change me mind."

They were given plenty of blankets, and a lantern made of etched horn to light their way. As they walked across the dark yard, leaving the growling dog behind, Florrie let out a loud sigh and clung to Adam's arm for real.

As they reached the barn's interior and shut the door, he peered at her. "You are bothered by something?"

"Bothered?" she echoed in disbelief. "Why should it bother me to lie to two nice people?" She leaned closer and lowered her voice. "Mistress Ascham thinks I am born noble, and that you are a common soldier I fell in love with, and that's why we are running."

"Oh," he said, setting the horn on a table near the ox's stall. "A plausible reason."

"But if anyone questions them about us, and it comes out that I am a noblewoman—"

"A noblewoman in love," Adam interrupted. "You were convincing enough."

"I thought *you* were," she said stiffly.

"My thanks."

He grinned, and in that moment, she saw even more of a resemblance to his brother.

His amusement faded, and he said with intent, "You have done well this night. You think very quickly."

The swelling of pride she felt at his words gave her a moment's unease. She should not want to please him so much. She changed the subject. "What about Robert and Michael?"

"I am certain they saw what happened, and the result. They will keep watch on our surroundings and make their own camp nearby."

She almost felt guilty for being under shelter when they were not, but she silently chastised herself.

"Can you climb into the loft without my assistance?" he asked. "I will feed and groom the horses."

She frowned at him. "I may be crippled, but I was a champion at climbing trees."

"You are not crippled," he said.

He spoke with enough force that she raised an eyebrow. He turned away too quickly and went to the horses.

Florrie was already snug beneath blankets in the loft by the time Adam climbed up, carrying the lantern. With their blankets, and the heat rising up from the animals below, she knew that they didn't need each other for warmth. Adam must have had the same realization, because he laid out his blankets several feet from her, then blew out the lamp. Slivers of moonlight showed her that he lay with his hands behind his head as he looked up at the ceiling.

"Today you told me about your childhood," Florrie murmured, lying on her side as if she could see his expressions in the dark. "But you really never said how you felt about it."

"Felt?" he echoed, seeming confused. "It was what it was. I was grateful. What more needs be said?"

"You were not angry or confused?"

"I probably experienced every emotion when I was young and immature, but I do not dwell on it now. What is the point?"

"But . . . talking can make you feel better."

"I disagree. Talking makes one remember, rather than leaving it in the past."

"Where it can fester. Obviously your resentment against my father has only grown."

"Of course it has. He committed a crime and has not been punished. I need justice."

"Or vengeance," she said softly, sadly.

"If so, 'tis my right. Is this a female thing?"

"What?" she asked in confusion.

"Talking about feelings."

"I forgot—Robert did hint that you saw few women."

He said nothing, leaving her even more curious.

"Talking resolves problems," she said.

"Not this one. The only talking I will do to your father will be offering a challenge."

"But if you talked—"

"What would be accomplished?" he demanded, sounding even more irritable. "This is a man who killed two unarmed people—one of them a woman. There can be no resolution without justice. If you are trying to save him from me—"

"I am not!" she insisted. How could she tell Adam that she wanted to save *him*? "Women are creatures who believe talking helps to resolve emotions. For instance, I can say all I want that my father will not be coerced in any way by you having me under your control. I am not important enough to him."

"I do not believe that. Are you saying this to somehow make me change my mind?"

"I would be happy if you would, but only because I do not wish to see you harmed in any way."

"Me. Not your father," he said doubtfully. "What point are you making?"

"Oh, nothing." She wanted to tell him about her father's recent illness, but it would affect every plan Adam had spent years formulating. Would he do something worse in desperation?

"If you do not wish to talk to me about such things, I understand," she said. "You can talk to me about something else."

He gave a heavy sigh. "I can think of other things to do rather than talk."

"We'll sleep in a moment. I have a military question. I heard Master Ascham say we are near Bosworth. Is that not the field where King Richard was killed in battle last year?"

"Aye, it was, but be careful. There are many who

believe he wasn't even the true king, and that his death was just."

"My father quietly supported King Henry, but did not do so openly until the battle was over."

"He was not the only one," Adam said dryly.

"What about you? Which side did you support?"

"I was not allowed to choose sides."

"Not allowed?" She wished she could see his face. "Who did not allow you?"

"My conscience," he said.

She didn't believe him. She wondered how strong Sir Timothy's hold still was on Adam. Could he have coerced Adam to seek his vengeance on her father?

"The political differences made the situation too murky," he continued. "I am more interested in helping innocent people, rather than assisting those corrupted by power. Unless it is necessary."

"So you do not serve the king?"

"Of course I do," he said with exasperation. "If he called on my service, he would have it. But last year, Henry was not the king; Richard was. And his supporters betrayed him in the end. I was in Scotland at the time."

"Oh, what were you doing in Scotland?" she asked with interest.

"Traveling."

His tone of voice made it clear he would not elaborate, and she knew she'd pressed far enough.

But she could not help saying, "The Ascham boys appreciated those horses you carved. 'Tis an impressive skill."

"The time limited what I could do."

"I can tell you possess even greater skill than that. I surmise you had little else to do, since there were no women about when you were young."

She heard the hay rustle beneath him, as if he'd turned to look at her, but he made no response. She hadn't thought he would, for he was a man who'd rather withhold a truth than lie about it.

Thinking of him made her far too wakeful, and curious, and—

"Adam?"

It was a moment before he said, "Aye?"

"If Master Ascham returns before we're awake, will he not wonder why we sleep separately?"

" 'Tis summer."

"I do not think that a good enough reason."

Without waiting for his permission, she got to her feet, bringing her blanket with her as she shuffled through the hay. She lay her bedding down beside him, feeling bold and uncertain—but adventurous. She didn't want to think too deeply about what she was doing. She lay down, her arm and shoulder brushing against his.

He said nothing, although she thought he might have sighed. She remembered his kisses, and the way his hands had touched her body, bringing on such feelings of pleasure. She shouldn't dwell on such things, but they seemed to sweep through her body uncontrollably, and she wondered what she was supposed to do about it. She knew she wanted to distract him from his mission, save him from himself, but was this the way to do it?

When he didn't turn onto his side, she did, curling her hips back against him.

"I cannot get comfortable," she murmured, rolling back to face him.

"Perhaps, 'tis because you're sleeping in a hay loft." He spoke impassively, staring at the roof.

He seemed tense, and she knew she was affecting him. She felt guilty—and exhilarated—all at the same time. What an adventure!

She found herself stealing glances down his body, looking for the clues of passion he'd explained to her. But sometime during their conversation, he had pulled the blanket up loosely about his waist, and she could see no telltale . . . bulge. Not knowing what to do next, she found herself fingering the sleeve of his tunic.

Suddenly Adam took hold of her, and in one smooth move, pulled her on top of him. She gasped at the impression of heat and hardness beneath her, his body seeming so big against hers. She didn't know what to do with her legs, only knowing that the more she moved them, the more she wanted to spread them wide, feel him deep against her, as she had when she'd thrown herself naked at him.

"Is this the other thing you wanted to do, besides sleep?" he said, his voice almost a low growl.

She was embarrassed by her earlier naïveté. Of course there were many more things people could do in the dark of the night besides sleep. To her mortification, she wanted to experience them.

"I did not mean to tease you," she whispered.

"What did you mean to do?"

His face was so close; moonlight etched its severity in dark relief. His lips were a thin line, as if he pressed them together to keep from . . . kissing her, she thought with longing. Aye, she wanted to experience his kisses again.

"Are you waiting for an apology?" he demanded.

"An apology?" she echoed, feeling dazed. Her hair had loosened from her braid in their struggles, and the strands fell against his cheeks like a curtain.

"For how I behaved last night, when I . . . kissed and touched you inappropriately."

She heard his words, but they seemed so distant compared to the almost painful press of her breasts against his chest. But the pain crossed the line into pleasure, confusing her.

"I . . . had wished for you to do it," she answered truthfully. "No man has ever . . . wanted me, before you."

"More fools they."

And for those sweet words, she leaned down and kissed him, feeling uncertain, but growing bolder. She parted her lips, exploring the curves of his, daring to taste the undercurve with her tongue. It rasped almost painfully against his whiskers, but that only reminded her more that he was a man.

As if his erection pressing into her stomach weren't proof enough.

He slanted his head, diving deeper into her mouth, coaxing her tongue into playing with his. The taste of him made her shudder, made her thighs part even more, but her skirt was hampering her. His hands slid smoothly up and down her back, then along her sides, to the outer curve of her breasts. She moaned.

Against her mouth, he said hoarsely, "We need to stop."

She made a mindless "Mmm" sound, as her hands cupped his face, then slid down beneath his jaw. Even the tendons of his neck seemed erotic to her. She'd lost any sense of restraint, responsibility—or propriety. His groin pressed into just the right spot, low on her belly. It set off an ache she only thought of as . . . hunger.

Suddenly, he rolled until she was on her side, bewildered, lost.

"Adam?"

"Go to sleep," he commanded, turning his back.

She stared at its broad width, hugging herself, feeling bereft and lonely and needy. It was a long time before her body quieted.

But as she fell asleep, her thoughts kept dwelling on his not being allowed to choose sides in a war. Not allowed by whom?

Chapter 11

All the next day, they remained far west of the normal roads to London, hoping to mislead anyone who might have picked up their trail. Florrie felt that her three companions—she was starting to forget to think of them as her kidnappers—seemed preoccupied, as if their close call with the farmer had made them even more wary.

But since she had them to care for her, she tried to keep relaxed and positive about what she could accomplish helping Adam in the time remaining to her. Every time she pointed out a flowering bush or how the green of grain fields dotted the rolling hills in multicolored squares, he looked at her in confusion so complete that it was comical. Had he never before noticed the glory of the countryside? It was so very different from the barren moors of her home. She was determined to enjoy every moment that she could.

But that night, everything changed. They were not able to find an adequate barn or shed before nightfall, and they were forced to camp in a small copse of trees. Adam was obviously uneasy with this, and he forbid the use of a large fire. They ate cold meat left over from the midday hunting, and cheese that had been crushed into a damp lump at the bottom of a saddlebag. After dark, Michael took the first shift of scout duty and disappeared from the encampment.

With all the tension, Florrie had a hard time falling asleep, and couldn't have been asleep for long when she heard a muffled oath. Adam was no longer behind her. She saw shadows and movement, but nothing made sense. She gasped as someone leapt the fire. *Adam.*

The sudden clash of steel on steel at last told her what she was seeing. They were being attacked, and she was a liability, she knew. She scuttled backward until she was at the base of a tree, needing to stay out of the way. Her heart pounded with fear, but not just for herself. If these were her father's men, they would kill Adam and Robert. And what about Michael, who had been on guard? Was he already dead? Her throat tightened with tears, and she dashed at her eyes angrily. There was no point crying over the unknown.

Both Robert and Adam were defending themselves from two masked men dressed all in black. By the cut of their clothing and their skill with a blade, these men were not thieves. Robert and his opponent were fighting on the far side of the clearing, but Adam was nearby, as if defending her. His sword moved with incredible speed, flashing in the firelight. His expression, though strained with concentration, betrayed no doubt, no fear. He had been well trained to fight, to conquer. He jumped a slashing sword aimed at his legs, then boldly attacked, driving his opponent farther away from Florrie.

She not only felt frightened for him, but also mesmerized by his skill. She knew he fought a man of equal talent, yet Adam was winning. His size and his speed made him one of the best swordsmen she'd ever seen. And besides simple admiration, she felt deep inside her a frisson of dangerous excitement, that a man like him desired her.

His sword at last connected with the man's arm, and she heard a grunt of pain. The man dropped to his knees, one arm cradled in the other. Chivalrous to a fault, Adam backed several steps away, his sword at the ready, even as he glanced in Robert's direction.

As Robert backed up several steps, meeting each slash of his opponent's sword with a strong parry, he stumbled over wood stacked near the fire. Adam rushed to his aid, and in that moment, Robert's opponent gave him a sudden push, sending Robert colliding into Adam.

Though Florrie feared for the brothers, her gaze followed their attackers. The injured one lurched to his feet, the second man caught his uninjured arm to help, and they disappeared between the trees.

Adam steadied Robert. "Stay with Katherine."

Even under stress, he did not use Florrie's name where it might be overheard, she thought in amazement.

"I am fine," she said to Robert when Adam was gone. "Go to help him."

He looked at her as if she'd spoken another language. "Disobey him where you are concerned? I may be his brother, but his wrath would fall even on me. Do not fear for him. He can take care of himself."

She rolled her eyes in frustration and came to her feet, feeling shaky. When she took a limping step toward the fire, Robert tried to help her.

"Did they touch you?" he asked, searching her face. "Are you injured?"

She shook him off. "Just the same old injury from childhood. I am well. Can we rebuild the fire? After all, my father's men have already found us."

"There were only two men," Robert mused, gazing out into the darkness.

"And they'll be reporting back to whatever small troop has fanned out over the countryside."

Robert didn't answer, only stoked the fire with more branches.

In a shared tense silence, the two of them waited. Florrie kept wondering about Michael's fate. The man was not as easy to converse with as the two brothers, but he had treated her kindly, and now he'd defended her. Was it just for the money, or did he feel a loyalty to Adam for some greater reason?

And was he even now lying dead? The fact that the two men had gotten by him did not bode well for his condition.

She shivered, rubbing her arms, suddenly feeling the cold. Robert put a blanket about her shoulders, and she gave him a distracted smile of gratitude.

At last, they heard the sound of shuffling footsteps. Florrie rose to her feet, then found herself pulled behind Robert, whose sword was now held threateningly in his hand. She peered around his broad back, yet could still see nothing.

After an unusual call of a bird at night, Robert's shoulders relaxed, and he lowered his sword. Ah, they were signaling to each other again, she thought. Adam came out of the trees, with Michael's arm across his shoulder. Florrie felt a rush of giddy relief that Michael was doing his own walking, uneven though it was. And Adam looked unharmed.

"They escaped." Adam bit off the words in obvious frustration.

He helped Michael to sit beside the fire, and she rushed to them, seeing the blood on Michael's face.

Michael tried to stop her hands from tilting his head. "The bastards only hit me. I did not even have a chance to draw my blade."

"Let me see to it," she commanded.

To her surprise, he stopped fighting her, though he gave Adam a sullen look.

"Wet a cloth in some wine," she said. When Robert had done her bidding, she parted Michael's red hair and wiped gently at the wound. "The bleeding seems to have slowed." She pressed down on the cloth. "Hold this to your scalp firmly." When he followed her orders, she stepped back and looked at Adam. "Forgive me if you've already figured this out, but if these attackers had been my father's men, wouldn't Michael be dead?"

Adam and Robert exchanged a look, even as Michael stiffened as if he were affronted.

"They were not your father's men," Adam said at last.

"And they were not thieves," Robert added.

Adam scowled at him.

Robert spread his hands wide. "She had certainly figured that out already."

"I had," she interjected. "What do you think is going on? Who else would be after us?"

"This is not your concern," Adam said calmly.

"Not my concern?" she cried in disbelief. "It would very well have been my concern if you'd all died and left me here alone, at God's mercy. I could not even have found my way back to the Aschams. You are using me against my father, and I am not fighting you. You owe me not just the truth, but even what you suspect."

The brothers once again exchanged a look as if they could read minds.

And then suddenly, a memory returned to Florrie. "When those men found our camp after we had already gone, you were worried that they were from the League of the Blade. Has tonight confirmed your suspicions?"

Adam opened his mouth—then closed it again, rubbing a hand down his bearded face.

"You cannot keep waiting for me to fall asleep before you discuss such things," she pressed. "I'll only pretend to sleep so I can listen."

Adam sighed. "Aye, I believe the League of the Blade has become involved on your behalf."

She gasped in surprise that he'd actually told her the truth. "How would the League—?"

"We cannot discuss this now. We have to leave, and we will remain silent while we travel."

Even Michael moved quickly, and they were on the road again in the dark of night. The moon was just beginning to wax from half toward full, and although it occasionally was hidden behind clouds, it lit their way well enough. To her surprise, they retraced their journey, heading north, away from London, which would not be expected by anyone attempting to follow them. They even rode several hundred yards in the center of a stream, to make tracking them even more difficult.

Although Florrie soon slumped in exhaustion in the saddle, her mind continued to whirl. The League of the Blade wanted to help her? She'd always heard that they appeared in a desperate person's life to right wrongs and bring about justice. And now they considered *her* a worthy recipient of their services? She could have giggled over it in disbelief, since she'd spent her childhood fantasizing about their exploits. But the League's appearance meant danger now, and she did not want Adam and the others killed.

Yet the League hadn't tried to kill them, as Michael's survival attested. If they thought she was being held against her will, perhaps for a ransom, wouldn't they consider Adam and his men expendable?

Unless . . . there was even more going on than she already knew. Several things began to come clear in her mind: when Adam said he hadn't been "allowed" to choose sides in a war, as if he had to be impartial; the way he and the League attackers had seemed so perfectly matched in skill—as if they'd been trained the same way; and their attackers trying not to kill them.

Was Adam a Bladesman?

She shivered in growing wonder. That would explain so many things.

But by kidnapping her and intending to challenge her father, he was going against the League of the Blade. How could he possibly succeed?

As Adam rode at Florrie's side, he could practically see the gears turning in her mind. He knew he would have to answer her questions later, but right now his own brain was churning all on its own.

The League was after him.

How had they discovered his plans? On his twenty-first birthday, they'd granted him the knowledge of his vast inheritance, though he'd known since childhood that he was an earl. But they would not speak the name of the man they suspected as his parents' murderer. He'd been furious that they would withhold something so important. That night, he'd seen sympathy and guilt on his foster father's face, and Adam was able to coerce him to reveal the identity of the killer. Sir Timothy had understood that power and wealth mattered little to Adam next to justice for his parents. Adam had promised his foster father that he would do nothing while the enmity of civil war still surged across the countryside. And of course, although he'd spent his life planning for justice, he could not leave his brothers, nineteen and eighteen, too young to defend themselves, not yet ready to face the world as Bladesmen. Adam had four more years to train them and expand his own experience.

But he had kept all his plans against Martindale secret even from Sir Timothy, knowing how the League would feel about him challenging a marquess. And then he'd left, as if setting out on his own. But he hadn't gone to his ancestral lands, as the League expected, and they hadn't known his plans—unless they'd coerced Sir Timothy into revealing that Adam knew Martindale's name.

And then, of course, Lady Florence Becket had gone missing. That had given the League all the proof they needed.

Still, Adam had a right to challenge a man who'd harmed his family, and he was furious that the League would not trust him in this. Aye, he'd kidnapped a woman, but they'd raised him, so they damn well knew he was honorable enough not to hurt her.

Weren't they supposed to dispense justice? Then why not for *his* family? For the first time, he felt that their pure purpose seemed . . . tarnished, especially after this attempt to capture him. His brother Paul had never trusted the League, had angrily told Adam he was foolish to believe in them. Had Paul been right all along? Adam felt like his world was beginning to shift.

Several hours later, they slept in an abandoned shed. If it had been raining, they'd have been drenched due to the holes in the roof. But Adam felt more secure being out of sight. He did not know how seriously wounded the one Blades-man had been, and he knew the second man would attend to the first, even see him to safety while waiting for reinforcements. The League had always trained their men to work in pairs when they could, rather than alone. Adam and his men had some room to breathe, to choose ways to London that no one would suspect.

He knew the League and its methods better than most other Bladesmen. No one was going to stop him.

They headed due east first thing in the morning, still not in the direction of London, and Florrie recognized that once again, they were trying to do something no one expected.

Adam seemed in a grim mood, his gaze scanning the road that was barely more than a farm path. Robert and Michael were taking turns riding far in front and far behind, scouting for anything suspicious.

Florrie needed answers, and now she had some privacy. She glanced at Adam. "So how long have you been a Bladesman?"

His expression didn't even change. He was trying to intimidate her, but she was not so easily fooled anymore. He *was* a Bladesman, a man deemed worthy to be one of the best, a defender of innocents, a bringer of justice.

No one had brought justice for him—he had to do it on his own. Inside her she felt an ever-increasing softness for him that was getting harder and harder to ignore.

But ignore it, she had to. Though he was honorable, loyal, honest where he could be—he was not a man for her. She was not foolish enough to think so. That dependency would only get her hurt, something she'd fought against her whole life.

"You can ignore me all you want," she mused, "but it does not change the truth. You and your opponent both fought with much of the same skills and techniques last night. And they were trying not to harm you—otherwise Michael would be dead, as you said yourself. Why would the League care about men who've kidnapped the daughter of a marquess, unless they care about you personally?"

He thinned his lips into a flat line.

"And then there was your revealing statement of not being *allowed* to choose sides in a war. Who would not allow such a thing—but the League?" She leaned closer to him, holding herself in the saddle with the pressure of her thighs and her foot in the stirrup. "I already know so many of your secrets, Adam. Why withhold this one?"

"Are you withholding secrets from me?" he asked.

She straightened. He was focusing on her now, his dark blue eyes alive with intensity.

"I know not what you're talking about," she said, trying to look innocent. "I have been your prisoner for days now, yet I've been *helping* you. Do not my actions speak for me?"

He looked at her as if he were trying to see *into* her, as if he could read everything in her soul by what showed in her eyes. There was a moment where she actually considered telling him more—as if she could trust him.

She was a fool. She had learned long ago not to give people the ability to hurt her.

At last, he sighed. "You can never in your life speak of this to anyone."

She tensed, shocked that he was going to trust her with something so secretive. And the fact that he was trying to prove *he* deserved *her* trust made her . . . distrust him. That was better for her peace of mind.

"So you *are* a Bladesman?" she practically whispered, even though there was nothing but rolling barley fields as far as the eye could see.

He nodded.

"And is it true that you had to do some great heroic deed for them to choose you?" She wondered if he would tell her what it was.

"For most Bladesmen, aye, there has to be something that brings one to the notice of the League. You cannot find them or contact them."

"But as a Bladesman, *you* can. You used their messengers to take your missive to London so quickly."

He nodded.

"You said *most* Bladesmen come to the League's notice. But . . . not you?"

"I came to their notice, aye, but when I only had six years."

She inhaled swiftly. "When your parents were killed."

"The League took us in to protect us."

She nodded, her thoughts coming so fast she had to sort through them. "You said you lived isolated to protect you from—my father. But . . . could not the League have placed you with a family?"

"We presented the League with an unusual situation. Three brothers with no family. Several members of the League council decided to try a bold experiment they'd only been contemplating: raising and training Bladesmen from childhood. Sir Timothy, our foster father, did not like it, but a vote was taken and he was outnumbered."

"So you were like . . . little soldiers to them?"

He took a deep breath, his head lifted with pained pride. "It was an honor never before granted to anyone. From what I'm told, it was not so very different from other young men raised to be knights in noble households."

"From what you're told," she echoed, feeling suspicious.

He glanced at her, one corner of his lips curved up. "I have had long conversations with Michael, who was raised on the outside. From childhood, we learned the fighting techniques that other Bladesmen never learn until they're accepted into the League. We had access to the best education— history and languages and mathematics."

She felt a pang of envy that she quickly squelched. He'd also had so many disadvantages. She guessed he was only just beginning to learn that.

"But Robert said there were no women."

"He did not say that."

"He hinted, and that was enough. No women, Adam? Ever? Not dairymaids or brewing mistresses?"

He shook his head, his expression rueful. "Nay, in those days there were no women admitted. But six years ago the League trained its first Bladeswoman."

"I am in awe!" she cried, feeling pleased for her sex. "And she fights with a sword?"

"She does. Another one is in training even as we speak."

"And you were there as they trained her? Was it so very strange?"

"I had already been on several League missions, so it was not so unusual to me. And Robert had already escaped to visit the nearest village and see women. But Paul . . ." His voice trailed off into sadness. "Paul was angry to have been so cut off from the female sex."

"I am not surprised," she said dryly. "You were not angry?"

His voice softened. "I was never angry with the League. Which made Paul angry with me. He thought I was blind."

"You thought any deprivation you suffered was worth it when people would be helped in the end."

He glanced at her with surprise in his eyes. "Aye, I thought that."

"And was it worth it?"

He looked away. "It was . . . for a while. To see the resigned sorrow in someone's eyes turn to joy—there is no better feeling."

"Perhaps that is how I'll feel when, as a nun, I can help people."

He shot her a sudden dark look, and she could not read his expression. He did not like hearing about her future? That was foolish, for it was inevitable.

"So have they found other children to bring into the League?"

He shook his head. "They deemed the program unsuccessful."

"Unsuccessful? Look at you! You are a fine Bladesman."

He grinned suddenly, and it almost stole her breath with its beauty.

"A Bladesman who kidnaps women?" he scoffed lightly. "I am certain the League is blaming itself for my downfall."

"You are your own man, making your own decisions. Any Bladesman would do the same. Why else do they think they failed?"

"My brothers and I had a difficult time out in the real world."

She winced at "the real world" as she thought of young boys being forbidden from a normal life.

"After Robert first escaped, the League realized that we might hunger for what we missed—and that we might stand out as different, which would make being a Bladesman difficult. After all, we're trained to be unnoticed when we want to be, but if we didn't know how people lived, how could we blend in? So we were given even more lessons about what a squire would learn, from how to play an instrument to serving the nobility at meals to dancing with ladies."

She had a difficult time restraining herself from gaping at him, as she imagined learning all these things without women. And then she wanted to laugh at the thought of a group of Bladesmen all learning to dance. But it wasn't funny. No wonder Adam seemed to find some of her behavior so curious. Women were a mystery to him!

Adam looked away toward the horizon with its endless fields of grain. She watched him study their surroundings, as if estimating their distance from the village that could only just be glimpsed far to the north. Even when he was talking, he was always aware.

"And people were . . . different from what I was used to," Adam mused. "There wasn't the same need for order. And so many people have no great honor in themselves or their work. I . . . did not understand them."

"But people are all different," Florrie said, wishing she could explain better. "Would not the world be a boring place if everyone were like the League?"

"In many ways, it would be better."

Then he turned those intense blue eyes on her,

and she felt the path of his gaze down her body as if he'd touched her.

"And in so many ways, it would be worse," he said in a husky voice.

She held his gaze, letting herself revel in his admiration and desire. She remembered his hands on her breasts, his mouth on hers, and the heat from memories alone warmed her body, made the depth of her belly clench.

"So women make the world a better place?" she asked softly, almost blushing at herself for wanting to hear his praise.

"Aye, they do," he murmured, his mouth tilting up in a small smile.

She wanted to kiss that smile, induce a moan of need from him. He'd been totally deprived of softness in his life, and now she wanted to give it to him—to experience it with him.

What did that say about her? she wondered, suddenly looking away.

Chapter 12

When they stopped to eat a midday meal, Adam stood as he munched his cheese and twice-baked bread, staring out at the countryside, wondering when the League would attempt to rescue Florrie again. Or would her father surprise him by doing the same? It was Michael's turn to scout the area, and he trusted the knight to alert them to anything suspicious.

He was concentrating so much on his thoughts that it took a moment for the conversation behind him to register. Then he turned around, frowning, to see Robert and Florrie leaning toward each other, talking.

"I cannot believe I would be capable of such a thing!" Florrie was saying in her dramatic way.

Capable of what?

Robert waved a hand in dismissal. "I am not proposing that you kill a man, just that you defend yourself, perhaps wounding him enough to escape." He held up a dagger. "Why are you so resistant?"

Florrie looked at the weapon as if it were a snake. "But . . . women are taught to be nurturing, to be loving. I pride myself on my ability to help others, to bring happiness into their lives. What kind of cynic would I be if I was prepared to harm someone?"

Curious, Adam sat down beside her, meeting Robert's nonplussed gaze before looking back to Florrie. "How is being prepared cynical?" Adam asked. "I would understand if in your everyday life you went without protection, but you saw what happened last night—what has happened before."

"You mean when you kidnapped me?" she said sweetly. "So if I'd have had a dagger . . ."

He shrugged. "You were so afraid, you'd have cut me without a second thought."

Unease clouded her green eyes. "And it would have been a mistake."

He smiled. "Really? You do not wish you'd never met me?"

She gave an exaggerated sigh. "I already told you that this is the adventure of my life, danger and all. I regret nothing."

"Then how can you regret learning to defend yourself?" Robert asked patiently. "What if thieves invade your convent someday?"

Whenever her future was mentioned, Adam felt the strangest feeling of unease. It wasn't his future; it wasn't his choice. But the thought of lively Florrie, wearing a wimple to hide her hair, having to be silent most of the time . . .

Florrie was watching his face, then looked away. "Very well," she said briskly. "Show me what to do."

Adam did not rise as they did, content to watch his little brother educate her. Robert, normally so amused, was full of respectful intensity, which pleased Adam.

As Robert began his explanations, Adam mulled his regrets. He hadn't liked confiding so much in Florrie, forcing her to keep even more secrets, giving her such power over him and his men. But he needed her confidence, and he thought he was slowly being granted it.

He smiled as Robert had to repeatedly reposition the blade in her hand, but he liked the quiet triumph of her expression when she finally mastered the position. Movement with the weapon was harder to master, for her uneven legs made timing even more difficult. Perspiration broke out on her brow, and after wiping her forehead twice with her arm, she bent over, grabbed the back of her skirt and pulled it forward between her legs, tucking it up into the girdle at her waist.

Even as Robert laughed, Adam's breath left his body in a rush. Though he'd seen her naked, it had only been a brief moment before she'd thrown herself into his arms. And at the time, his gaze had concentrated farther north. Now he was able to stare at his leisure, and he didn't even think of looking away. Though her legs might not be matching in length, they matched in smooth suppleness, with long lines that curved in and out provocatively from her dainty ankles to her willowy thighs. Strong-looking thighs that had already clasped about his waist.

He was suddenly glad for the tunic that hung to his own thighs.

But he didn't look away. Florrie was hesitant to thrust her dagger at Robert, obviously fearing to harm him. She didn't realize that Robert had been trained to study facial expressions, to anticipate movement, and could adjust his response so quickly that it seemed magical.

She rounded on him after staggering past where he'd just been. "How do you do that?"

"I am talented," he said, shrugging.

She tried again, and this time he caught her from behind, easily taking the dagger from her. When she was free, she stamped her foot in frustration.

"'Tis only your first lesson," Adam said mildly, crossing his arms as he leaned back against a tree. "Robert had a dagger in his hand when he was five."

Her frustration changed into a brief expression of pain. She was a woman, and she would not like to imagine young boys with weapons. But how else did boys become men?

"And who would a child of five train with?" she asked skeptically.

"Me, of course," Adam answered.

"And that made you . . . seven?"

He nodded.

"Well, seven is so much older," she said with sarcasm.

He shrugged, still amused. "I felt compelled to train, even then."

Looking at him, she slowly lowered her dagger and spoke in a soft, mournful voice. "Because of what had happened to your parents."

Elaborating would only hurt her, so he said nothing. After a moment of silence, Robert touched her arm, and they returned to her lesson.

After another half hour of frustration—with a bit of triumph at the end—Florrie rounded on Adam, again wiping her damp forehead. "I have a request, and I think it will help mislead anyone still trying to follow us."

He was on his knees, packing up their meal when she spoke. He glanced up at her. "Proceed."

"We should stay at an inn tonight."

"Impossible." He stood up to attach the bag to his horse's saddle.

"Please listen."

She approached him, and he almost said that if she wanted his full attention, she should hide her legs, but she didn't seem to notice his distraction.

"After the recent attacks, no one would ever guess we would openly stay in a village inn," she said. "No one would think you would allow such a thing. Am I correct?"

Though Robert met his gaze, he only whistled and went to tighten the girth on his horse's saddle. After all, it was Adam's decision, his nonchalance seemed to say.

"Of course I wouldn't," Adam said. "Nor will I allow us to stay in the open."

"We will play husband and wife, and I will be so convincing," she said, a faint thread of pleading now in her voice. She laid her hand gently on his arm. "I have not had a true bath since this adventure began."

"And is that not part of the adventure?" he countered, but already feeling himself beginning to sway. If he gave in to her, risked notice, would she trust him even more? Perhaps he could at last discover if she was aware of any of her father's secrets.

She did not answer, only gazed up at him with beseeching eyes, her hand still touching him. He knew she was trying to manipulate him, and he allowed it—but only for the sake of her trust.

"Very well."

When she clapped happily, he put up a hand.

"Allow me to finish. I will discuss it with Michael and Robert, to best determine our course. And you will abide by our decision."

"Aye, sir!"

She almost skipped to her horse, a slightly out of balance move that was far too endearing. He turned away, disappointed in himself.

Robert came to his side even as Florrie mounted her horse.

"Adam?"

"Aye, I know it might be a mistake," Adam said in a low voice. "But she still might know something about her father. The more relaxed and happy she is, the more she might tell us."

"I understand," Robert said.

"But will Michael?"

Robert gave him a confused look. "Do you not know he would do anything you wanted? You are his liege lord."

"Quiet," Adam murmured, glancing at Florrie. But she couldn't have heard, for she'd guided her horse to the edge of the path, and was watching as Michael approached through the fields.

Adam had spent his whole life learning to disguise himself as other people, but those skills had always been used against a villain. How was he to manipulate Florrie? Real life had more subtleties than he'd ever imagined. Once again he found his confidence in the League shaken, since they hadn't even given him the skills to face a woman like her.

Adam was both impressed and uneasy at the way Michael took to the challenge of finding the right inn. They rode far too close to Rockingham, a royal castle begun by William the Conqueror, in hopes that none of their pursuers would assume them so bold. They went past it to the market town of Corby in Rockingham Forest, with its wooden, two-story inn near the market cross. Both Robert and Michael would remain outside the town, taking turns scouting for the enemy.

Florrie looked disturbed when she heard about the two men's assignments as their party entered the outskirts of the town. "But I thought we all could enjoy a night of comfort."

"I thank you for your kind thoughts, my lady," Michael said, nodding to her, "but I would feel better knowing that you and— Sir Adam are safe."

Adam refrained from rolling his eyes at Michael's hesitant use of his assigned title.

But Florrie only nodded solemnly. "How kind of you, Michael."

Robert, riding at her side, doffed his cap. "And me, my lady? Do I have your good wishes?"

She leaned between their horses, her seat secure, and patted his arm. "Of course, Robert. My husband and I appreciate your service."

And though she laughed at Adam, her eyes merry, he began to remember what it was like having to play her husband. This time, instead of a hayloft in a barn, they would be sharing a single room, sleeping together in a bed—and bathing.

Perhaps some of his uneasiness transferred to her, for after they entered the stable yard through a tunnel beneath the upper story, she became far more animated than normal. She held his arm possessively—though he realized this allowed her to mask her limp; quite intelligent on her part. After grooms led away their horses, they went into the entrance hall, where she spoke more to the innkeeper than he did, prattling on with sunny happiness about their first year of marriage, and their journey east to visit her mother.

It was only when the manservant left them alone in their chamber, with promise of a hot supper within the hour, that she grew quiet. It was a small room, with a coffer, a table, two chairs—and the bed.

She lifted her chin with determination, smiled at him, and began to unpack her saddlebag.

"Hand me your dirty garments, Adam. After my bath later, I will wash them."

"I can see to my own garments," he said.

She rolled her eyes. "I am your wife tonight. We cannot forget that."

As if he could forget. A wife for the night. In her innocence, she could not know what that implied.

He gladly reached for the pitcher of ale left by the servant and poured himself a tankard. He sat down by the fire, for it was a cool night. He *should* look at the embers or out the window—anywhere but at Florrie. But her precise, feminine movements drew his gaze until he finally stopped fighting it. She hummed as she worked over the saddlebags, laying out her second dress, frowning over a tear in the hem.

"Perhaps I can borrow a needle and thread,"

she murmured, almost to herself. "Surely some of your garments could also use mending."

This was a domestic scene totally unfamiliar to him, and it rendered him strangely melancholy. "I can repair my own garments." He almost winced. He hadn't meant to reject her gracious offer so abruptly.

But she seemed to understand where his thoughts lay. "Ah, since there were no women, they taught you to sew."

"In a limited fashion," he amended.

But she gave him a soft smile. "Let me do this for you."

He opened his mouth, but didn't know what to say. At last, too confused, he asked, "Why do you want to help me like this?"

She stopped near him, refilling his tankard. "But this is what I do, Adam. I help people. It has always given me great fulfillment."

"Because you've had no other kind," he said darkly, thinking of the way her family treated her as a servant.

She tilted her head, her expression wry. "What other fulfillment is there for a woman in my position?"

For a frozen moment, he thought of the fulfillment he could give her in that bed. He would seduce a woman's joy from her body, give her pleasure she'd never imagined.

Give *himself* pleasure. And that was too selfish. She was no strumpet to be used for a night. She was the daughter of his enemy, bound for the convent—and how many more times could he repeat those excuses to himself?

To his great relief, a manservant arrived with a covered tray and left it on the table for them. After asking the servant for sewing supplies and seeing him to the door, Florrie busied herself setting out each wooden plate with its thick trencher of bread, and chunky stew poured over the top.

"The table could use flowers in a vase," she murmured, as if to herself.

"Why?"

She glanced at him in surprise. "For something beautiful to look upon."

He simply stared at her, because he wanted to say that she was beautiful enough to look at. Concentrating grimly on his food, he began to slice it into smaller bites.

When she had seated herself and begun to eat, he said, "You like making things look pretty. Why?"

"Because it makes me feel happy to see beauty."

"But . . . it is not a function of the meal. All we need to do is feed ourselves, to help us stay strong."

"Can we not feed our minds, our happiness, too? I think that is much of your problem, Adam."

He swallowed his food and waited warily.

"You are not happy," she continued.

"I am *content*," he said, feeling foolish for being

tense. Although he did take satisfaction in using her own word back at her. "Happiness will come later."

"You cannot live your life like that, or happiness might never come. You have to be happy in the moment, as well as content. Let me help you learn that lesson."

He frowned at her. "One cannot learn to be happy. One has to make such a reality happen."

Softly, she said, "And happiness will happen when my father is dead?"

"Nay, not happiness," he said. "Justice."

"And that will make you happy."

"Aye, it will."

"What if you do not receive the justice you expect?"

He watched her intently. Again, she seemed to know more than she'd revealed. Or was she simply following this silly line of reasoning about happiness?

"I will make it happen," he said with conviction.

"You cannot control other noblemen or the king. What if after all you've done, you cannot succeed?"

He leaned toward her across the table. "I am strong-willed, my lady. I can make *anything* happen."

And in that moment, their conflict was forgotten, and Adam knew his words could refer to the simmering desire between the two of them.

She blushed in the candlelight, creamy skin, pink cheeks, and eyes so bright and green he could see a summer's day in them.

There was another knock on the door, and she rose to her feet, bumping the table in her urgency. Two menservants carried in a wooden bathing tub, followed by more servants with steaming buckets that were used to fill up the tub. Florrie's face shone with more pleased excitement than Adam knew *he'd* ever inspired, he thought wryly. One man handed her sewing supplies, and she beamed at him as if he were her savior.

And then they were alone and her smile faded as she looked between him and the tub.

"I cannot leave you unprotected," Adam said, "but I can turn my back and finish eating. Will you trust me?"

She nodded quickly and began loosening the laces at her neck before he'd even turned around. Adam faced the wall in disgruntlement, not certain if she had really learned to trust him—or she was simply desperate to bathe.

He continued to eat, almost able to ignore the rustling of her clothing. After all, she'd washed herself every night in water nearby. He was used to it, he firmly told himself.

Then he heard a splash, and a low moan of pleasure. He jabbed himself in the lip with his spoon.

"Oh, Adam, this is . . . heavenly," she murmured. "Thank you so much."

He put down the spoon for fear it would shake

in his hand. He had to think about something else. "So you offered to mend my clothing. I understand that women normally sew much of the day?"

"Aye, there is a whole chamber in the castle for sewing. With so many residents, 'tis a never-ending chore. I am very good with the loom, too," she added with obvious pride, "and I'm known for the patterns I can create."

He thought of her doing such domestic things, and it made a soft portrait that pleased him—better to think of that than her naked so close to him, hands full of soft soap, rubbing her body . . .

"What else does a woman do?" he asked too forcefully.

"A woman must supervise everything domestic that happens within the castle, from the brewing to the butchering. Of course there's always wool to be carded and spun. I have been taught the use of herbs as well, so people come to me for healing. And then there is so much to do in the gardens or in the dairy."

"I am tired just listening to it all," he said with amazement. "Anything else?"

"Well, my sisters never cared much for the business of running the castle, so when my father was gone, I consulted with the steward and made all the decisions, including anything involving our soldiers."

He was so shocked, he looked over his shoulder, and saw the back of her head and her wet, glistening shoulders rising from the tub. He quickly turned back to the wall. "You—women learned to manage the business of the estate?"

"Of course. The men are often gone to London, waiting on the king's pleasure. It was usually months before my father returned. And once, on a tour of his other properties, he was gone fifteen months."

"And he wants to put *you* in a convent?"

"He has an heir to see to his commands now," she said with no bitterness, but a sigh in her voice.

"Claudius Drake."

"Aye, you've mentioned that you researched my family well. Now that he is married to my sister Matilda, he lives with us. I do not like him."

"But I thought you wanted everyone to be as happy as you are," he said with cynicism.

"Claudius *should* be happy with all that he has received—a wife, a second child on the way, his future as the marquess of Martindale. But he seems . . . greedy for more. When my father isn't looking, Claudius eyes him like a hungry wolf. Matilda once confessed to me that he'd . . . taken her innocence before their marriage. She thought it was because he loved her so, but I secretly suspected it was to ensure that he received the marriage—and the dowry—that he wanted."

"Why, Florrie, who could have guessed you could be so cynical?"

She hesitated. "Is it cynical not to lie to oneself?

'Tis simply the truth as I see it. But it does not pertain to me, so I have put it from my mind, hoping that Matilda does not suffer."

"And is she suffering?"

"As I said, she is with child again," Florrie said wryly.

He smiled. "It does not sound like she's suffering to me."

"The children will be within a year in age. That can be difficult for a woman."

"And you know this how?"

She blushed. "I . . . have heard it said."

"Now on this you will have to listen to me. Your sister wanted this marriage, and you want her happiness. It seems like she gave herself every opportunity."

"She wishes to see her husband more."

Now she almost sounded sullen. Florrie sullen? She seemed to have interesting relationships with her family.

"Tell me of your other sisters."

"Agnes is married to a viscount and Christina is married to an earl."

"How illustrious."

"Christina, who is closest to me in age, has only been married less than a year. She lives near London. Perhaps I can see her before I return."

To the convent.

The unspoken words lingered in his mind. And they made him angry with her family. "Are you finished with your bath?"

She gave a loud sigh. "I cannot soak in it longer?"

"Only if you want to share it with me. 'Tis my turn to bathe."

She gave a little squeak, and with a grim smile, he began to remove his tunic.

Chapter 13

Shocked, Florrie glanced over her shoulder and saw that Adam was already pulling his tunic over his head. She stood up in the water, and even though he was keeping his promise not to look at her, she almost fell reaching for a bucket of fresh water to rinse herself. She dumped it over her head, letting the warm water take away the last bubbles of soap. After wrapping a linen cloth around her body and putting another about her hair, she held on to the edge of the tub as she stepped out.

She almost gave another foolish squeak when she saw that Adam had removed his shirt. She should have looked away—but she couldn't. She'd seen his naked back more than once. Now in the light, she could see scars she hadn't noticed before, a slash mark on his shoulder, a puckered ridge along his bicep, and more. He had fought hard for his life—and for the lives of others. That made him so appealing to her.

Yet tonight they were alone, indoors, pretending to be man and wife.

And he was about to bathe right next to her.

Perhaps it had not been so wise to do her own bathing right beside him. Had he felt as uneasy as she now felt?

"D-do you not want fresh water?" she asked.

" 'Twill take too long."

"Very well. I will keep my back turned," she promised. "Please do not look this way, for I must dress."

He nodded, but his attention was focused now on the tub. He was loosening the laces that held up his breeches. She whirled away and went to look for the clean smock she'd laid out. She pulled it over her head before removing the towel beneath, and only then did she feel a bit better.

She heard the splash of water as he entered the tub, and then his sigh of contentment.

She shivered, feeling all strange inside. This was desire again, she knew. She could not escape it where he was concerned. He was lying in water that had only recently touched her own body. It was . . . wicked . . . and too exciting.

She had to stay out of his way. He had a dangerous look in his eyes whenever she only wore her smock around him. Sitting at the table, she toweled her hair dry, but the damp ends made long wet marks on her thin garment. She shivered.

"Go warm yourself before the fire," he said.

Without thinking, she glanced over her shoulder at him. His upper body didn't fit into the tub, so she had an almost safe view of what she'd seen before.

"You were not supposed to look at me," Florrie said primly.

"You'd already had plenty of time to dress."

She said nothing else—she sounded petulant enough as it was. Quietly, she limped to the hearth, carrying Adam's comb, and began to work it through her hair in the fire's warmth.

She was directly in his line of sight now, and she knew he watched her. Water rippled softly as he soaped his body. Her flesh felt feverishly hot, and her hands trembled as she dried her hair. She'd never imagined that she could feel even more aware of him. She wanted to look at him, to see if it truly was his gaze making her feel so unsettled. Struggling against her urges, she deliberately stared at the embers of the fire, then added a few more twigs. But still, she wanted to look at him.

At last, she did. And he was watching her, his hands slowly soaping his chest. His eyes, usually so impassive, seemed to smolder with intensity. She couldn't break away, only helplessly let herself be caught. She almost said she would leave until he was done, but he would only vault from the tub to stop her, to keep her safe. And she did not want to see him nude.

Though he'd seen her in such a state.

But she was not a woman to ignore things and hope they'd go away. She had to talk, but couldn't bring up the feelings so tense between them.

"You . . . seem at ease with this situation," she said at last, almost strangling on her words.

He arched a brow. "At ease?"

She nodded before he could go on. "Though you were sheltered growing up, you have been a man on your own. Have you been . . . naked around other women?"

He stopped washing himself and just blinked at her. "Are you asking if I have been intimate with women?"

She didn't think she could blush any hotter, but it now seared her cheeks. "Nay—aye—oh, I do not know what I mean. We need to talk about something, or . . . or . . ."

He sat forward. "Or what?"

His voice was low, almost gravelly.

She shivered. "Please." Her word was but a whisper.

At last he leaned back again and worked the soap down one arm. "If talking will help this . . . awkwardness, then by all means. Aye, I was sheltered, and saw few women as I was growing up. But once I began to work beyond the League compound, there were women available to me."

"Of course there were," she murmured, embarrassed. "There will always be such women who need the coin to survive."

"I did not pay anyone to bed me."

She glanced quickly at him. Though his smile was tight, it was there.

"I—I did not mean to insult you," she said.

"No insult was taken."

Now she found herself too curious, and though she turned to sewing to keep her hands busy while her hair dried, she had to ask, "So women simply . . . offer themselves to you? When you do not even know one another?" She could not imagine it.

"There are women who do not like to be alone," he said slowly, "women who do not have your confidence, or your ability to be content. They need reassurance."

"And you provided it?" Ooh, she should not have spoken, for she sounded almost . . . catty.

He gave a low laugh.

Before he could speak, she quickly said, "Nay, do not respond to that."

"I am a man, Florrie. There has never been a woman long in my thoughts. So when one who appealed to me suggested an evening in her arms, I did not object. It did not happen more than a few times. Though it satisfied a physical need, it did not make me happy or content, all the things you prize so greatly."

"Love would do that."

He said nothing.

She could not help it—she looked at him, needing to see his expression. "You have never been in love with any of these women?"

He only shook his head.

"Do you want to be in love someday?" She hurried to add, "I only ask because marriage is something a man pursues, unless he enters the priesthood. For we women, 'tis more difficult."

"It can be just as difficult for a man, especially if he has little money or property to offer in dower."

Oh, she had not imagined that he might be poor. No wonder the League took him in, and he stayed even after he knew the truth of his parents' murderer.

"I guess 'tis not so different between men and women," she murmured thoughtfully.

"Do you not want to be in love, Florrie?" he asked.

She smiled. "'Tis not to be. I have known that most of my life." She took a deep breath and put on a smile, even though she didn't look away from the fire. "So you have heard what I do with my days. When you are not training, what do you like to do?"

"Besides look for available women?"

She gasped, feeling prim, even as she heard his low chuckle.

"I enjoy educating myself," he said. "There is much knowledge to be had in the world, and I have been fortunate that the League has granted me access to it."

"Books," she murmured wistfully. "We only had a few. I am looking forward to reading more of them in the—"

"Do not say it," he interrupted.

She looked at him again, and found him watching her solemnly.

"I cannot imagine a woman as vibrant as you imprisoned behind stone walls forever. Every time you talk about your future, something inside me grows dark with anger that your father is forcing such a life on you."

"I can make any life a good life," she said quietly.

"I hope that my future actions enable you to make your own choices."

"You mean by killing my father?"

He said nothing, although she could see a muscle clench in his jaw.

"I do not think that will make you happy and content, Adam," she said, lifting her chin. "But I cannot make you see that. And as for my father deciding my fate, if he were not there, it would be Claudius, a man I distrust. And would I be better off if he insisted I remain to be handmaiden to his wife, my sister? I think not."

Something in his gaze softened. "Florrie—"

Suddenly, someone pounded on their door. Before she could even draw in a breath, Adam vaulted from the bathing tub. She saw his naked buttocks, water streaming down his legs, even as he pressed himself against the door to listen.

He motioned brusquely for her, and she caught up a linen cloth as she passed the tub. He grabbed her arm and pulled her behind him. She should be afraid, she knew, but he was there to protect her. She realized she trusted in his protection implicitly. The thought was more frightening than who was at the door.

She was pressed up against his wet back, but she pulled the cloth up between them, holding it to his hips with her fingertips, trying not to touch his smooth flesh, hoping he'd wrap it about himself. But he ignored it.

"Who is there?" Adam demanded in a harsh, cold voice.

"Ye've had the bathin' tub long enough," a man said. " 'Tis me wife's turn."

She felt some of the tension leave his back. He even took the cloth and wrapped it around his waist, making her feel a little better.

Adam said, "The servants are coming back for it when I leave our linens in the corridor. 'Twill not be long."

"See that it is not!" The grumbling faded down the corridor as the man stomped away.

Adam turned around to face her, opened his mouth, but said nothing, and she realized his gaze had dropped lower. She'd pressed so hard against his back that his wet flesh had dampened her smock in two circles over her breasts, allowing her to see the vague shadow of her nipples—and he could, too.

She gasped and fled across the chamber to the fire, where she plucked her garment away from her skin and prayed the heat would dry it quickly.

"So we are safe?" she asked over her shoulder.

"It appears that all we have to fear is an angry, dirty wife."

The cloth rode low on his hips. He held it bunched at the front, as if he was hiding—

She turned away. "I will not look as you dress," she said, leaning even closer to the fire, so she would at least have a reason for her red face. "Then I will wash our garments."

"Let me rinse my body and shave first."

She kept her back turned as he got into the tub to remove the last of the soap. But once he was moderately covered in a cloth again, she watched as he used a small hand mirror of polished steel that the servants had provided, standing over the tub to soap his face. With a dagger, he neatly sliced away the last of his dark beard, making him look younger—and letting her see the dimple in his chin. Even that made her feel all strange inside.

She did her best to ignore him as she washed out her two dresses and the other smock. To her surprise, he took each from her one at a time, and squeezed the last water out of them far better than she could have, then laid them across the table and chairs positioned near the fire. The muscles in his arms bunched and flexed as he moved, and

she thanked God he did not lift his head to see her
mouth agape at the splendor of him. How could
anyone think only women were beautiful?

They worked in silence washing her garments
and then his until he reached for his saddlebag.
"I have a clean shirt and breeches. You wear my
shirt and wash your second smock."

When she started to protest, he only said,
"'Twill cover you as well as a smock."

At last she nodded. He turned around, she
turned around, and they both began to change.
They were going to be naked at the same time, she
thought, far less mortified than she expected to be.
She didn't know what she was feeling, but it was
almost . . . excitement and trepidation and wonder
all mixed together. She slipped off her smock and
slid on his garment, trying not to inhale, because
it might have the scent of him. It would be too
easy to remember being held in his arms, made to
feel desired as a woman.

Shirtless, Adam dumped all the dirty bathing
linen into the corridor, and within minutes, as if
they'd been ordered to wait, the menservants returned to remove the bathing tub. She donned her
cloak to keep herself decent. Then she was alone
with Adam, and the only thing left to do was go
to bed. He blew out the candle, leaving the chamber glowing by firelight.

He reached past her for the extra coverlet that
lay across the end of the bed. "I shall take this and
sleep in the chair."

"You will not!" She spoke without thinking, but she didn't have to. "How can you sleep in a wooden chair? And both are covered in wet laundry."

"Then the floor—"

"Stop it! I have slept in your arms for over a sennight. And we can do so again." She lifted the coverlet to reveal the sheets—and stared at them with longing. "Though the sheets are rough to the touch, they still make me feel luxurious." She slid in on the stuffed mattress and moved to the wall.

Adam hesitated only a moment, then he sat down beside her. When the bed sank beneath his weight, she grabbed the edge to keep to her side. Stiffly, he lay on his back, their shoulders touching. Each tried to move away, but the sagging mattress drew them back.

She sighed heavily, and heard it echoed from him. They looked at each other, then laughed uneasily.

"Should I lie on my side with you behind me?" she asked. "We might feel as comfortable as we do on the road."

"I am never comfortable like that," he said, coming up on his elbow and resting his head on his hand to look down on her.

Her shoulder brushed his chest. "But— I know we are usually on the hard ground . . ."

" 'Tis not that." He looked as if he meant to say something, and instead he rolled onto his back again. "Enjoy your sleep, Florrie."

"And you as well," she murmured.

Their shoulders brushed with any movement, so she tried not to move at all. She stared at the beamed ceiling of the room, which flickered as the fire cast its glow. Though she was warm, and more comfortable than she'd been since the journey began, she was too aware of the man at her side.

But . . . the thought of eventually sleeping alone someday almost saddened her. This adventure would have to end. When it was over, would she have had some effect on him? Could she convince him that killing her father would harm Adam's very soul?

There was a bird singing insistently out the window. That was the first thing that penetrated Florrie's deep, comfortable slumber. And then the incredible feeling of heavy warmth.

Heavy?

Awareness came back to her slowly, and she realized that sometime in the night, she and Adam had become entangled in the narrow bed. He yet slept on his stomach, but his upper body lay half across hers, his arm flung across her chest, his head on the same pillow as hers. He faced her in his sleep, his dark lashes resting on his cheeks. He was relaxed, his expression peaceful rather than wary, as if nothing weighed on his mind, not revenge, not kidnapping.

His body pressed her into the mattress, but it

was not uncomfortable—in fact, even though her breast was flattened beneath him, the sensation was . . . pleasurable. More than pleasurable; it made her want to rub up against him.

Suddenly his eyes blinked several times and opened, and they were nose to nose, staring at each other.

He said nothing to her; he must be noticing all the places they were pressed together. Then slowly, he leaned his head to hers, his lips but a breath away, as if waiting for her to refuse.

She couldn't—she didn't want to. She lifted her head to meet him, pressing her mouth to his over and over, as if making up for what they'd held back from the night before.

He moved then, sliding over her, first his entire chest, then one leg riding hers, and dipping between. His hips followed, his erection prominent, pressing down on her, until she eagerly parted her thighs to accommodate him. He was wearing breeches; she was wearing his loose shirt, well down past her knees, but that wasn't much between their bare flesh. He slanted his head for a bolder kiss, even as he sank between her thighs and rolled his hips. The shock of his body so intimately against hers made him groan as if he ached.

She returned the sound against his lips, sliding her hands up the hot skin of his arms, then across his back, with its firm muscles and the ridge of his spine. She held him against her, thinking of nothing but the pleasure he gave her, the way they moved as one. Every press of his hips made her push up against him. She wanted more, she wanted the passion promised, the way it stretched out before her toward some culmination she could only imagine.

The bird was still singing insistently out the window, and Adam at last lifted his head, his expression suffused with comprehension. He gave a piercing birdcall of his own, startling her; the other "bird" went silent.

" 'Twas Robert?" she whispered.

He nodded. And although they both knew that this madness could not continue, she wanted to wrap her legs about him, hold him to her, make him share what a man and woman would share together. She wanted to know everything, before she never saw a man again except for a priest.

But did she want to be one of the women he eased himself with, the desperate women who needed a man for the night? That wasn't how she saw herself.

When he rolled off her, she didn't stop him. They didn't speak as they dressed, their backs to each other. A moment had been lost, she knew, but she'd also overcome a temptation.

Adam was both glad that his brother had interrupted him, and angry. The temptation of Florrie was beginning to overwhelm him. What would he have done—what would she have allowed him to do? Lying between her thighs, feeling the heat of her beneath him, had made him forget every promise to himself to keep her safe. He'd almost lost himself without even being inside her. He felt like an immature boy again, one who wanted to prove himself to a woman.

He didn't want to use Florrie like that. His few sexual encounters had been exciting, but hurried, more about immediate need, both his and the woman's. With Florrie, he wanted to take his time, explore every inch of her. He needed to watch her face when he gave her the ultimate pleasure. The fact that he was more concerned about her than himself struck him hard, for it did not bode well for his future. He did not want to feel something more for Florrie, but he feared it was already too late.

Out in the stable yard, where Robert and Michael waited to make their report, Adam called on every bit of his skill at presenting an impassive face. When Florrie wasn't looking, Robert nudged him from horseback, grinning, and Adam gave him a cold stare that had his brother's eyebrows rising.

Florrie handed out the food they'd purchased within, with bread still soft and warm instead of hard and cold. She'd spread it with butter, and the other two gave her appreciative thanks for the rare treat.

"Sir Adam," Michael said, "neither Robert nor I found anything unusual in the night, but I could not discount my feelings of unease."

Florrie's happy expression faded and she listened intently.

Robert sighed as they began to ride across the yard, into the tunnel beneath the inn, and back out into the sunlight. "I know not what he's talking about."

Michael gave Robert an impatient frown. "We must not discount our intuition, Robert. We have been followed before. The League—"

"You know it will take time to send fresh men," Robert said dismissively.

"Then we'll continue to the east," Adam said. "London can wait. I overheard a group of travelers in the public room this morn, heading out. Let us ask to journey with them."

"Could we endanger them?" Florrie asked.

"Not if we leave them before dark. Someone traveling far behind us might be misled by so large a group." He looked at her, trying to give her a ready smile, when he was still trying to banish the scent of her hair from his thoughts. "My lady wife, are you prepared to soften their mistrust of us?"

"She should ride with you upon your horse to give the appearance of frailty," Robert suggested. "The traveling party surely could not refuse that."

Even though it was a good idea, Adam sensed that Robert had other motives for keeping Florrie so close to Adam. What purpose did his brother serve? Did he not understand that a woman like

Florrie would do her family's bidding? Robert could not change that.

Florrie met his gaze with serenity.

"Will it bother you to ride with me . . . Katherine?" he asked softly.

She shook her head, her eyes suddenly big as she watched him. "Nay, Edmund."

"Take your feet out of the stirrups," he said.

She did so, obviously thinking to dismount. Instead, he lifted her from her saddle and settled her across his thighs, just behind his pommel. Her hip pressed into his groin.

"Forgive me if this is uncomfortable," he murmured, unable to stop looking into her eyes. "I do not have a pillion for you to sit upon behind me."

"I do not mind," she said, sounding almost breathless.

It was going to be a long day.

Chapter 14

Florrie thought it was both difficult and easy to ride sheltered within Adam's strong arms. It was easy, because it certainly helped them overcome the reticence of the small group of travelers they asked to ride with. It was an extended family—two brothers, Ralph and Godfrey Boorde, their wives and five children, as well as two men-at-arms. The Boordes did not hide their suspicion about three strange men joining them, but the women's expressions softened when they looked on Florrie. She kept her head against Adam's chest as if she didn't have the strength to lift it, but she smiled at each person with gratitude.

And of course, riding with Adam was difficult, because it was hard to forget how wonderfully their bodies had moved together in a different way just that morn.

The elder brother in the traveling group, Ralph Boorde, tall and lean, wearing a grim frown, asked, "Is she ill? We cannot be riskin' our families."

She was about to fall back on what had worked before, but Adam was quicker. His large, warm hand slid over her stomach. She glanced up to see him grin with pride.

"My wife is early on with child," he said. "'Tis no sickness you can catch—unless your wives do."

The women laughed and the men looked chagrinned. But Florrie knew that she and Adam had won them over. He might think that the League had not taught him how to blend in with people, but he'd learned well on his own.

"And we will only be with you for part of the day," he continued. "Then we head south."

That seemed to ease even the doubters.

Their small party joined the tail of the larger group, composed of horses, a donkey, and a cart carrying the smaller children. Michael and Robert were positioned at the end. Throughout the day, the two of them would take turns dropping behind to keep watch.

The horse ambled slowly, and Florrie rocked with its gait, safe and content within Adam's arms. Quietly, she asked, "Have you ever been to London?"

He shook his head. "Have you?"

"Nay, but my sisters have, and their descriptions defy even my imagination. The number of churches with spires touching the clouds is awe-inspiring, and their bells are like music when they all ring out at once. When you travel on the Thames, you float by palaces of the very rich."

"So you will see your father's home for the first time," he said softly.

She didn't want to think about Adam's reasons for this journey, so she only answered, " 'Tis not so grand or on the river, according to Matilda. There are others far finer. She also said the streets are full of more people than you can count, and you can buy anything you need at little shops, or right on the streets. And people actually live on London Bridge, so massive is it! Their businesses are right beneath their homes. And at the docks, there are ships from all over the world. I will be glad to see that."

She did not say "before I enter the convent," knowing how he seemed to dislike the reminder. She felt some of his tension leave him.

"Perhaps, when this is all over," she mused, "you can begin to look for a wife there."

His arms stiffened around her, and she looked up to see him frowning.

"I do not wish to speak about a wife with you, *Katherine*." He emphasized her alternate name mildly.

"And why not? I have spent my life hearing about courtship and marriage, and knowing it would not happen for me."

"You are a woman, regardless of how they treated you. It cannot have been easy to hear about something every woman expected."

"Not at first, but sometimes I thought it was easier to be me, with no pressure, no fears of my future. But you will need a wife to make you happy. You cannot spend all your days doing the work of . . . your brethren."

She was a looking for a word to disguise the League of the Blade, but perhaps she'd chosen wrong. After all, "brethren" could also mean his own brothers, whom he'd helped raise.

He seemed to understand her meaning, for he smiled. "Fear not for me, Katherine. I understand how the *brethren* work. I will only be with them once a year. If they choose to have me back. Other than that, I will live my own life."

"Ah, then you definitely need a wife. Only a woman can make you truly happy."

It should hurt to talk about another woman spending every night in his bed, but Florrie was practical; she could not let hurt pierce her deeply. It was obvious that Adam needed gentle companionship by the way he was drawn to her. She wanted him to be happy—did she not?

When he made no reply, she said, "I believe you do not think of a wife, because you do not consider your future at all."

"Katherine, I have spent my life thinking of the future."

"But the moment you've concentrated on for so long is almost here. What happens then? How will you support yourself once you no longer live with . . . your brethren?"

"I have land. 'Twill be good to finally reside there."

"Oh, so you have a home!" she said, feeling relieved that he would not live in poverty.

"I have not seen it in nineteen years."

Though his words were stark, stripped of emotion, she felt it all for him. Because of her father, he'd been torn from his home. It had surely been deemed too dangerous to risk the three brothers living there.

There was a lump in her throat that she could barely speak around, but she forced herself to say, "Land will appeal to a woman and her family. So now you have to consider how to appeal to a woman to earn her favor. Much as some marriages occur regardless of the feelings of the bride and groom, 'tis always better to be pleased with one's marriage partner."

He gave her a dubious look.

"I have not had much experience personally, but I have watched my sisters for many years. Most of all, a woman wants your respect and consideration." She frowned. "I am not certain Matilda succeeded there, but she cared more about being a marchioness than anything else. A woman who marries you will not be looking for a title, of course, but you are a powerful, landed knight. You will not have difficulty."

"I am please you think so," he said dryly.

"You must offer to assist her in even the smallest thing, whether it be helping her from her horse or walking with her up the stairs."

"And of course, those things allow a man to

touch a woman, and see if there is that intimate awareness of each other."

She hoped he did not look down to see how red her face had become. "Now you are thinking correctly," she said. "A woman also likes to know that you can protect her, and 'tis obvious just looking at you that you are well trained."

"It is?" he countered pleasantly. "And how can that be if she has not seen me in battle or training?"

"Oh, well . . . your shoulders are . . ." Her voice faded away. How did a conversation about appealing to women lead to the width of his shoulders and the strength of his thighs? ". . . adequate."

"Adequate shoulders? Such a compliment will send a man's head spinning."

She elbowed him lightly in the stomach, and he grunted.

"At court, I hear that dancing is important," she continued brightly. "You have already told me that you'll have no problem with that. It still surprises me that they bothered with dances in your . . . training."

"Not if you look at it from my *brethren's* position. They wanted me to blend in with other people, wherever I was. It was important to them that in so many ways I behave normally. They just did not consider . . . anything else."

That made them both think of the League again, and she slumped back against him, biting her lip.

Suddenly, she felt his mouth against her ear, and his breath made her shiver.

"There are more intimate things to speak of that are important in a marriage," he whispered.

Guiltily, she looked around lest her companions—or their children—hear Adam's words. But she couldn't speak.

"Should you not explain what would please a woman in her wedding bed?"

She gave a little choked cough. His deep laughter reverberated through her. Perhaps they'd exhausted this topic.

It was not long later when they reached the banks of the River Nyne. Even to Florrie's eyes, she thought the bridge they'd meant to use looked unsteady. It was made of wood, not stone, and barely wide enough for the cart full of children. There were gaping holes in the planks where the horses would tread.

"The horses will need to swim the river," Adam said.

Michael drew his to a halt at their side. "'Tis deep water here. We should go north."

The two Boorde brothers obviously agreed with Michael, because soon the party headed north beside the Nyne. Michael offered to be the one to occasionally ride into the river to check the depth. After time passed, it was decided to take the risk and swim the horses rather than journey any farther out of the way. The cart would float.

Florrie found herself very nervous, which dismayed her. She trusted Adam to see her safely across to the other side, but she kept looking at the cart full of children. Only one mother rode in it, along with the three smallest children, who could not safely hold on riding with an adult. One was only an infant, held in her arms.

"We have done this before," Godfrey Boorde said, as he exchanged places with one of his men-at-arms to take his turn driving the cart.

He was not as grim as his elder brother, who'd been so suspicious of Florrie and her companions.

"Can all of you swim?" she asked, knowing how few people ever learned.

"Nay." He gave Florrie a cheerful gap-toothed smile. "But the cart is like a little boat."

She nodded and smiled in return, but it felt forced. She watched the first of the riders cross, and saw that the horse kept to the riverbed for quite a distance out, then only had to swim for ten or fifteen yards. The horse labored successfully. Everyone breathed an audible sigh of relief when the animal touched ground again and began to stride through the current.

At last it was time for the cart. Robert rode north of it, to try to break the force of the water before it reached the cart. The woman riding in it eyed the river with wide eyes, but she gave Godfrey Boorde a grim smile before he began the journey across. The cart bobbled over the stone bed of the river, and the two children clung to her knees, while she gripped the baby. One started crying, then eased to little hiccups rather than sobs, when at last the cart's labored progress eased as it began to float. The horse pulled strongly as it swam against the current, and Florrie knew it would only be another moment or two before the horse reached land again.

And then a little boy, with perhaps only two years, staggered from the women and leaned out as if to touch the water. The woman reached for him, the uneven current dipped the cart, and the boy fell in.

Florrie found herself dumped so quickly from Adam's horse that she collapsed to her knees. And then he rode into the water. Ralph Boorde's horse was in water up to his chest behind the cart, not yet swimming, yet resisting Ralph who tried to turn it downstream. Robert was already on the far side, and he and Michael, still on the near side, took off at a gallop along both riverbanks, outracing Adam. The two men-at-arms had also ridden their horses into the water, but it was Adam who flung himself from the horse's back and started swimming powerfully for the child.

Florrie lurched to her feet and ran with her awkward gate, her breath soon coming in gasps. She could see the child's head bob to the surface and then disappear. She frantically pointed, as if Adam could actually see what she was doing while he was swimming. Behind her there were screams and cries, and she knew that Godfrey Boorde had to get the cart to safety before anyone else was hurt.

And then Adam dove under water, and something inside her froze to ice. It was summer; the water couldn't be too cold for swimming. Surely that wasn't the problem.

And then he reappeared, and she realized he was looking for the little boy. He dove again.

She saw that farther downstream, Michael had already come to a halt. He had a length of rope in one hand, and was quickly attaching it to an arrow, which he fitted to a bowstring. He shot it across the water, the rope trailing behind.

Robert, on the far side of the river, flung himself from his horse to retrieve the fallen arrow. Without speaking, they seemed to know what each other would do. Had they been trained in even something such as this? Between them, they tightened the rope hard, then lowered it until it skimmed the uneven surface of the Nyne. Grimly, they faced upstream to await Adam.

One of the soldiers on horseback had already passed Robert and guided his horse right into the water, a fallback position should the rope not work.

Florrie saw Adam again, but she no longer saw the little boy. Her lungs burned from her staggering run. She could only imagine what Adam was feeling.

And then he surfaced again, and this time, she saw the dark head of the little boy cradled near his chest.

"He has the child!" she screamed to whomever could hear her.

She was getting closer to Michael now, who was squatting to keep the rope low, his gaze focused on Adam. Heart-stopping moments later, with one hand, Adam caught the rope, then positioned it beneath his arm. The water swirled around him, but slowly he made his way along the rope toward the near shore. Michael and Robert pulled hard, and she could see Michael's grimace, even as his head fell back with the strain. If he dropped the rope—

But then Adam got his feet beneath him, sparing Michael and Robert some of the tension. Adam still held the rope until he was waist deep, and then he subdued the screaming, thrashing boy with both arms tight about him.

Florrie was laughing and crying at the same time as she approached. Ralph Boorde had already galloped past her, and now he flung himself from the saddle to take the little boy, who'd begun to scream, "Papa!"

Adam staggered, water dripping from him in sheets. He put a hand on Michael's shoulder, exchanging a relieved grin with the knight, then turned to wave to his brother on the far side of the river.

Florrie stood alone, hugging herself, her smile so wide it almost hurt. He'd saved that little boy, forgetting his sworn mission, regardless of the danger to his own life. And then she flung herself into his wet arms and just held on.

Adam tried to hold her away after a moment. "You shall be soaked through!" He spoke between gasping breaths, then bent over and began to cough.

She pounded his back. "You might have swallowed the whole river! You were beneath the surface so long, I thought—I thought—" But she couldn't say what she thought, so much did those emotions terrorize her.

The little boy had stopped crying, and now was sucking on his thumb, breathing in little uneven breaths. He lay contentedly on his father's chest.

Ralph Boorde put out his trembling hand, and Adam gripped it. "Sir Edmund, I will never be able to repay ye for what ye've done."

Adam pushed his wet hair from his eyes. "No repayment is necessary. You would have done the same for us."

"But whether we would 'ave succeeded or"—he eyed Michael—"thought of yon rope across the water, well, ye've taught us a fine lesson."

"But we still have the rest to get across the river," Adam said.

"We'll tie the child to me. He screams somethin' fierce, but he's lost the choice."

Not long after, the entire company reunited on

the far side, and Ralph's sobbing wife held her little boy, who looked like he had no idea why his mother was hugging him so tightly.

Florrie watched Adam's chagrin as everyone praised him.

At last, he looked down on her. "You are crying," he said in surprise.

She quickly wiped away a tear. "'Tis glad I am to see a babe reunited with his mother. I feel the woman's fear, 'tis all."

But that was partly a lie. She felt her own fear, and knew a profound confusion. She had not wanted to lose Adam. That meant he was becoming too important to her. She never allowed such a thing to happen, not even with her own family.

They had their midday meal near the half wall of a sheep enclosure on the far side of the Nyne, and everyone was in good spirits. Adam wished they'd all stop thanking him. He felt so . . . exposed, as if these people would speak about him to others, and someone coming along would recognize him.

But it felt good to know he'd saved the child.

He found himself reluctantly entertained by Florrie's antics. She offered to share some of their abundance of cheese with the other party, and as she limped to the two women, Adam knew that any suspicion on their part was long gone. She continued to play the part of his wife admirably, glancing at him occasionally as if he might need her, bringing him the choicest piece of cold pheasant offered by the Boordes.

If they were going to play man and wife, he might as well enjoy it. In dry clothes now, he put his arm around her when she reached his side, even as he took the meat from the linen cloth and began to eat. She smiled up at him and coyly batted her long eyelashes.

"So women flirt with their husbands even after they've gotten the marriage they want?" he asked with amusement.

"They should."

She relaxed against him, one muscle at a time, almost reluctantly.

He let his fingers gently play with her earlobe, then his thumb rode up and down her neck. "Am I doing this correctly?"

"I—I think so," she breathed.

"Come, let me walk you over to the trees where you can see to your needs."

Arms about each other, they walked past the rest of their companions, who smiled or nodded, even as they went back to sharing food with their families. More than one person was walking about, easing stiff muscles, so Adam had to lead her farther away than he meant to. The voices faded behind them.

When she would have pulled away, he held her still, speaking softly against her ear, where he could inhale the sweet scent of her. "When I am courting, how close can I be with a woman?"

She didn't look up at him as she spoke hesitantly. "You should hold her hand."

He kept his arm around her shoulders. "Might I lean near to her, so that I can smell the way she perfumes her skin?"

She didn't answer. He tipped up her chin, forcing those mysterious green eyes to meet his.

His mouth was just above hers. "Am I permitted to kiss a woman whom I am courting?"

She watched his mouth, her own lips parted. "Here? Only in moments of deep privacy, with a woman he is already betrothed to, should a man—"

"But now we are pretending to be married," he interrupted.

And then he kissed her, not with the passion and need she'd aroused in him at dawn. Now he wanted her sweetness, her goodness, and he could taste them in the gentle trembling of her parted lips. For only a moment, he let himself imagine that they were other people, not separated by warring families and revenge and opposite destinies. He was supposed to be a married man, with a child on the way, and he took full advantage, sliding his hand over her stomach as if to feel the babe—but letting his fingertips briefly brush a bit too low. She jerked in his arms.

He didn't care who watched, for all thought them newly married, caught up in the joys of impending parenthood. But not Robert and Michael. That thought doused his passion, made him glance up and see both an amused Robert and an impassive Michael watching them. Did Adam look as much the fool as he was suddenly feeling? Teasing Florrie served no purpose except his own amusement. She didn't need this from him; she was only trying to help out of the goodness of her heart.

A wife, indeed. As if he were even thinking of such a thing, when his loins were overruling his head.

Or was he thinking about it *because* of Florrie? That was an unsettling thought.

Florrie put a hand on his chest, and he looked down at her once more. Her expression was bemused, troubled, and he knew he'd done that to her.

"Ad—Edmund," she corrected herself, then whispered, "I know not what you want of me."

He didn't know either, so he only kissed her hand, and led her back to their traveling companions, who were preparing to depart.

Chapter 15

Adam tried to devote his attention to the dangers of the road. According to Michael, they were entering Huntingdonshire, and they would soon cross Ermine Street, begun by the Romans over a thousand years before. It was the most heavily traveled highway in the country—the last place he wanted to be. If someone had spies looking for them, this road to London would be the perfect place to keep watch. But all they had to do was cross it quickly, and head farther east.

As they approached it, with its old Roman mile markers, Adam debated pulling up the hood of his and Florrie's cloaks. But it was summer, and that might be even more suspicious. Going north or south, he could see several lone riders, perhaps messengers by the speed they rode, and a line of mule-driven carts loaded with covered goods. He felt tense as they rode onto the packed earthen road, letting the horse pick between the holes that pockmarked it from centuries of use.

Since they were nearing the wet fens, the ground here supported an abundance of trees. Someone could be hiding anywhere to watch the travelers. Adam felt like he had a giant target on his back. He must have held Florrie too tightly, for she looked up at him with a confused expression.

"Forgive me," he murmured, looking up and down the road, then feeling relieved to leave it behind.

"'Tis very busy here," she said. "Do you think we've been seen?"

He shrugged. "I hope the size of our party is misleading."

But it must not have been, for an hour later, in broad daylight, Robert came riding up fast behind their party, chased by four men, their swords raised.

"To arms!" Robert shouted.

There were gasps and cries among the Boordes, and almost immediately, as if they'd known to prepare for robbery on dangerous roads, Ralph, Godfrey and their men-at-arms began to draw around the women and children, protecting them. Adam only had a moment to release Florrie to their care. He looked down on her anxious face.

"Oh, do be careful!" she cried.

He gave her a grim smile. "Others have more to fear. Trust me."

She nodded.

He, Michael, and Robert, along with the two men-at-arms, rode away from the party to meet the assault head-on. With a slash of his sword, Adam turned aside the first man, who lost his own weapon before tumbling to the ground.

Another villain avoided the main defense and headed for the women and children. Adam chased him, saw the man vault from the saddle, elude one of the Boorde brothers, and raise his sword as if he meant to harm innocents. To Adam's shock and fear, Florrie came forward with her dagger raised. Adam was trying to get near, but with his focus on her, he didn't notice that one of the attackers had come too close. He heard the movement of air as the sword slashed at him, and he flung himself from the saddle, feeling a sharp sting along his ribs.

But he was on the ground now; between the Boordes and him, they killed the coward who'd threatened the women.

Adam turned back to the rest of the battle. Michael had already sent his opponent fleeing on horseback. Another attacker fought Robert on foot with both sword and dagger. The last villain realized that he faced two men-at-arms and Michael. The element of surprise was obviously lost. He yanked hard on his reins, fleeing the scene while riding low over his horse's neck, even as Robert buried his sword in the final man.

"Should we give chase?" one of the soldiers shouted.

Adam started to speak, then remembered he wasn't in charge.

Ralph Boorde shook his head. "The cowards be dead or gone. We must flee this place soon before they return."

In fury, Adam drove the point of his sword into the dirt and leaned on the hilt. How could such villains be from the League of the Blade? One had targeted the women and children, perhaps even Florrie herself! Or would her own father instruct his men to do such a thing? He had to know one way or the other.

"Master Boorde, take your families and move on," he said. "My men and I will see to the bodies."

"We cannot ask ye to bear such responsibility alone!" Godfrey Boorde replied.

"I would feel better if you were all safe. We needed to turn away from this eastern path eventually, and will take the opportunity now. If we split our party, this might confuse any returning villains."

"But after all ye've done for us—"

"Nay, please go with God, and know that we have appreciated your company."

Though the children cried and the women looked wide-eyed with shock, at last the Boorde families rode away. Adam turned to Florrie, who stood with her arms about her and looked almost lost.

She looked at the two dead men and shuddered. "Thieves?" she asked weakly. "Surely they could not be Bladesmen."

Michael and Adam searched the two bodies, then shook their heads to Adam.

"What were they looking for?" Florrie demanded.

He sighed. "Identifying tokens that mark them as Bladesmen. They carry none."

She put a trembling hand to her throat. "Then they're from my father . . . ?"

"Nay, we cannot say that for certain. They could very well be thieves."

"And with all the travelers just behind us, they choose *us*?" she demanded bitterly.

"The road was crowded, but we had left the safety of its numbers." He put an arm around her shoulders, and she let him draw her against him, though her body remained stiff with tension. "You know not their purpose, Florrie. Even if they work for your father, they are far from London and his control. They might not care who they killed as long as they were paid, and he could have no say in that."

Biting her lip, she nodded. Suddenly a frown lowered her brows, and she stepped away from him, looking down at a smear of blood on her upper sleeve. Adam stiffened. How had she been hurt?

"What is—" she began, then touched his side. Her fingers were stained red. "You are bleeding!"

Adam looked down at the gash in his tunic. "I barely felt it," he said. "I will help Robert and Michael hide the bodies, and then—"

"Nay, you will not," Robert said sternly. "We're near the fens, and surely it will be easy to weigh down two bodies and have them sink. You let Florrie see to your wound. We'll return quickly, and then we can depart."

Annoyed, Adam watched Robert and Michael put the bodies across a horse, then ride away, disappearing into a path between trees.

Florrie was already picking at his tunic where it stuck to him. "You need to remove this."

"Not right in the open. We'll ride to the trees."

Only when they were sheltered from prying eyes, did Adam reluctantly remove his tunic.

"I do not have many garments," he said in disgust, as he saw the tattered, bloodstained slit.

"I will mend them," she said distractedly. "Now remove the shirt."

He was tempted to tease her about such an order, but her expression was so full of concern and determination—and guilt.

He took her arm, made her look at him. "Florrie? What causes you such pain?"

Her eyes welled up. "Is it my fault they found us, Adam? I insisted on going to the inn."

"Nay, do not fear, my lady," he murmured. "We already suspected we were followed. The inn might have given us one more day free of attack. I fault myself, for not realizing they would so boldly attack by day. I could have cost those good people their lives."

"You did not know!" she protested.

He caught her face in his hands. "Neither of us could know. Do you understand?"

They stared at each other for a moment, and at last she nodded. "Very well, then. Remove your shirt."

He pressed his lips into a thin line to keep from teasing her. When the shirt was gone, she made him hold his arm up so she could better see the wound. It spanned across his ribs, front to back.

"The blade skittered across bone," she said, shaking her head. "One inch higher or lower . . . Tell me, do you have herbs with you, perhaps yarrow?"

He shook his head.

"We could find the nearest monastery and purchase some," she said with hope.

"Nay, we are not alerting anyone else to our presence. We will wash the wound and bind it. I'll tear up the remains of the shirt for bandages."

After he'd made strips of cloth for her, he laid back on the blanket she'd spread for him. She soaked several in wine and began to dab at his flesh. Her fingers were cool and gentle, and she worked over him with a faint furrow in her brow. She was born to nurture others, but it made him almost uncomfortable, as if he were a child.

Or was it that he could see her caring for a child? The child she'd never have?

Robert and Michael returned during her ministrations, and Robert gave him a smirk. At least his brother resisted teasing him right in front of Florrie.

"The blood yet flows," she finally said, looking up at him with concern. "Binding it might not—"

"Then burn it," he said.

Florrie inhaled sharply, her mind suddenly full of images of Adam's charred flesh. How could he bear the pain? Then she remembered the other wounds upon his body—the wounds upon his soul. He'd borne terrible pain his entire life, more than she could imagine.

And yet he was going to add more pain to his soul by trying to kill her father. She was trying so hard to lighten his life, to make him happy. Yet always his ultimate goal never left his thoughts.

Without speaking, Michael built a fire.

A grim Robert set out their meal of dried apples and cheese. "I'll see if I can snare a rabbit," he said. "Food will help heal you."

Adam only nodded, expressionless, as he stared at the fire. Florrie followed his gaze and saw Michael put a dagger into the flames.

She couldn't seem to catch her breath. She had performed this very technique herself; what made this different? Perhaps because Adam wouldn't have been wounded at all if he hadn't been trying to save her life—again.

Michael came forward, and under the gloom of the trees, the dagger seemed to glow in his hand.

Florrie stayed at Adam's side, and when she tried to take his hand, he gave her a strange look.

"I—I want to be of help," she said, feeling that it was a lame excuse. But she had to do *something*.

"I might grip you too hard," he said, refusing her touch. Then he looked at Michael. "Do it quickly."

With precision born of practice, Michael laid one side of the dagger along half the wound, and Adam stiffened, throwing back his head. He made no sound. Florrie only heard her own tortured gasps. Michael laid the other side of the dagger on the rest of the wound, and it was done.

The flesh was charred, and the bleeding had stopped. Adam breathed deeply through his nose, eyes closed. His rib cage expanded and contracted powerfully. Florrie wanted to gape at him, to twist her fingers, to beg him to say that he was well. Instead she used the wine-soaked linen once more on the wound, and flinched when he flinched.

"I wish we had a salve to protect it," she said, shaking her head. After covering the injury with linen, she wound several strips around his waist to hold it in place. "You need to rest now."

To her shock, he sat up, then got to his feet. He didn't even stagger, although his jaw was obviously clenched.

"Nay, we must go," he said through his teeth. "Will you bring me another shirt, Florrie?"

"But . . . Robert is bringing you a rabbit. We need to cook it, and you need to eat it."

Michael put up a hand. "We can spare an hour. We are hidden in the trees. If the villains return, they'll assume we fled."

Adam obviously wanted to disagree, but Michael was already ignoring him, beginning to build a wooden spit for the rabbit. While Florrie helped him into another shirt, Robert returned with the promised meal. During the time it baked, little was said, and Florrie found herself glancing repeatedly at Adam.

He looked at her at last, and gave a tight smile. "Aye, my lady, it hurts, but I will survive."

She rolled her eyes melodramatically, hoping to amuse him. But inside she couldn't help her worry. She needed her healing herbs, and felt panicked that she'd had none for a poultice to draw out the bad humors.

"Should we . . . wait until the morn to leave?" she asked, looking up at the darkening sky, and the faint pink streaking out from the setting sun.

"We'll go south for several hours tonight," Adam said. "There are no clouds to block the full moon."

When no one protested, Florrie stifled her own worry. The roads they'd been journeying on were terrible, and they did not improve. After only a few hours traveling by moonlight, Michael's horse stepped in a marshy hole and broke its leg. They had to kill the poor animal, leaving them with only three horses. As they made camp, Florrie tried not to watch Adam with too much worry, praying he would not be unable to go on, like the horse. Once more they slept entwined, and he fell asleep immediately, which she was thankful for. He needed to heal.

She herself found it difficult to relax at first. The worry she was feeling was new to her; she was usually so good at taking things as they happened, not creating new fears in her own mind. But for so long she'd thought of Adam as invincible, a man trained to do fantastic feats.

But he was human, and a sword could bring him down. Once again, she reminded herself that they were using each other for specific purposes, that when this was over, they would separate. She couldn't care too much, couldn't need him this much.

When Florrie awoke in Adam's arms, she felt the deep dread of something wrong. She lay still, trying to sort through her confusion; and then she realized that Adam felt too warm to her.

Instead of healing, his wound was becoming inflamed, and his body with it.

Sitting up, she rolled him onto his back and tried to pull his tunic up, but it was held in place by his hips.

Groggily, he opened his eyes. "Florrie, what is amiss?" Then he gave a crooked grin. "My charms have at last succeeded in captivating you."

Robert came up on his elbow to blink and stare. Michael was gone, keeping his turn at the watch.

Florrie smiled at Adam as naturally as possible. "I need to see your wound."

He grimaced. "Cannot a man rise to face the morn first?"

She shook her head and tugged on his tunic. Sighing, he lifted his hips, and she was able to slide up his tunic, as well as his shirt. As she suspected, the bandage appeared crusted with unhealthy pus.

Adam was looking at her face. "Not so good, I believe."

Smiling, she put a hand on his forehead. "How do you feel?"

He shrugged, not quite meeting her eyes. "Wounded. It will pass."

"Not without medicine, it will not," she said.

"Florrie, I already told you—"

"You are fevered now, are you not? That means the wound is inflamed. We must find a healer."

"Nay." He sat up, pulling down his garments. "'Twould be too dangerous, and not just for us. I have harmed enough innocents."

"And saved them, too," she said crossly. "Lie back down, so I can change the dressing."

To her surprise, he reluctantly did so without further comment.

But when they were riding south, skirting near the reeds of the low, damp fens, mud sucking at the horses' hooves, Florrie could feel that he was not holding her weight across his lap so easily. She convinced him to allow her to ride astride, with him behind her, and it was a mark of his illness that he did not fight too strenuously. They left the fens behind at last, and the countryside had more woodlands and meadows and farm fields. By midday he was slumped against her, heat shimmering between them, dampening her back. She called a halt at the edge of a stand of trees.

Adam lifted his head. "What is it? Is someone following us?"

She looked at Robert, whose usually cheerful face was now shadowed with concern.

"Adam—" Robert bit off his words.

"I am fine," Adam said. He tried to dismount, and almost missed the stirrup, gripping the saddle hard to help him down.

Before Florrie could dismount, he took the horse's reins and led them deeper into the woods. At least he was still in his right mind.

But perhaps not for long.

When Robert and then Michael joined them, Adam was already kneeling by a stream, drinking water from his cupped hands, then splashing his face.

She looked at the other two men. "He needs rest and medicine. This infection will only worsen."

Robert hesitated, watching as Adam waved a hand dismissively.

"Feel his fever!" she cried at last.

Robert narrowed his eyes but did so, inhaling swiftly. "Adam, she is right, you are truly ill."

Adam only laughed, leaning back against a tree

stump to look up at her. "Florrie, what happened to all of your optimism? 'Tis what I admire most about you."

"One can be an optimist without being a fool," she said. "I am not a fool. You must listen to me, Adam, or your future plans will dissolve into ash."

"'Tis too dangerous to involve anyone else," he said, his voice sounding tired.

"So you've said," she replied, "but I have been thinking. The castle of my sister Christina's husband is north of London. Surely we cannot be too far. She might be persuaded to give us aid and comfort. And of the men following us, who would ever think you would take me, your captive, to the home of my own sister? This is the perfect place to hide and heal."

"Nay, we will not risk it," Adam said. He started to get up, then collapsed back on his butt, frowning.

Florrie stared at Robert, who at last sighed. "Do you think you can persuade your sister to help us?"

Before Florrie could speak, Adam angrily said, "Robert—"

"Nay, you are no longer in charge, big brother," Robert said. "Until you're well, I am in command, as you trained me to be."

Adam blinked at him, but said nothing.

"And we will attempt Florrie's plan," Robert finished.

She suddenly felt nervous, responsible for what she'd proposed. She looked at Michael. "I know not where it is. Her husband is the earl of Standon, in Hertfordshire."

"Ah," Michael said, looking to the south. "With enough time to rest the horses, we could reach her by midafternoon on the morrow."

"Do you see?" Florrie said with excitement. "This will be perfect."

"'Twill be dangerous," Robert said before Adam could speak. "The roads are far more crowded now that we're near London. And how can you know that your sister will help us? You have not spoken with flattery of your family."

"She is the sister nearest to me in age," Florrie said. "Of all of my family, I trust her the most."

Chapter 16

They traveled as much as possible through the outskirts of forests as they sojourned through Cambridgeshire. Florrie understood the danger; she could see how much more populous this county was. Michael had told her that Ermine Street was only a league away in the west, and the large town of Cambridge a league away in the east.

She glanced again at Adam, now riding against his brother's back. He slept, but his face grimaced with his dreams. The dread in her stomach grew tighter.

Robert smiled at her. "He has been injured before, Florrie."

"But not because of me," she said darkly. "This whole journey is the fault of my family."

"He made his own decisions. He knew the risks associated with kidnapping you. Do not forget, he put you in danger as well. And you're an innocent in all of this."

"And are you saying you blame him?" she said in a stunned voice.

"Nay, how can I?"

Robert glanced over his shoulder at his brother. There was a fondness there, a love that Florrie had never seen in her own family. A cold feeling of worry swept through her at the thought of begging her sister Christina for a dangerous boon on the morrow.

"He is my brother, Florrie," Robert continued. "He is doing what he thinks best to restore our family's name and position. Our parents were unjustly murdered, and he needs the truth to come out."

"Would you do the same in his position, challenge my father to a combat to the death?"

Robert's hesitation said it all. But at last he spoke. "I am not the eldest, with the weight of this on my shoulders. 'Tis a burden to him, but one he bears without regret. I do not always understand him, but I can admire his determination."

She nodded and looked forward again, across more endless pasturelands where cattle roamed. She thought again of Robert calling her an "innocent." How could she be innocent, when she knew why her father had committed such unspeakable crimes? She was so afraid to confess the truth, for she couldn't know who would be hurt the worst.

She glanced again at Adam, her gaze lingering in warmth and fear. She had begun this journey in terror, then in anticipation of an adventure. Now it was full of danger and confusion. She would not be the same when it was over.

* * *

They rode through part of the night, then the next morning, but it was slower going with only three horses. Michael and Robert took turns bearing Adam's weight, and Florrie saw to his comfort whenever they stopped. At first, he was alert often, grouchy with having to be coddled, but resigned to being her patient. But the closer they were to Christina's home, and the more ill he became, weakness overtook him. By late morning, it had begun to rain, and the men had to take turns tying him onto their backs. Never in her life had Florrie felt so ill with concern, her fear making her glance at Adam at Robert's back again and again.

The hood of her cloak hung wetly on her cheeks, but she'd stopped trying to push it out of the way. At last, she said, "Talk to me, Robert, or my thoughts will drive me mad."

"I do that to women," he said, nodding in resignation.

She groaned.

He laughed. "Of what would you have me speak?"

Her eyes touched Adam again, yet she hesitated. How transparent was she to Robert, with all her focus on his brother? But why fight her inevitable curiosity?

"He told me how the three of you grew up," she said slowly. "It must have been very difficult."

" 'Twas all I knew, and for a boy, it was exciting. And I had Adam."

"He is only two years older than you!"

"Perhaps it was only our temperaments that made it seem like so much more." Robert grinned. "He was the serious, studious, focused brother. Paul was much like him, especially when we were younger. But I . . . I did not feel the same goals in life that Adam did."

"Yet you're here with him."

"Not at his request," Robert said dryly. "But I do have my honor, and I could not let him do this alone."

"You love him."

"Men do not like to talk of such things, Florrie," he teased. "But aye, how could one not love someone who puts your welfare before all else? Even when he was a young boy, he understood his role as the eldest. No adult had to tell us to go to bed at an appropriate hour, not when Adam was around. My favorite part of the day was training at the tiltyard, but Adam made sure I saw to my studies as well."

"It sounds as if 'twould be easy to resent him."

"Only on occasion. He never made one feel bullied or inferior. I knew he only wanted what was best for me." His amusement faded. "Just as I knew the terrible things haunting him, the images that made him as driven as he was.

She said nothing, feeling sick.

Robert wasn't looking at her. "He saw their lifeless bodies, and it never left him. I remember him screaming with nightmares, but in the end, he was the one who comforted me."

She could not imagine having such a sibling to count on. She had never been close to her sisters, who treated her more as a servant than a friend.

"I . . . I hope that time and separation have helped bridge my relationship to Christina," she said. "I always thought that once they lived away from home, my sisters would understand that we shared a bond that shouldn't be dismissed."

"I cannot help you there. I would have thought Paul would feel that toward us, but he's been gone many long months, and we've heard nothing from him."

Robert's voice was sad, and it surprised her that he had such feelings within him. Not a fortnight ago, she would have thought he never took anything seriously. Everyone hid their truths beneath a mask, it seemed. She'd never thought that of herself, but now she wasn't so sure.

"Though I think going to Christina is our best plan," she said softly, "I admit that I fear asking for her help. What will I do if she refuses? What will happen to Adam?"

"Florrie, I have no doubt in you whatsoever." He gave her his cheerful smile. "Look how you've manipulated us, your kidnappers. You're practically in command now. And you have Adam doing whatever he can for you."

Blinking in astonishment, she gave him a slow nod of thanks for the encouragement.

But in command? How could that be possible?

By late afternoon, Standon Castle reared above the trees of the surrounding woodlands. It had towering curtain walls, with a gatehouse, and a drawbridge over an old-fashioned moat. The moat was mostly marsh and reeds, but the fortress was impressive nonetheless. And inside, the main keep rose above it all, crenellated with battlements along the top.

They found a wooded copse nearby, where the three men would await Florrie.

Adam sat on a wet log, his hands braced on his knees. His eyes looked bleary, but lucid, his face ruddy with fever. "I like this not."

Florrie put her fists on her hips as she confronted him. "You know it will be best if I go in alone. I shall be as any other villager, especially now that my gowns no longer look refined." She spread her skirt. "The hems are ragged and the fabric stained. Who would think me otherwise?"

"But—"

"And if I have a strange man looming over me, will not my sister think I'm being coerced or threatened?" She put a hand on his shoulder and squeezed. "This is Christina, older than me by a year, closest to me of all my family."

"That is not necessarily comforting."

"She will help us," Florrie insisted. "And then I will return for you all."

She stared at his flushed face, and the way he kept his hand on his wound, and felt a flood of worry and tenderness overwhelm her. She could no longer deny that she cared for him, that he mattered deeply to her. How did a temporary adventure dissolve into something that could change her life? If she fell in love with him, how would she ever be able to resign herself to her old life—or the one in the convent she was destined for?

She stepped away and pulled up her hood, then was shocked when Adam reached to grab her arm. She stared down at him in surprise, seeing the urgency in his gaze.

"Be very careful," he said quietly. "Flee if you feel even one bit of suspicion."

"I promise I will. But you need not fear. This will work."

She put her hand over his and held it there for a moment, suddenly wanting to kiss him. But she did not have the right, and would not embarrass herself before Robert and Michael. She prayed to God that Adam's illness would not worsen while she was gone.

She turned away, tugging the hood even lower over her forehead as she moved swiftly through the trees. The wet ferns lashed at her legs, and dripping branches splashed her face. But at last she left the line of trees, and was able to fall in line behind two men pulling a cart of hay toward the castle.

She was tense crossing the drawbridge, but the guards on duty only let their gazes slide right over her, as if she were of no consequence.

Following the muddy road up through the inner ward, she passed the tiltyard in use by the soldiers even as it rained. There were wooden structures built against the curtain walls, housing everything from the garrison of soldiers to the dairy to the blacksmith's shop.

But it was the great keep that drew her attention, rising up to overpower every other structure. She wondered about the people inside, the people now ruled by her *sister*. It was a strange thought.

Then an even more daunting thought occurred to her. What if her sister were not in residence? She looked up and saw that the earl's banner was not flying over the battlements, so he was gone. Her heart began to race. If Christina had traveled with her husband, who would help Adam?

But no sooner had she entered the great hall of the castle, than she saw her sister speaking to a servant. All around her valets dismantled the trestle tables used during dinner. And Florrie's stomach growled, as she realized she'd eaten nothing since that morn.

Florrie stood beside a tapestried wall, waiting for her sister to be alone. Christina was unchanged, which wasn't surprising since she'd only been married less than a year. Her sandy blond hair was piled high beneath a flattering head-dress, and she wore an expression that could only be called . . . mature. She was four and twenty, after all, finally married to the man—and his ti-tle—that their father had wanted for her. Florrie prayed that she was content.

At last, Christina was alone, but to Florrie's dismay, she turned immediately and started through an arched doorway. Florrie hurried after her, but she'd never been as fast as her sister. Once she was in the torchlit corridor, she saw her sister turn the far corner, and she tried to increase her speed before Christina could disappear.

Florrie caught the edge of the wall as she took the turn, and there was Christina, opening a door latch.

Her sister looked up in surprise, then frowned, ducking her head as if to see beneath the stranger's hood. Florrie let the hood drop.

"Florrie?" her sister cried, gaping.

Florrie put a finger to her lips, limping forward. "I must speak with you," she whispered. "'Tis urgent and requires the utmost secrecy!"

"But . . . how did you get here? Who else is with you?"

Florrie motioned to their door. "Can we speak privately in there?"

Christina slowly shook her head. "Nay, 'tis the sewing chamber. Follow me."

They continued down the corridor, going up a circular staircase built into the corner of the keep.

On the next floor, Christina hurried past several doors, then opened one, drawing Florrie in before closing it quickly. "This is the bedchamber I share with my husband."

For the first time, Florrie let some of the stiffness leave her frame. Christina had been surprised—but not dismayed—to see her, and so far Florrie was undiscovered by anyone else. She let herself study the impressive bedchamber, with its whitewashed walls between wooden panels. There were woven mats on the wooden floor, and a wide bed hung with luxurious curtains. Several coffers lined the walls, as well as cupboards displaying a collection of glass bottles.

And then suddenly Christina hugged her. Surprised, Florrie patted her back.

Christina looked almost embarrassed as she stepped away. "Forgive me for such a display, but you cannot imagine how good it is to see you. It can be rather lonely here."

"You need ask no forgiveness," Florrie said, smiling. "'Tis good to see you, too."

Her sister smoothed a hand down her gown. "Did you notice anything different?"

Florrie shook her head, feeling guilty that her thoughts were too filled with Adam.

"I am with child! The babe will not come until the end of the year, so perhaps that is why you did not notice."

"Oh, Christina, I am so happy for you!" Florrie said with honest enthusiasm—and guilt over her own preoccupation. "Your husband must be proud."

"And relieved. His mother is relentless about the future succession, and his heir right now is a cousin no one likes who. . ." She trailed off, studying Florrie at last. "You seem . . . different. And you said you need to speak with me in secret."

Florrie nodded, feeling uneasy again now that the moment was at hand.

"Whom are you traveling with?" Christina asked.

"I have come to you alone," Florrie said, moving closer to take her sister's hands in her own.

Christina's eyes widened. "Alone? How is that possible? Father never even permitted you . . ." Sudden comprehension lit her eyes, which were as green as Florrie's. "He does not know that you have come to me."

"Nay, nor does anyone else know." She took a deep breath, ready to repeat the lies she'd concocted—and feeling surprisingly guilty about it. "I am having an adventure the likes of which I had never imagined. There is a man who—"

"What?" Christina cried, then quieted when Florrie winced and glanced at the door. "A man? A strange man?"

Florrie nodded. "He is one of the guards escorting me to London."

Christina smiled with relief. "Father allowed you to visit at last?"

"Aye, he did, as long as I promised to enter the convent when I return."

Christina's happiness faded. "I had so hoped he would change his mind."

"You know he will not," Florrie said. Her usual optimism and contentment was suddenly hard to fake.

"Surely there would be a man somewhere who wants you."

Florrie winced, though she knew her sister meant well. "Not without a dowry, Christina." She did not need to say that most of the money had gone to her sisters' marriages. She saw the awareness and guilt in Christina's eyes. But it wasn't Christina's fault, so Florrie hurried to say, "Right now it matters not. Allow me to tell you my tale."

With excitement, Christina led her to a cushioned bench near the bare hearth. "I'm listening—and I will not breathe a word!"

Florrie hesitated before sitting down. "I do not want to ruin your furniture."

Christina at last took in Florrie's wet cloak,

filthy hemline, and shoes. Florrie removed the cloak, and Christina gaped at the rest.

"What has happened to you?"

"I told you—an adventure that I will never regret." She sat down on the edge of the bench. "I am being escorted by three knights. They carry a missive for Father, which must be delivered with all speed. But yesterday, we were attacked."

Christina gasped and covered her mouth. "Oh, 'tis so dangerous to travel! And the thieves so bold!"

"These weren't thieves. They wanted that missive, but Father's men defeated them. One of our soldiers, Sir Edmund, was injured in the battle, and the men fear we are yet being followed. I brought them to you, because I knew not what else to do." Florrie wrung her hands together as if at a loss. "Sir Edmund needs healing, but we cannot let anyone know we're here. I would not want to bring notice of you to our enemies. Can you help us?"

Florrie hated to even say so much, but she needed her sister to understand the danger—and see the need for silence. She waited, holding her breath.

Christina didn't hesitate. "How can you even think you need to ask? Of course I will help you! And though 'tis dangerous, the adventure must still be so exciting for you!"

Florrie was surprised—and touched—that her sister understood even that much of her. She smiled warmly. "Aye, it is. 'Twill give me wonderful memories for the rest of my life." She sobered. "But I can delay no longer. I need to bring Sir Edmund inside before his injury worsens. Let me tell you my plan."

Chapter 17

Adam had never in his life felt so weak. Even riding through the countryside had taxed everything within him, and he was mortified by how much he slept, propped up against the backs of his men. He'd always been the oldest, the strongest, and now watching Robert—and Florrie—make all the decisions was frustrating.

Robert was certainly competent enough, Adam knew, from having been involved in his training. But Robert did not take life seriously, and there was a deep part of Adam that worried about trusting him. It was just . . . this illness that made Adam feel so strange. His body was hot one minute, dripping with sweat, then cold enough to shiver the next. Though Michael took care of the horses while they waited for Florrie, Robert had little to amuse himself but the wood he was carving. So he watched Adam too much, making Adam feel like an invalid everyone had to tiptoe around.

"She should be back by now," Adam said, for what had to be the fifth time. Even feeling bleary, he knew he was repeating himself.

Robert sighed. "I understand your concern for her, but this is her sister's home. Nothing will happen to Florrie. It might happen to us, of course," he added nonchalantly.

"Florrie will be able to convince her sister," Adam insisted.

Robert grinned. "See? There is nothing to fear."

Adam wanted to pace his frustration, but the last time he'd tried that, he'd found himself staggering into a tree trunk. It was humiliating to be so humbled.

He suddenly heard Michael's birdcall, the sign that all was well. And then Florrie came from between the trees, and Adam remembered how to breathe. She was smiling with such belief in herself that he was jolted. How had she become this magnificent woman, raised as she'd been?

She came right to him, and instead of hugging him or taking his hand, as she would a man she'd shared intimacies with, she felt his forehead.

He ducked away in annoyance. The world seemed to tilt, and then both Florrie and Robert had his arms. Feeling shaky, Adam let them help him sit, then shook off their concern. "How did you fare?" he asked Florrie tersely.

"Christina will help us. She believed my story of the three of you as Father's men, escorting me to London. But I was still worried about drawing attention, so I told her I would only bring you in, Adam."

Robert heaved a good-natured sigh.

"We will not be long," Adam said.

"You need at least a full day's rest," Florrie scoffed. "Robert, we will contact you by the day after tomorrow at the latest."

Michael had approached silently, and now spoke. "Until then, we will keep watch."

"What excitement," Robert said dryly. "If I would have known I would miss all the good things, I would have stayed home."

"And what good things will you miss?" Florrie demanded. "The part where I keep your brother in bed?"

Adam joined the others in staring at her, trying to hide his amusement.

Her face flushed, and she rounded on Adam. "You are too ill to be up and about. You know what I meant."

Robert chuckled. "I will miss seeing the women of your sister's home. Perhaps she has beautiful ladies-in-waiting."

Florrie folded her arms over her chest. "My sister likes to be the most beautiful one, so I doubt it." Then she glanced at Adam. "Have you removed your spurs? We cannot walk in there looking like we suspiciously left our horses."

He wanted to rise to his feet, to use his height to intimidate, but his illness didn't allow it. She was growing bold, and though he liked it, right now it irritated him.

"Aye, my lady," he said with sarcasm. "Is there anything else you command, that I might be too foolish to realize?"

He saw the hurt pass over her face, but it was gone quickly. She was too used to hiding her feelings. He felt like a monster. Not caring that his brother and servant watched, Adam caught her arm and pulled until she was sitting on his knee.

"Forgive me," he said softly. "My temper seems uncontrollable, and I say things without thinking."

" 'Tis the fever," she murmured, her expression once more concerned and tender.

"You have done a wonderful deed, braving an unknown castle for me."

" 'Tis my sister's home," she demurred, eyes downcast.

But he'd pleased her, restored her spirits, and that was all that mattered. He let her go, then rose to his feet, putting a hand on her shoulder when the weakness overtook him again.

He glanced at his men. "I will return soon, and we will finish what we started."

Both men nodded, but Adam noticed that Florrie looked away.

Though he wanted to walk unassisted, Florrie slid beneath his arm and took it across her shoulders.

"Let me help you through the trees," she said. "Because once we reach the road, it will look too suspicious for you to be seen in such a weakened state. The guards might think we bring the plague to them."

"You are getting very good at disguises," Adam said, giving her shoulder a squeeze. He had to think about that, rather than the way the entire length of her body was pressed to his. Even ill, he couldn't stop wanting her.

Before she could answer, Robert called, "I have been teaching her much while you've been unconscious."

Adam rolled his eyes while Florrie giggled. At last they began to walk through the trees. They had to skirt low-growing brush and step over tree roots, and he found himself reluctantly thankful for her sturdy support. He really must be weaker than he thought. Surely time should have assisted his recovery, but it had not. He had accepted Florrie's suggestion for medicine and healing, because he could not allow himself to fail. He kept telling himself that, but inside he felt growing doubts that he did not want to heed.

When they approached the main road to the castle, Adam stepped away from her and had to pause while weakness made him unsteady. The road to the drawbridge and gatehouse seemed interminable, and with every step he took, he felt ever slower. Florrie kept looking at him with worry, and finally, he stopped glancing at her. It was like seeing his weakness in her eyes. He wanted to be strong for her, to protect her from danger. But she was the one protecting *him* now, and that confused him.

Or perhaps it was the fever.

As they passed beneath the gatehouse, where darkness briefly descended, he imagined the portcullis concealed in the ceiling above them. With one cry of alarm, the guards would lower it, and the sharp metal points would plummet.

But no one seemed suspicious. Several guards were standing together as he and Florrie passed. With her hood down, she even gave the men a smile, and one guard elbowed the other.

Adam gritted his teeth and kept moving, his legs as heavy as if he walked through water. Surely they were being watched the whole way across the inner ward, for his back felt as hot as a target.

But it was the fever. His strength continued to ebb, and Florrie seemed almost far away at his side. He found himself squinting at her in confusion.

She put her arm around his waist. "Adam, how do you fare?" she whispered. "'Tis not much farther. Christina will have a chamber for us."

He only shook his head, for words seemed too difficult.

After that, events slid together. He knew by the sudden coolness that they'd entered the great hall of the keep. Florrie murmured something about finding the garderobe as if she had to relieve herself, and his befuddled brain remembered that that had been part of the plan for them, as two strangers, to leave the great hall. Down a corridor, he saw a woman waiting for them. She gaped up at him, and he wondered if this was Christina, and if she already regretted her agreement.

But she beckoned them onward, and he wanted to groan. He did not think he could walk much farther, and already Florrie labored beneath his weight. But at last they were inside a bedchamber with a bed. He staggered toward it, and it rushed up to meet him.

Florrie gave a soft cry as Adam fell forward. Even though he landed on the bed, she feared for him. "Christina, help me roll him onto his back."

Her sister nervously came forward. "He is so much . . . bigger than I imagined."

"He is a knight," Florrie said distractedly. She felt absurdly proud of him.

Between the two of them, they helped him onto his back. Adam murmured something unintelligible, and Florrie prayed that he would not reveal anything important. She wanted to brush the hair from his face, see if his fever had worsened—but her sister was here, watching her too closely now, and Florrie knew she had to pretend only friendship and concern, not betray the absolute fear and worry that consumed her. Adam was unconscious now, his chest rising and falling too swiftly.

" 'Tis difficult to imagine you alone with him," Christina said.

Florrie wanted to demand the herbs and the peace with which to work, but she could not risk offending her sister. "Is that because you seldom saw men pursue me?"

Christina blinked at her in surprise. "I . . . had not thought of it that way, but I imagine you are correct."

"Well, Sir Edmund is a knight," she said, using Adam's false name. "He was hired for this assignment. But he is a good man, and to see him like this . . ." Her voice failed her, and it took every bit of her restraint to keep from crying over his condition.

"Then we must make him well," Christina said firmly. "You need him to take you to London, so you can see all the wonders therein. I brought you my supply of herbs."

Florrie gave her a grateful smile. Over the next hour, the sisters worked side by side. Florrie stripped Adam of his tunic and shirt, and though she caught her sister's surprised glance, Christina said nothing. How could Christina be surprised at her efficiency with the sick? Florrie had often been the one they came to for help, but perhaps Christina simply hadn't noticed.

She was noticing more than that now, and Florrie couldn't blame her. Adam's chest was wide and firm with muscle, his body well suited for combat.

But the sight of his stained bandage made Florrie forget everything else. While Christina was steeping willow bark in hot water for his fever, Florrie crushed the herbs yarrow and comfrey to make a poultice. After struggling to prop Adam on his side, she laid the paste over the long wound, then covered it with strips of cloth dipped in hot water. She repeated this over many hours, hoping to draw away the infection. Christina came and went, bringing food for Florrie and broth for Adam, which Florrie spooned to his mouth occasionally.

Once, he opened his eyes and seemed to really see her. He searched her face, his expression confused and even yearning. He lifted a trembling hand and touched her cheek. She wanted to cup it against her, hold him close. But his hand dropped back to the bed as he fell asleep again. She found herself wiping away tears of confusion and pain.

As the hours dragged by, Florrie lost focus of everything but Adam, and as she touched his cheek too tenderly, murmuring, "Get well, Adam, please," she forgot that her sister had come back into the bedchamber.

"Adam?" Christina echoed in surprise. "I thought you said his name is Edmund."

Florrie kept her gaze on Adam, knowing her sister would read the truth in her eyes. "Forgive me. I am so tired I do not know what I say."

"Nay, you knew what you said," Christina replied, taking her arm and pulling her to the far side of the chamber.

Florrie found herself trembling more than when she'd been physically attacked. Adam was defenseless, and she only had her own wits to see them through.

"I cannot talk about this, Christina," she said forcefully. "Father gave him specific instructions for our journey to London that have nothing to do with me. He has a special mission to fulfill."

"But he has two names."

Florrie only shrugged.

"And I saw the way he looked at you."

Florrie narrowed her eyes. "I cannot help what he does in this state. But I can only take your meaning as one thing. A man shouldn't look at me at all. Do even *you* think I belong in the convent?" She held her breath, praying that she was handling this the right way.

Christina's face crumpled into concern, and she gripped Florrie's upper arms. "Nay, do not think that! I am hoping this journey to London leads to a better life for you. Though I've spent my life feeling the pressure of father's expectations, I think in many ways it was so much worse for you, because he had no expectations at all."

All the stiffness went out of Florrie in a rush of amazement.

"And yet . . . I always envied your ability to let nothing bother you," Christina admitted, looking guilty. "And sometimes I was angry at you for that."

Could it really be true that Florrie had never understood her sisters at all? Or at least Christina. Or was it maturity that made them both look at their childhood in a different way?

She hugged her sister hard. "Trust me, my dear," she whispered into Christina's ear. "I cannot tell you everything, but I promise to someday."

"Then I will accept that," Christina said as they separated.

They looked at each other, smiling, and then Florrie heard Adam groan.

"Tend to him," Christina said. "I will see you on the morrow."

When Adam awoke, dawn had already passed, by the light piercing through the window shutters. Though he felt exhausted, for the first time in a while his mind seemed to be functioning. With his head propped on a cushion, he was able to see the small chamber—and Florrie, standing in the center of the room, wearing only a cloth wrapped around her. He froze, not quite certain what was going on. She looked more exhausted than he felt, with smudged shadows beneath her eyes. Taking care of *him* had put them there. He told himself that she would take care of any ill person, but that did not stop the feeling of tenderness that tightened his chest.

But now she was taking care of herself. There was a basin of water on the table, and he realized that she was standing on a towel. She rinsed a facecloth in water, dabbed it in a crock of soap, then began to wash first one arm, and then the other. She did not look at him, so he was able to stare at her from beneath lowered eyelids.

He knew he should speak, should alert her, but words were stuck in his parched throat. Instead, he watched her lift her arm, slide the wet cloth down it, then across her shoulder and neck, and to the other side. Water glistened on her skin, ran in tiny rivulets to be captured in the cloth covering her.

Arching her head back, she washed her neck and face, then braced one leg on a chair and began to torture him with smooth strokes along the length of her calf and thigh. Adam's breath was tight in his lungs, his body reacting powerfully to the eroticism of watching her bathe. When she switched legs, the cloth gaped at her hips, and he saw the shadowed recesses of the depths of her body. His eyes could see little, but his mind could imagine.

He should say something, he knew, but then she turned away from him, dropped the facecloth into the basin—and lowered the concealing cloth and fastened it at her hips. The long, slender lines of her back enticed him with a show of feminine strength. As she lifted her arm to wash along her ribs, the round swell of her breast seemed to peek at him, still mostly hidden by the turn of her body, and the shadows in the chamber.

Now he was truly wishing he'd spoken sooner, for this was torture more severe than he'd imagined being able to tolerate. Though he couldn't see the front of her body, he knew she was washing her breasts, her hands sliding along what he ached to touch.

Would she soon stand totally nude before him? he wondered desperately.

Instead, when she finished with her upper body, she maneuvered the cloth back to its original position, then reached beneath to finish the more private recesses. He gave a choked sound, and she froze, dropping her facecloth to the floor.

"Adam?"

Her voice cracked on the word, as if fear had haunted her through the night. Guilt slithered through him like a serpent.

"I am well, thanks to you," he murmured hoarsely.

Her smile was tremulous, and she turned her head away for a moment. Composing herself? Had she feared so much for him? Had anyone, but his brothers, ever cared like this?

"How long have I been asleep?" he asked.

She came to him, removing the poultice to look at his wound. It did not appear nearly as inflamed as it had yesterday, and he knew that she was relieved. Her ministrations had helped him. She put another cushion behind him, so that at least he was not lying as prone as an invalid. She understood him too well already.

But during all her concerned care, she wore only the cloth, fastened roughly at her breasts. He could not take his gaze away from the smooth line of her cleavage. She most certainly noticed his pointed stare, because she gave a beguiling blush and didn't meet his gaze.

"I brought you here yesterday afternoon," she said, then glanced at the shutters. "It looks to be morn."

"I remember arriving, but little else. All is well?"

She nodded. "My sister helped me with your care. I am sure she will return soon with a meal to break your fast."

"Good. I am hungry."

With a grin, she said, "That is a sign of returning health. But although you may feel much improved, you need rest to fully recover. As I told your men, we will contact them tomorrow."

"Tomorrow?" he repeated, frowning. "In several hours, I will be able to—"

"Nay, do not argue," she said firmly. "You are returning to health, but you are not there yet. Eat and sleep more. Let the medicine heal you. London—and my father—will still be there."

He said nothing as their gazes held.

At last he sighed. "I need a moment's privacy." And then he thought of the night, and imagined her caring for him in such a way.

She smiled. "You actually demanded your privacy last night. You managed well enough alone."

He exhaled in relief.

"Close your eyes so that I can don my gown."

He heaved a loud sigh, causing her to giggle, but he did as she requested. His breathing was far too rapid as he listened to the rustling of her garments.

"I will be outside in the corridor if you need me. The chamber pot is beneath the bed."

He did not have to call for her, but he was surprised at how weak and light-headed he felt just standing up. She was right; he needed rest. He just hated to admit it.

When she returned, she was not alone. The other woman with her was dressed in silks, obviously the countess of the household. She carried a tray covered with a piece of cloth.

Though he was sitting propped in bed, Adam inclined his head toward her. "Lady Christina, thank you for your generosity."

She looked a bit like Florrie, especially through the green eyes, but with none of Florrie's open joy at life. Lady Christina watched him with wariness, her hands clasped together after she set down the tray. He kept his movements gentle for fear of startling her.

"*Sir Edmund*, you look well this morn," she said, glancing at her sister almost nervously.

Then Florrie looked guilty. Why the emphasis on his false name? Unless her ladyship *knew* it was false.

"I feel much better, although my nurse insists I'm not," he said dryly.

"You had quite the fever," Lady Christina said. " 'Tis well that you rest."

"Yet we do not wish to cause you problems."

She shook her head. "My husband is not in residence, sir. I can easily offer you our hospitality. And you have been taking care of my sister on her journey to London, which I appreciate."

She seemed to be accepting the story for what it was, making Adam relax.

Florrie took the tray from her sister. "I do not wish to keep you, Christina. If you could bring me some sewing to pass the time, I would appreciate it."

"And how will I pass the time?" Adam asked.

Florrie raised an eyebrow. "Sleeping."

After Christina had left, Florrie brought the tray over and sat on a chair at his side. With the tray resting on her knees, she slid away the cloth to reveal a large bowl of pottage, two spoons and knives, a tankard of something, a loaf of bread, and a crock of butter.

She nodded. "You will not be able to eat much, so we can share this."

"I beg to differ, Florrie, but—"

She lifted a spoon to his mouth, and with his outrage, she was able to put it between his lips. When she pulled the spoon away, he took it from her hand.

After swallowing, he said, "I can feed myself."

She put the tray in his lap, smiling enigmatically. A short while later, he had to admit she was right. Though the food filled the hollow in his belly, he wasn't able to eat much of it.

At last she stood above him, hands on her hips. "'Tis time for you to wash, but I fear you are still too weak. I will have to do it."

He was about to protest his fitness, then realized his foolishness. Meekly, he said, "Whatever you think best."

She rolled her eyes and gave a little snort that made him smile. After leaving the chamber briefly, she came back with a clean basin of water and fresh linen. All brisk competence, she folded his blanket down to his waist, laid a drying cloth to protect the bed, and began to work, beginning with his face. He must be feeling better, for all he could think about was her fingers touching him and her concerned face so close to his. She kept glancing up at him from beneath her lashes, and he didn't look away, which seemed to fluster her.

As she moved on to his neck and shoulders, he realized that she was trembling.

"We should talk about something," she finally said, then bit her lip.

"We should?" he answered softly. As she wiped farther down his chest, brushing a nipple, he gave a jerk. "I think if I open my mouth too much, I'll moan."

"Oh." She hesitated, holding the dripping cloth just above his stomach. "Should I stop?"

"And allow me to repulse you with my uncleanness?"

She narrowed her eyes. "You *want* me to continue."

"I am a man, Florrie. How could I not? But I will try not to respond in any way."

He closed his eyes and steeled himself against responding, knowing he'd frighten her away. It took every bit of his control not to shudder when her cloth moved along his side. When she had him roll to his side so that she could reach his back, he felt a little more distant and calm. But then she folded the blanket back from his legs and began to work on his lower body, starting at his feet and moving up. Try as he might, all he could imagine was doing the same to her. If she removed the blanket completely, she'd see how the ministrations were affecting him.

At last, when there was nothing left to do that was not far too intimate for a virgin to contemplate, Florrie hesitated. He waited, wondering how bold she would be.

When she touched the blanket at his waist, he

caught her arm and pulled her down so that she pressed against his damp chest.

"I will finish," he said huskily. And then he kissed her, a hot, passionate kiss meant to show her how she affected him, how much he wished they could continue. Every moment they were alone together made it harder and harder for him to resist her.

At last she lifted her head, her mouth wet, her breath coming in shallow pants. "I should . . . apply a fresh bandage."

He grinned and closed his eyes, surprised by how tired he suddenly felt. "You do that."

Yet he barely remembered her ministrations. He slept on and off through the morning, reluctantly admitting to himself that he still needed time to recover. Later, he saw her sewing by the window, and he didn't even remember hearing someone arrive to bring her the cloth and supplies.

By the midday meal, he decided it was time to test himself, so he ate with her at the table after donning a clean shirt and breeches that had been left for him. Standing up was easier than he'd thought it would be, and she smiled her encouragement.

Florrie studied him as they sat facing each other, and she looked thoughtful.

"Ask your questions," he said at last. "But I cannot promise long answers. I feel ravenous—another good sign?"

She grinned and nodded. "Tell me, after London, what do you do next? Do you continue your work with the League?"

"If they will have me." He ate a bite of roast lamb. "But the League does not demand year-round service. They only ask for a man's service once a year, for perhaps a few weeks at most. They want us to have a normal life. And other people are less likely to be suspicious."

"And you will live at this home you have not seen in almost twenty years."

He nodded as he buttered a piece of bread.

"Will you miss the place you grew up in?" she asked hesitantly.

He shrugged, chewing his bread before speaking. "Of course I will miss the friendships formed there, but there were not many of us there all the time. After several months of initial training, most Bladesmen never came there again."

"So it will be as if you start a new life," she said softly.

He sat back, his belly full at last, regarding her. "Many people are forced to do so. I've seen this in my work for the League. The few assignments I've been on have shown me that the world can be a cruel place, and people are often dealt tragic blows. But they survive them, just as I did. Just as you'll survive whatever happens to your father."

It was a cruel thing to remind her, and he saw the stunned look she couldn't hide. But she had not yet told him all of her secrets, and he could not let her forget them—or what they meant to him.

He stood up and began to move about the chamber, pacing from the window to the hearth, from the door to the bed. Although he was not at peak strength, he felt well enough that they would certainly be leaving by dawn on the morrow. His wound occasionally gave him a twinge of pain, but it wasn't bleeding.

By late afternoon, he was restless and bored. He kept looking at Florrie, who seemed to be plucking out more stitches than she sewed. More and more he was thinking about the bed, and Florrie, and the privacy they'd have for one more night. He really must be feeling better, because she was dominating his thoughts.

He stopped above her to examine her work, and she didn't lift her head. He looked at the fine hairs curling beneath her ear, and the way her fingers delicately touched the cloth. He'd spent a night with her hands on him, and he couldn't remember any of it, which was frustrating.

"Do you want something, Adam?" she said, at last looking up at him.

He put his hand on her shoulder, and the silence stretched out between them. Her eyes widened and grew softer, and she glanced at his hand, so close to her face.

Then there was a soft knock on the door, and he stepped away.

Christina entered. As she closed the door behind her, she looked between the two of them curiously, then focused on a blushing Florrie. Adam wondered if perhaps Christina understood her sister more than Florrie ever thought she did.

Christina leaned back against the door. "I wanted to let you know that we have a guest who knows you, Florrie."

Florrie rose to her feet. "Who is it?"

"Our brother by marriage, Claudius Drake."

"I thought he was in London," Florrie said with a growing frown.

"He was, and he returns again on the morrow. He was been visiting people in the countryside, or so he says."

"So he says?" Adam echoed.

Christina glanced at him, as if surprised he had spoken. Of course, she thought of him as nothing but Florrie's guard.

Florrie said, "Christina and I never quite trust what Claudius says."

"He has been caught too often in convenient . . . mistruths," Christina agreed.

The sisters exchanged smiles.

"Do not let him stop you from disguising your- selves and sharing the evening meal with us," Christina said. "There will be dancing afterward. Surely you are tired of being confined here after your exciting journey."

"Nay, we cannot," Florrie said before Adam

could even open his mouth. "I thank you for thinking of us, Christina, but 'tis imperative that we quietly leave on the morrow."

"Imperative, why?" Christina asked.

Adam said, "The missive I carry needs to be delivered, Lady Christina."

"But do you not work for my sister, who needs to recover from the strain of caring for you?" Christina's voice was a little sharper now.

Florrie walked to her sister and took her hand. "He works for Father, Christina. In London, I will have time to relax and enjoy myself."

"But will you, Florrie? Do you promise not to allow Father to shorten your stay?"

"I promise."

Christina glanced at Adam again. "Since you are better, Sir Edmund, perhaps my sister should stay with me this night."

"I am sworn to protect my lady," Adam said. "I will not leave her side."

"'Tis all right, Christina," Florrie said. "I will be safe with him."

When a reluctant Christina had gone, Adam said, "It seems you and your sister have come to an understanding."

Florrie, who'd been staring thoughtfully at the door, now smiled over her shoulder at him. "Amazing, is it not? It seems distance and time do help. Perhaps it will be so with you and your brother Paul."

He gave her a gentle smile. She was always so

concerned for him. Surely she was that way with everyone, he told himself. But he couldn't believe it. He found himself walking toward her slowly, waiting for her to back away.

But she didn't. Though her gaze remained confused, it never left him. She looked at his mouth. Did she want him to kiss her? Did she understand that after all they'd been through, all they'd come to mean to one another, he wouldn't be able to stop with just a kiss?

And then Florrie licked her lips, and it hit him like a kick in the gut. He had no more control where she was concerned. But he had to try, for her sake, even if they had to take a risk to distract themselves.

"We need to leave this chamber, even if only for a while," he said in a low voice. "Your sister said there was music and dancing. Shall we go watch in secret? Did I see a gallery above the great hall? With a screen?"

She cleared her throat. "You did. I did not think you were so aware."

He shrugged. " 'Tis the training. Shall we go?"

She nodded her agreement, but part of him thought she was disappointed with his suggestion. Did she really want to risk being alone with him—and accept the consequences?

Chapter 18

Florrie did not know what was wrong with her, but this breathless sensation, this awareness of Adam, had been building all day. Or to be honest, ever since she'd known him. Everything was conspiring to make her lose her head where he was concerned: the illness she'd feared would take him from her, their proximity to London, and the end of their adventure. Did she want to end with regrets? Did she want to risk her future for a chance encounter that might have meaning only to her?

She was relieved when Adam turned from her and began to pace again. He seemed so healthy and strong that it was difficult to remember he was still recovering. She went back to her sewing, trying not to look at him—trying not to look at the bed.

Christina brought them a tray of food before her own supper, looking between them with bemusement, but saying nothing except that she'd see them on the morrow. Adam had told her to come at dawn, or they would already be gone, and Christina nodded almost sadly. To Florrie's surprise, she thought Christina would miss her—and she'd miss her sister, too. She'd never thought she'd have people she'd regret leaving behind when she went to the convent. But that was no longer true, and it made her feel almost . . . angry. Anger was an emotion she seldom allowed herself, for it affected and hurt no one but her.

She and Adam ate in strained silence, and she was grateful when he did not change his mind about watching the dancing. Sitting alone staring at each other for the entire evening would prove too tempting. They ascended a floor, then Florrie led him back in the direction of the great hall. The corridors were eerily empty as all enjoyed their meal. Gradually, they could hear a cacophony of voices growing ever louder, and at last they reached the gallery running along the top of the great hall. Part of it was screened in, with peepholes disguised within the decorative front of the screen, so that servants could watch from above and see when their master might need them. But the master had departed, and the servants were all below, enjoying the conclusion of their meal.

Florrie stood almost shoulder to shoulder beside Adam and looked through a peephole large enough that she could watch with both eyes. As the trestle tables were folded away, the musicians began to warm up their instruments on a dais in the far corner.

"Did you dance often?" Adam asked quietly.

She kept her gaze on the people below. "Aye, I did. It was one of my favorite things. My limp makes it awkward, of course, but sometimes the right partner knows how to help me feel like it doesn't matter."

"I imagine with you in his arms, a man wouldn't care about something so unimportant as a limp."

Though she shouldn't pay any heed to his flattery, she blushed with pleasure. He was just being kind, she told herself.

The music began to play, and her toes tapped to the rhythm.

"You said you knew how to dance," Florrie said. "How did you learn without women?"

"I learned the steps, but I've never danced *with* a woman."

Her eyes left the peephole then, and she met his solemn gaze. He'd spent his life without so many of the things people took for granted. She ached for him with a sweet longing she could not deny.

"Dance with me?" he asked softly.

She nodded and put her hand in his. They moved together and apart with the steps of the dance, but always their gazes remained locked together. She felt a rising inevitability, knowing that she could no longer deny her complicated feelings for him. To a crescendo of music, he lifted her into the air, his hands circling her waist, and she gasped with the pleasure of it. He lifted her again, and this time he did not put her down immediately, but let her body slide against his. The sensation in her breasts and loins felt shocking and overwhelming, and she wished she could be suspended here forever. Before she touched the floor, he caught her with his arm beneath her buttocks, staring up at her, his customary mask of impassivity gone. There was yearning and tenderness—and hunger in the blue of his eyes. They'd both been denied so much in their lives, but they had this night to share.

Her resistance gone, she cupped his face in her hands, felt the masculine stubble and the lean strength of his square jaw. She kissed him, her desperation making her just as hungry as he was. Over and over she let her lips meet his, each kiss a little deeper. He murmured her name against her mouth, his voice with a husky timber that satisfied her. She'd never imagined being the source of a man's desperation, and it thrilled her.

He suddenly turned her in his arms until he was carrying her, one arm behind her back, the other beneath her knees. She put her arms around his neck and clung to him, still kissing him passionately.

He lifted his head at last. "If we go back to that bedchamber, Florrie . . ."

She smiled up at him. "Aye, let us go back, and quickly."

"You know what will happen?"

"I know." And she wanted it, every adventure she could share with him.

He grinned and kissed her hard, then walked through the empty corridors carrying her, displaying such strength it was as if he'd never been wounded. But when they were at last alone, the door closed between them and the rest of the world, she could not stop her worries about his health.

"Adam, what if you are not sufficiently recovered?" she asked, gazing up at him.

"You have seen to that, my sweet, in more ways than one."

He set her down gently next to the bed. Although the window was open, the sun was setting on the far side of the castle, leaving the bedchamber full of gloom but for the lone candle on the table. Suddenly Florrie felt awkward. She wasn't sure what she was supposed to do.

Then Adam loosened his tunic and shirt and pulled them over his head. The bandage tied about his ribs was yet clean, without the mark of infection. The last of Florrie's worries about his recovery faded away. She had healed his body; how she longed to heal his soul. She could give of herself this night, and perhaps a miracle would happen.

She reached behind her back for her laces, but Adam was there, tugging at them gently, loosening her gown. She lifted her arms as he pulled the gown up over her head, not even feeling embarrassment, for even her smock seemed like too much clothing. And he'd—briefly—seen her in less.

The smock loosened with a single lace at the gathered neckline, and she swayed against him as Adam spread it wide. It slid down her shoulders, then caught at her breasts, as if for a moment offering her a chance to change her mind. Adam waited, too.

She shrugged her shoulders and the smock fell down her body to the floor. She stood proudly before him, letting him look at her.

"You are more beautiful than I'd imagined," he whispered at last.

Finally, she blushed. "You have seen me naked before, when I thought I saw a snake in the river."

"Before you, I'd never seen a woman totally without garments."

She stared up at him in surprise. "But—"

"My encounters with women were always hurried. I've never even slept in a woman's arms, as I've done with you for so many nights."

His heated gaze moved over her, and her desperation rose higher. "Touch me," she whispered.

"Not yet. Lie down."

With a moan of regret, she did so, lying back against the bed cushions, her knees demurely together. She wanted him to remove his breeches, but couldn't imagine asking such a thing.

He lifted up the candleholder. "I need to look upon you."

To her surprise, he came down on his knees beside the bed, then held the candle near her body.

The yellow circle of light moved over her, almost as intimate as if he'd caressed her. The light lingered on her breasts, on her belly, then on the hair that covered the deep secrets of her body. She felt admired and cherished, something she'd never experienced before.

"Spread your thighs," he whispered hoarsely.

She gasped, her head falling back until she could search his eyes. She was shocked by the open need he didn't hide from her, so without speaking, she did as he asked, feeling the heat of a blush sweep up her body.

At last he rose to put the candle on the table, and without thinking, she began to close her legs. He stopped her. Silently he slid his breeches off, leaving only his braies, the cloth riding low about his hips. And then he removed that, and seemed to hesitate, as if his engorged penis would make her change her mind. But her sister Matilda had long ago confided many details of the wedding night, and Florrie knew what happened between men and women. And she wanted him to know that she would never be afraid of him.

She reached out and touched the smooth head, feeling its heat and strength, and to her surprise, he shuddered.

"I hurt you?"

Giving a rough laugh, he shook his head. "Your touch is so far from hurtful. Let me show you so that you can understand."

She expected him to climb into the narrow bed

with her, but he went back to his knees. Leaning back amongst the cushions, she arched her back, reveling in the hot way he looked at her, wishing he would touch her breasts again as he had so many days ago, before things had changed between them.

To her surprise, he lifted her foot in his hand and placed a kiss on the inside of her ankle, his gaze never leaving hers. She smiled, feeling wicked, watching as he pressed his lips in a trail up her calf, then behind her knee. Her smile faded as he didn't stop at her knee, his lips following a hidden path ever higher. She couldn't breathe as he parted her thighs, as his head brushed against her woman's mound. She moaned softly, trembling, anticipating—

And then his mouth traced up over the outside of her hip and to her waist. The air rushed from her lungs, leaving her feeling weak.

He smiled up at her, and it was shocking to see his face just beyond her breasts.

"Disappointed?" he asked.

"Never. Every touch is . . . wondrous."

His smile faded, and that soft look returned to his eyes. He pressed kisses across her belly, dipped his tongue in her navel, moved ever higher, to where her breasts trembled, their peaks hard and tight with wanting.

She groaned as he ran his tongue along the lower curve of one breast, then up between them. He traced little wet paths toward her nipples, but never quite touched them. By this time she was practically writhing beneath him, her breath coming in little pants, trying to hide the sounds of her pleasure. At last she touched him, smoothing her hands over his shoulders, sliding them through his dark hair.

Then his mouth hovered over her nipple, and she found herself whispering, "Please, please," not caring how desperate she sounded. For she *was* desperate, longing to be one with him.

He suddenly licked her nipple, and the shock of intense pleasure made her convulse beneath him. When he took her into his mouth, suckling her, teasing her with his tongue and lips, she bit her lip rather than cry out. Pleasure suffused her body, moving in hot waves across her skin, but it was centered deep between her thighs. She felt an ache of what could only be hunger, and she wanted more.

He moved more urgently now, spreading kisses back down her belly and beyond. His head dipped between her thighs, and he kissed her there, shocking her, but not embarrassing her. Nothing seemed wrong when they experienced it together. She felt his tongue part her and press deeper, stroking and circling. When his fingers rubbed her nipples, it was too much. Everything inside her rose to a fevered pitch, as she felt the approach of a new bliss. And when it swept over her, it changed everything, shuddering through her body, shocking her with a pleasure she had never imagined.

And then he joined her on the bed, rising up over her, settling between her thighs. Once again, she felt uncertain, but only because she wanted to please him as much as he'd pleased her, and she didn't know what to do.

As her thighs cradled him, he leaned down to kiss her mouth. She tasted the saltiness of herself on his lips, opened herself up to the thrust of his tongue, enjoying the weight of his body against her. She felt his erection rub along the depths of her, and that set off another wave of pleasure through her body.

And then he was there, at her entrance, and she instinctively lifted her knees to give him better access. She was rubbing her body against his, wanting all of it, wanting all of him. He lifted his head and looked down on her, and she saw his hesitation, his worry that he would hurt her in the end.

"Do not stop," she cried, clasping his hips in her hands, lifting herself up to him. "I know it will hurt the first time. I have married sisters."

With a groan, he thrust home. The shock of pain was brief, a burn that quickly subsided.

"Aye," she said again, still unable to remain still. "More."

When he moved, she felt as if she understood the world in a new way. She felt a part of him, caught the rhythm of his movement and responded to it, giving herself up to the wildness within him. He slid out and entered her again, over and over, each press against her body encouraging the explosion rising up within her. And he must have felt it, too, for he groaned against her lips as he kissed her, hunched so that he could reach her breasts again with his mouth. She caressed him with fervor, brushing his nipples with her inquisitive fingers, glad to see that she was able to pleasure him in more ways.

The bed shook beneath them as once again he gave her the ultimate in passion. With a groan he joined her, shuddering over her body, thrusting deeper and deeper, until at last the fever left him.

But he did not leave her. He came down on his elbows, his chest to hers, and looked into her face. They were still joined exquisitely together, and every little movement by him sent answering ripples through her body. Their breathing quieted together. She found herself looking into his eyes, and suddenly the magic was lost for her. She would never be one with him again. Those blue eyes, filled with tenderness, would soon turn impassive as a mask, as he went off to challenge her father. She hadn't succeeded in changing him, in making him happy. And though sex had, it was temporary.

This experience was only another part of her last adventure before the convent. She tried to tell herself that she could now retire to a solitary life having experienced the ultimate passion of a woman. But her soul didn't want to hear it.

Adam frowned, even as he leaned down to kiss her. "Florrie? Did I hurt you?"

She shook her head, then said wryly, "I am having trouble breathing, though."

He lifted himself off her body, and it was suddenly so sad. She was alone again. Rolling onto her side, she made room for him behind her. For so many nights he'd slept against her back, his hips intimately against hers. But she had no idea that the true intimacy of nudity changed everything. His erection was now cradled against her backside; the hand that had lain across her waist for so many nights now cupped her tender breast. The hair on his chest teased her back. And he was so very warm.

And she was so very angry.

Chapter 19

Adam had never felt such peace before. He lay with Florrie, after having shared the most intimate pleasure of his life. She had been open with her body and her joy, as he always knew she would be. But now she seemed . . . too quiet.

"Florrie? Is something wrong?"

Her pause was too long, and she only breathed the word, "Nay."

"Tell me what you're feeling."

"Sated."

He frowned, lifting up on his elbow to tuck her hair behind her ear. He could see her profile now, and she looked anything but happy. His talkative Florrie suddenly didn't want to talk? The peaceful exhaustion that had comforted him was now gone.

"I know you were a virgin," he said, "and if it was not all you expected, I wish you would talk to me about it."

Suddenly she pushed away from him and sat

up. Reaching for her smock on the floor, she pulled it over her head before standing up to pace.

He did not know how to respond to her anger, so he tried the mild approach. "That is a new garment."

She frowned, but did not look at him. "My sister gave it to me. She was appalled at the condition of my clothing."

He sat up and reached to touch her, but she pulled away. Unease and dismay swept over him. Was she so very unhappy that she'd made love with him? He'd wanted to show her how much he cherished her, and instead he seemed to have driven her away from him.

"Could you put some clothing on?" she asked.

He pulled on his braies and breeches. He didn't remain standing, for it would hurt him too deeply if she cringed away from him.

"Florrie—"

"Stop trying to appease me!" she cried, whirling to face him.

He'd never seen her angry like this, and he imagined that if she had felt it at other times in her life, she had always suppressed it to make everyone else feel happy.

"I thought this night would help heal you," she continued, "would change everything between us, but I quickly realized that I do not have that power. Only you do, but you will not do anything to change."

"Change how?" he asked tiredly.

"I am sick of your need for vengeance!"

He stiffened. "You mean justice."

"You continue to tell yourself that, and though justice is part of it, the rest is simple, ugly vengeance."

He shot to his feet. "Whatever you wish to call it, am I not justified?"

"Do you *want* to feel this way, forever angry and bitter, forever wanting *something* to make you feel right again? I've been trying to make you see that we create our own happiness, that we cannot control the world, only ourselves."

"Florrie—"

"I have been trying to make you happy, so that you would forget this mission, not commit murder—and not get killed."

"I thought you understood what I needed to do!"

"Understood? Aye, rationally, in my head, but in my heart—" Her eyes were full of hurt and confusion, and she briefly turned away from him as if fighting for control.

"You've been trying to make me happy," he said slowly, thoughts rushing through his brain so quickly he almost couldn't sort them. "Was that also the purpose of our lovemaking? Was it only your attempt to manipulate me?"

"Nay!" she cried, throwing her arms wide. "What we shared was special to me. I entrusted my body and soul to you!"

He winced. "How can you speak of trust?"

She blinked at him in confusion, and he watched some of the anger leave her eyes, only to be replaced by sadness.

"You are right," she whispered, hugging herself. "I have been keeping the truth from you, but no more. It cannot be about me, or my father, but only about you, Adam. I had hoped you would change your mind, give up this mission on your own, but I can see now that after a lifetime of waiting, you could not. So here is the truth. I think I know what my father would kill for."

He clenched his fists and his jaw, waiting, tense with the need to know.

"Did you believe that I knew?" she asked quietly.

"Nay, but I had hoped you might become aware of a clue, an event, that might be helpful to me. I wanted you to come to me freely."

She gave a bitter smile. "And I wanted you to do the same for me. So it will be I who surrenders. Your strength has surpassed mine."

"Just say it." At last he would know what was so important that Martindale would kill an un-armed man—and his wife. He should be glad and relieved, but instead he felt sick inside.

" 'Tis not easily said," she began, pulling out the hard-backed chair to sit down.

Adam did the same on the edge of the bed.

"Several years ago, I was caring for my father when he was ill. Nights were the worst, when he did not want to be alone, yet he suffered through terrible fevers. In his ragings, he kept saying that no one could know about the document, and he swore me to secrecy."

A document? Adam thought in surprise.

"I thought him delusional with illness, but at last, I came in one night to find him clutching a piece of parchment which must have been torn from a bound book. He would not be calm until I agreed to put it back in its hiding place in the false bottom of a coffer." She stopped to bite her lip. "But I read it," she admitted at last. " 'Twas the parish record of my grandmother's death, as well as the death of her unborn child. I could not understand why this was so important, until it dawned on me that my father's birth date was two months later. So another woman—probably my grandfather's concubine—had given birth to him, and his father claimed him as the legitimate heir."

"But . . . why would they not lie about his birth date?" Adam asked in confusion.

"I thought of this at great length. The child must have been a newborn when he was introduced as the heir, and they were unable to claim him as two months older. My grandfather had much property scattered through England—I always thought it would have been easy for him to keep his wife secluded until she had the boy he so obviously wanted. And when that did not happen—it would be simple to cover the truth with money and intimidation to the few servants who knew. Even death," she said, shuddering.

It was sad that a daughter should think her grandfather capable of such a thing. "And somehow your father discovered the secret of his birth."

"I know not how. But the parish record was torn away, and I fear for the priest involved so many years ago." She met Adam's gaze. "'Tis the only secret I can think worth killing for. After all, if my father were ruled illegitimate, he would have lost the title and all the lands and wealth. My sisters' chances at good marriages would have been gone."

"And you said nothing after your discovery," he said in a tight voice.

She stared at him. "If my father had never been the marquess, the title would have descended through my cousin Claudius's branch of the family. And already he is my father's heir. I thought that by giving my father no sons, God was returning the title to where it belonged, and everything would work out. Why would I speak up, when the only people to be harmed would be my sisters?"

Though Adam understood this, part of him was bewildered. He'd never imagined his Florrie could keep such a truth hidden. "Yet we do not know for certain that anyone else discovered this secret."

She shook her head. "But I have never seen my father act as he had that night. He seemed . . . crazed, and it was not just the fever. That parchment obsessed him. He even said he could never destroy it, that he was haunted by the priest of the parish where the marchioness had died. My father said the priest would not allow him."

"So that meant the priest was dead."

She shrugged. "If you can trust my father's word. He was . . . not making sense."

"Do you think your father killed him?"

"Killed a priest?" she whispered.

He saw the fear and sadness in her expression. "How else would he have the parchment from the parish records?"

"Perhaps he simply stole it."

He nodded, trying to imagine how his parents might be connected. Without Martindale's confession, he would never know. And what were the odds of that, he thought with rising anger. And would the League even think this a good motivation for murder, if it could never be proved?

"Adam?" She said his name in a small voice.

"Aye?"

"You asked if I was trying to manipulate you through sex. Were you doing the same with me?"

"Nay, my feelings for you go deeper than that. But I am still angry. You were trying to change me so that I would not kill your father. I thought I'd won your loyalty more than that."

"And at the same time you believed I was keeping something from you?" she asked sadly.

She was right. How could they even understand what there was between them emotionally, when their families had been at war, and making the two of them a part of it?

Florrie could not seem to stop trembling. She'd told her father's secret, and much as it gave Adam a motive, they could not connect it with certainty to his parents, except to imagine they'd somehow discovered her father's illegitimacy.

Yet still she was holding back, hoping that something that she'd said or done could convince Adam to back away from this foolish plan to challenge her father. If Adam knew her father was too ill to fight him, he'd be thwarted from combat—but not through his own choices, his own change of heart. She wanted him to feel free of the past, not to live in bitterness. She still hoped he'd change.

It wasn't normal for someone to be angry with her. She was too used to making people feel better. But this time she would stand her ground.

Suddenly, there was an urgent pounding on the door. Both Florrie and Adam shot to their feet, but neither was fully dressed. Before they could even respond, Christina burst through the door, her face wild with concern. She slid to a stop, and Florrie knew at once what they must look like, the bed rumpled, neither of them wearing their outer garments.

Christina's expression changed to confusion and then outrage. Florrie winced.

"Christina—"

"I need to speak with you, Florrie," Christina

said. She saw the gown in a heap on the floor, then picked it up with dismay. "Put this on quickly."

Florrie turned to Adam, who had already pulled his shirt over his head. She gave him a helpless look and did as her sister asked. "Christina, can we not speak here?"

Christina shook her head and opened the door. When Adam stepped forward, Christina held up a hand and begrudgingly said, "I understand that it is your duty to protect her . . . and that you take it seriously. But I am her sister, and I wish to speak with her in privacy. We will not go far."

Florrie saw Adam look at her, as if he wanted her to object. She couldn't; this was her sister. "I will not be gone long," she said softly.

Christina gave an exaggerated sigh. "We will be two doors down on the left. 'Tis an empty bedchamber."

"You have my thanks for the information," Adam said.

Florrie turned away. She knew Adam was truly concerned for her welfare. If only she could trust that it wasn't about more than that.

After a short, hurried walk down the corridor, Christina opened another door and walked into a deserted bedchamber, gloomy because the shutters were closed. Florrie sighed, waiting for the inevitable scolding.

Christina took both her arms. "Oh, my goodness, Florrie, is it true?"

Florrie blinked in confusion. "Is what true?"

"Claudius was in London when Father received the news. He told me you had been kidnapped!"

Florrie gaped at her in shock.

Christina clasped her in a hard embrace. "Oh, my dear, and now to see that you've been . . . that he's forced you to . . . satisfy him. Why, 'tis rape!"

"Nay, oh, Christina, do not think such a thing!" she cried, disengaging herself to step back. "Adam is the most gentle man I know."

"So 'tis Adam, not Edmund."

"He would never force me to do anything I didn't want to!"

"He kidnapped you!"

"Oh, well, there is that. But he had a good reason!"

"A good reason for a kidnapping?" Christina demanded. "Now this you must explain."

And Florrie didn't know what she *could* explain. "He was only going to use me to convince Father to meet him in combat."

"Father? Our father? Does he not know—"

"Nay, he does not! I did not tell him. I wanted him to change his mind without knowing the truth. 'Tis . . . a long, tragic story, but suffice it to say, he is demanding justice for a terrible crime."

"And you're going to let him kill our father."

"Of course not! Even Adam does not plan such a thing. But an honorable combat cannot occur, and I desperately want him to realize that before we reach London." She took her sister's hands.

"Oh, Christina, he is such a good man, one who's been treated badly throughout life. If he lets himself become bitter . . . 'twill harm him in ways he cannot imagine."

"You know this, because you never let yourself become bitter," Christina slowly said.

"Bitterness kills a person's spirit. I have always refused to live like that."

Christina pursed her lips. "Another reason I always envied you," she said dryly. Then her expression became worried. "But, Florrie, I was so shocked by what Claudius said, I may have reacted in a . . . confused way."

Florrie stiffened. "What do you mean?"

"I hope I did not make Claudius suspicious about what I might know of you."

"Oh," Florrie breathed.

Christina suddenly gripped Florrie's arm. "Hear you that?"

Florrie frowned, but in a moment's silence, she heard what Christina was referring to. A man was calling Christina's name.

Their gazes met in shared fear.

Florrie gasped, "Is that—?"

"Claudius!"

"Oh, he cannot see me, Christina!"

"Hide beneath the bed. I will try to stop him."

Florrie nodded, only having time to squeeze her sister's hand with gratitude. She dropped to her belly on the floor, then slid beneath the bed, disregarding her clean, new gown. She hoped the shadows hid her, because she could still see the partially open door.

"Christina!"

She cringed at the arrogance and demand in her cousin Claudius's voice.

She heard her sister farther down the hall—closer to Adam's bedchamber. Did he hear what was going on? Would he hide as well? She prayed that he had not gone out the window, thinking he could cling to the ledge with his Bladesman strength. He was not strong enough for anything right now—except lovemaking, she thought with a wince.

"Christina, what are you doing here?" Claudius demanded.

"I am in a corridor of my home," she said.

Florrie was impressed by how even her voice sounded.

"Why did you disappear from the evening's festivities?"

"I had a sick member of my household to attend to," she said. "I will return in a moment."

"You care for every lowly servant yourself?"

"Aye. And does not your wife, my sister Matilda? We were taught together the healing arts."

"She has been much preoccupied with our child."

"That is a shame, for people are more loyal when they're also grateful for one's help."

"Who is this sick man you tend to? And does your husband know?"

Florrie held her breath, straining to hear as they moved past the door.

"Of course he does, Claudius. Do not think me a fool. What are you doing?"

"I am going to meet this man you tend so diligently, to the detriment of your guests."

"Do not disturb him. I tell you, he is ill!"

Florrie covered her mouth and closed her eyes to pray.

Chapter 20

A dam heard the raised voices in the corridor, as well as Christina's defense of her "patient." But he did not hear Florrie, so he had to assume she'd somehow escaped Claudius Drake's notice. He quickly stripped his shirt off and climbed into bed, pulling the blanket only to his waist, so that the large bandage was evident. He closed his eyes, took a deep breath, and forced every muscle in his body to relax, as if he were unconscious. He heard the door open.

"There he is," Christina said in a haughty, furious voice. "Surely you can see that I was telling the truth."

Adam heard footsteps, then a man's breathing. Drake must be standing right over him. Would the man rip off the bandage to see if Christina, his cousin and sister by marriage, was lying to him?

Drake sighed. "Aye, I can see the truth before my eyes. How did he do this?"

"An accident on the tiltyard. And then it became inflamed, and he needed my care."

"He is getting well now?"

"He is," Christina said, her voice becoming more reserved, but less furious.

"You cannot blame me for my suspicion. You were acting . . . in an unusual manner. And since I am your father's heir, I am responsible for you as well."

"I thank you for your concern, but my husband is responsible for me. Now I need you to go, for at last this man's fever has broken, and he needs his rest."

They walked to the door, and Adam heard it open and shut. He waited a moment, then slowly looked up beneath his lashes—and saw Christina staring at him angrily from across the room, hands on her hips.

She marched toward him and spoke quietly but firmly. "My brother by marriage told me you kidnapped Florrie. What do you have to say for yourself?"

He came up on his elbows. "So that is what you needed to talk to Florrie about. And since you did not reveal me, she told you something to appease you."

She groaned. "Do not confuse the issue! She is an innocent—or she was until you!—and believes the best in everyone. 'Tis obvious you are her new project."

Adam raised one eyebrow. "Project?"

"She is trying to redeem you, and she believes she can succeed."

"She said that?"

"She did not have to. She will never admit it, but she can be so easily hurt, after how she's been treated by our family."

"By you, too," Adam said coolly.

She looked stricken. "Aye, by me, too."

"It has taken you a long time to realize it. Why did you not defend her, help her to be one with your family?"

Christina spread her arms wide. "You, a kidnapper, are taking me to task?"

"I am more than that to her now."

"You are her seducer," she answered bitterly. "Or should I say rapist?"

He felt the sting of that. "Is that what she would say?" he asked softly.

"You know 'tis not. And that infuriates me. She was innocent before God, meant to serve Him, and then you—"

"Perhaps we should simply stop accusing each other," he interrupted, "and let Florrie decide." But her words gave him pause. She was right—he had altered Florrie's life forever.

Florrie limped through the door a moment later, then leaned back against it, breathing heavily, looking between them with open worry. "Claudius accepted the ruse?"

"He did," Adam said. "But we must leave quickly, before he changes his mind. Also, your sister thinks I am using you."

"Well, of course you are," Florrie said, rolling

her eyes. "You have told me that from the beginning. And I am using you."

He did not know whether to laugh or simply shake his head. But they were at an impasse, and her answer would decide his fate. "I cannot force you to come with me, not now. What will you do?"

Florrie gave her sister an apologetic look. "And I cannot miss the end of my last adventure. I need to see London."

Christina looked stricken, but said nothing.

Florrie crossed to her. "Do you understand, Christina?"

"If you cannot stay to visit now, do you promise to return on your way home? The convent will always be there."

Florrie smiled. "I promise. But for now, I must leave in the morning."

Adam shook his head and stood up. "If Claudius's suspicions rise, he will be far too curious come the morn. We must leave tonight."

"I cannot ask the guards to raise the portcullis at night," Christina protested. "They would be too suspicious."

"We could climb down the walls," Adam mused, "but your guards might see that, as well."

Christina hesitated, looking between them. "There is a small iron door built into the wall at the rear of the castle, used for emergencies only. I have the key."

Florrie brightened. "And this is an emergency!" She hugged her sister. "Christina, thank you so much—for everything!"

As Adam followed Florrie through the dark landscape of the trees that skirted the castle, he found himself feeling confused. He wanted to be angry with her; she truly was trying to manipulate him, regardless of the fact that she thought it was for his own good.

The League had manipulated him as well, and perhaps that was why Florrie's behavior galled him. He had always thought the League's good motives put them above his reproach. Was he supposed to feel the same way about Florrie? Or would that make him just as gullible?

After alerting Robert and Michael with a birdcall, Adam led Florrie into their encampment. Both men were there, studying him, Robert with relief, Michael without surprise, as if he knew Adam could not be so easily killed. Sometimes it seemed difficult to live up to Michael's expectations of him, but apparently Adam had not failed to, so far.

"You look well," Robert said to Adam, while giving Florrie a quick hug.

Even by firelight, Adam could see the pleased blush on her cheeks.

"Our Florrie is a marvelous healer," Robert continued.

"With help from my sister," she quickly added.

"Martindale's heir, Claudius Drake, is inside, and he knows about the kidnapping," Adam said without preamble.

Robert's easy smile died. "So that is who arrived with a troop of men. But you are here, so nothing untoward must have occurred."

"He did not discover us," Florrie said. "Again, thanks to my sister."

"But we cannot remain here for the night," Adam said. "He turns toward London as well, and we do not want to be headed in the same direction at the same time. We'll break camp and put some distance between us."

Michael went to prepare the horses, while Robert began to pack up their blankets and supplies.

At last, Adam looked at Florrie, only to find her watching him solemnly. She had come to be with him when he faced her father. Adam could not read her thoughts, didn't know if she would still try to stop him. But he wanted to trust her, and wanted to earn her trust in return. Only a few hours ago, she'd trusted him with her body, and the memory of it made him poignant with longing.

He took the satchel of fresh garments from her. "I will put these in your saddlebag."

She nodded, but did not meet his eyes. Adam felt confused and sad, then angry with himself. He had to focus on his task in London; it was almost upon him. But thoughts of Florrie, and how his actions might affect her, simply wouldn't die.

To his surprise, a fourth horse waited with the others. He turned to the other two men questioningly.

Robert grinned. "I was bored. A farmer was glad for the coin. We helped each other."

Michael and Florrie took the lead, and Robert guided his horse beside Adam's into the rear.

"What happened in there?" Robert asked.

"Florrie told me more about her father and a possible motive for his crimes." He quietly explained about Martindale's illegitimacy.

Robert sighed. "That must have been difficult for her to admit, especially since she's in love with you."

Turning his head to stare at him in surprise, Adam frowned. "She is not. She is a woman who obeys her family."

"But she didn't, for you."

"How do you think she could love a man who's suffered because of her father? She's been trying to protect him."

"And protect you. She told you the truth. Put yourself in her position. Do you not think it would take a while for someone to convince *you* to go against your own father? For God's sake, you *kidnapped* her. It doesn't inspire trust."

"Because of Martindale, you and I never had any chance at all to know our father."

"Then draw from your life. You finally have doubts about the League and their mission where our upbringing was concerned. Yet you still cannot repudiate them. But you think it should be easy for Florrie to go against her family for you? Or is it that you want so desperately for her to love you, that every doubt of hers is like an arrow in your heart?"

"Maudlin poetry does not become you," Adam said, feeling surly.

Robert only shook his head, his face peaceful and amused beneath the waning moon. Adam found himself wishing he were more like his brother, unaffected by useless emotions. He had once thought himself impervious to them, caring only about logic, honor, and duty. What had happened to that man?

Florrie was exhausted by the time they made camp several hours later, just before dawn. They stayed well east of the main road to London, but the way had been dangerous and slow, due to the poor condition of the roads. Adam would have preferred to continue traveling by night, since they were less than ten leagues from London, but they could no longer risk the horses breaking a leg. So they would rest for the morn, and begin traveling again after noon.

Feeling chilled from the night air, and just able to see with the first gray light, Florrie stumbled through damp undergrowth and past a stand of trees to reach the stream Michael had pointed out. As she knelt down, she could hear the rustling of small animals in the brush, awakening to a new day. The stream gurgled over rocks, and she lifted a dripping handful of water to her mouth.

But it never got there. A man's hand covered her mouth instead. She stiffened in sudden terror.

The voice was unfamiliar, low but calm. "Come with me now, and you will not be harmed."

She had heard that before—and it had proven true. But her luck could not possibly bear a repetition.

While she hesitated, he spoke again. "I will explain everything. Sir Adam must be stopped."

The fact that he knew Adam's identity made everything worse. She shoved her elbow back hard and hit him in the stomach. He grunted, but did not release her, only dragged her to her feet and splashed through the stream, pulling her with him, his hand still covering her mouth. When she bit him, he stuffed a cloth between her lips and tied another about her head to hold the gag in place.

She could see him now, as the rays of the rising sun sent light through the trees. He was not an especially tall man, but he showed his strength by his barrel chest and large, gnarled hands. And he wasn't young. His brown hair was streaked with gray, and lines bracketed his mouth and eyes.

Softly, he said, "I do not understand why you fight me. I am rescuing you from a kidnapping, am I not?"

She glared at him, her only method of communication through her eyes.

The man sighed. "Ah, but Sir Adam is one with the confidence, bearing, and honor to convince men to follow him. He has swayed you as well."

She tried to kick him, but he neatly avoided her.

"I cannot allow him to use you in his quest," he said. "Without you, he might be foiled."

This man might very well work for her father, for they wanted the same outcome; but she realized that he was not Martindale's man, because he spoke almost fondly of Adam.

He must be with the League of the Blade.

And there was pride in his voice, too, which he couldn't quite hide. Was this Sir Timothy, Adam's foster father? She let him bind her wrists, let him continue leading her through the trees, away from her party. Adam would find her, she already knew. Or would he go on to London, before his deadly errand could be stopped?

At last they halted, and she stumbled with weariness. There were two horses waiting silently, well trained. Where was the other rider? Or was it for her?

Not resisting her captor, she beseeched him with her gaze, then touched her bound hands to her mouth.

" 'Tis obvious you will scream," he said.

She shook her head. They stared intently at one another, and at last he sighed.

" 'Tis not your fault what has happened. You are an innocent, even as Adam was—and still is, if he can be stopped. Do you promise not to scream?"

She nodded, eyes wide, willing him to trust her. At last he removed the gag, and kept his hand against her mouth.

Through his fingers, she said, "Sir Timothy?"

His eyes widened in shock. "You know of me?" he demanded hoarsely, letting his hand fall away.

"You are Adam's foster father. He speaks of you with great love and admiration."

He watched her with confusion.

"I am no longer his captive," she said. "I freely journey the country with him. Other Bladesmen tried to stop us days ago."

He winced at her use of such a secret word, but at last he said heavily, "Aye, and they returned defeated. I was forced to come in their place, to try to reason with my foster son."

" 'Twill not work," she said sadly. "I have tried myself, and by my actions, I only made him mistrust me more. He believes he needs to see this through."

"That was my conclusion, too. Which is why I've taken you. If he thinks he needs you to convince your father to fight him, then without you . . ."

"I am not sure even I matter anymore," she said sadly. "But let me ask you this. Four days ago we were attacked by a band of five men who almost killed me, and wounded Adam. Were they of the League?"

With eyes narrowed, he shook his head. "After the two returned injured, only I and my partner were dispatched. And never would I risk a lady—or Adam."

"I know. This only proves they were from my father, and how little he cares for my welfare."

Sir Timothy said nothing for a moment, his expression grave. "Then leave here with me, Lady Florence. 'Tis obvious you care for Adam. Between us, perhaps we can stop my foster son before the worst happens."

Was that the right thing to do? she wondered in desperation. Perhaps Adam really would come after her, instead of going to London. But then again, it might only delay the inevitable. Christina had urged her to stop—and now so was Sir Timothy, who obviously loved Adam.

"She's not going with you," said an angry voice through the trees.

Florrie stiffened and looked over her shoulder to see Adam emerging. She could not lie to herself—she was glad that he'd come for her.

She knew she had fallen in love with him, regardless of how it would change her life.

Chapter 21

Relief flooded through Adam at seeing Florrie safe. After capturing the other Bladesman watching his encampment, he'd known she was a prisoner of the League, which gave him some comfort.

He looked at his foster father grimly. Before he could speak, Timothy grinned.

" 'Tis good to see you, son."

"Under these conditions?"

"Under any conditions. And tracking us here, in the gloom before dawn—so impressive and rare. But you always did have the eyes of a cat."

Adam wasn't in the mood for fatherly praise. "Did you tell the League that you'd given me Martindale's name as the suspect in my parents' death?" He gestured to Florrie, and she immediately came to his side so that he could unbind her wrists.

Sir Timothy put his hands on his hips, not shirking away from the question. "Aye, I did, and it grieved me. At first I withstood their pressure, but young Rob disappeared, too, and then the Lady Florence. 'Twas pointless to deny that you knew Martindale's identity."

Adam nodded. "You know me better than almost anyone. How could I live with myself if there was no justice for my parents? And 'twas my fault that the pendant wasn't at the site of the murders to connect Martindale with the crime."

"Adam, you speak of the past as if you were a man full grown then, instead of a grieving little boy. Come to peace with yourself, son."

"That is where you misunderstand me, Timothy. I am at peace with this decision to challenge Martindale." Why did he sound as if he were trying to convince himself? Surely Timothy could see that, too. "He's not even truly the marquess. He's illegitimate, a secret he's been hiding for a long time. And I think my parents discovered it, which is why they were killed."

"Then you've learned the reason, and without proof, who will believe you—who will care?"

"But there's proof, a parish death record. If Martindale hasn't destroyed it already. He keeps it in his bedchamber." Adam wanted to rub his hands over his face. He was so tired. He looked down at Florrie, and she was watching him solemnly. Was Robert right—did she love him? And what was he supposed to do about it? For after all, she didn't trust him.

But the thought of her love gave him an unexpected pang of need. Was that not a weakness?

Timothy changed the subject. "Lady Florence tells me you were attacked by a band of men. I was the second team sent, so they were not Bladesmen. I know you think that makes them Martindale's soldiers"—he glanced at Florrie apologetically—"but I think not."

Adam stiffened. "Tell me what you know."

Timothy almost seemed uncomfortable.

Quietly, Florrie said, "You may speak before me, Sir Timothy. I want only the truth, and your good opinion matters."

Timothy sighed. "I believe those men cannot be Martindale's, because he sent a message for you, Adam."

Adam frowned in confusion. "For me? I only told him the name of one village where we could communicate, but there was no message waiting for me there."

"It came later, and the Bladesmen involved forwarded it to me."

Timothy fell silent, and Adam's unease grew.

"What did it say?" Florrie asked.

Adam heard a tremble in her soft voice, but as usual, she would face anything, however difficult.

Timothy said, "Martindale wrote that since you had taken his daughter"—he cleared his throat—"compromised her, that Lady Florence is yours now, without a dowry."

She gasped, putting a hand to her lips.

"Further, he said that you should be grateful he doesn't claim you as her rapist."

Adam thought of Martindale's motive for such a missive—was he trying to trade the silence of one crime for the other, as if Adam were expected to be a part of some kind of pact? Then he watched Florrie's face pale, saw the way she schooled her features, tried to dismiss her own pain. She'd spent her life doing that.

Even though Florrie knew she shouldn't be surprised at her father's open dismissal of her— he'd made sure she knew she didn't count—the pain of such an abandonment was almost too much to bear. After all, he didn't know Adam, or how she'd been treated. Adam could have been . . . a cruel monster. And her father didn't care.

She saw Sir Timothy watching her with the sadness of a parent who understood a child's pain. Her own father had never been that kind of parent. She was glad Adam had someone who cared so deeply about him.

Adam was watching her, too, and she saw an echo of her pain in him, but he seemed to put it aside just as she always did. They were more alike than he realized, she thought sadly.

"Timothy, go back to the League," Adam said. "You've delivered your message, and you've tried to do what they wished. Tell them to leave me alone."

Timothy watched Adam in surprise. "I hear . . . bitterness in your voice when you mention the League. It surprises me."

"It should not. I have been thinking much about my childhood, and much about how the League cared more about helping others than helping me find justice for my family."

Timothy winced. "We've been through all of this, Adam. But as for your childhood—"

Adam held up a hand. "We can discuss it at another time."

"Nay, listen to me. From the beginning I failed you. I allowed a vote by the League council to matter more than my opinion about how best to raise you. I wasn't a father; I thought I did not have the right or the ability to express my opinion."

"You did not fail him," Florrie said, feeling the tightness in her throat. "You did the best you could, and you raised three boys to honorable men. Not many can say that." She hated that she sounded bitter. That was not who she was.

"I can make up for a small part of it," Timothy continued. "I can warn you. Be careful, Adam, for they have men watching Martindale in London."

"If I make a public challenge, no one can—"

"Titles and crowns could be thrown into chaos by the simplest action. Make sure you understand what you do." He took a step toward his horse. "My partner?"

"He is with Robert."

Timothy led his horse forward. "My lady, would you care to ride my partner's horse? Adam can ride with you, and I'll take the lead."

She was suddenly so tired. Without speaking, she only nodded. Adam mounted and leaned down for her. She took his hand, then let him pull her up until she could reach the stirrup and slide her other leg behind him. Sir Timothy swung into his saddle, then led the way back through the trees.

Though she'd just been half dragged this way, riding back seemed just as long. She clung to Adam's waist, her anger with him forgotten, pressing her cheek against his broad, warm back. At last they reached their little encampment, where Michael was guarding their new prisoner. When Sir Timothy's partner saw him, the man heaved a sigh.

"Will you release him?" Sir Timothy asked Michael.

Michael looked to Adam, who nodded.

"Heed my words," Adam said, too quietly. "Go now and do not return. Make them understand that you raised me; therefore, they must trust what I intend to do."

Timothy stared at him thoughtfully, then nodded without speaking.

Adam dismounted, and Florrie followed him. Robert, smiling with chagrin, went to Sir Timothy, who reached down and touched his head as if he were still a child.

"I hope you understand my part in this," Robert said.

"I do." Sir Timothy smiled. "You are helping your brother. I hope you can understand—and forgive me—for my part . . . in everything."

The other Bladesman mounted his horse, and together the two of them rode away.

Florrie stood beside Adam as they watched the men disappear through the trees. "You did not settle anything with him," she said.

"'Tis not the time."

"Will you make time someday?"

He glanced down at her. "I will. But what of you? That was a terrible thing your father did."

She suddenly felt on display, knowing that Robert watched her curiously. Although Michael busied himself with a meal, he, too, was listening.

"I . . . I do not wish to talk about it right now. We will sleep through the morning?"

Adam nodded. "Do you want something to eat first?"

She shook her head, crawled into her blankets, and wished she could bury herself and not have to feel.

Adam had gotten several hours rest himself, then let Robert sleep while he stood guard. But he was watching Florrie too much. Her sleep seemed disturbed by dreams, for behind her lids her eyes moved too much, and the occasional frown chased across her sweet features.

How much more would she have to bear?

He found a patch of flowers and laid some beside her, hoping that seeing something beautiful would lift her spirits, as she'd taught him.

His parents had not been at fault when he'd been left orphaned; the same was not true of Martindale. He'd discarded Florrie as if she were nothing to him. How many more sins could such a man commit?

He thought again of everything Florrie had done to try to change him—to redeem him in Christina's words. At last it dawned on him that all this time, if Florrie had been triumphant in keeping his combat with her father from ever happening, she would have been sentencing herself to the convent, where her father wanted her.

How could anyone be so selfless? She was a woman who was trying to save Adam's soul more than save her father's life. Christina was right.

Except for Sir Timothy's awkward parenthood, such selfless caring had been rare in his life, and it had taken him too long to recognize it. With his ignorant stupidity, he'd hurt Florrie too many times. How could he be the one to hurt her again, when she felt herself abandoned in the world?

He realized at last that he could not challenge her father to combat.

The sudden absence of the goal that had driven him his whole life was like a void inside him. But he would find other ways to fill it. And he still meant to confront Martindale, and discover the truth. But Florrie did not want the stain of killing on his soul, and that was enough for him.

Was this love? he wondered. But how could he love a woman who was the daughter of his enemy, who didn't yet trust him?

He looked down at her innocent face, free of expression, as if in her dreams she'd found peace at last. But soon she would wake up and remember. He would give anything not to see the shadow of hurt that would come into those vivid green eyes.

Florrie came slowly awake as she heard the men move around their camp. She felt stiff and groggy, not rested in the least. And then she saw the white daisies beside her.

Adam had given her flowers?

She pushed herself slowly into a sitting position, then reached for the flowers. They were something beautiful, when the rest of the world seemed so cold and barren this morn.

She lifted her gaze and found Adam watching her solemnly. How did he feel, knowing he'd suddenly become responsible for her? She could not imagine allowing such an embarrassment. And she wouldn't. She had to make him understand.

He came over to her and knelt down. "How do you fare?"

She shrugged even as she gave him a small smile. "I will be fine. The flowers are lovely."

To her surprise, he ducked his head. It was . . . endearing.

"Foolish, I know," he said, "especially when things are so bleak. But you said you liked to look at pretty things."

"They certainly can lift a mood," she said brightly, knowing that today it wasn't the truth.

"Come with me," he said, taking her hand and helping her to her feet.

He nodded at Robert, who nodded back, looking amused. Florrie could have blushed at the picture they made, with one hand in Adam's and the other clutching daisies.

He took her back to the stream where Sir Timothy had captured her just hours ago. But in daylight, with the sun dappled through the trees, and more flowers peering between rocks and ferns, it was a place to soothe the soul. She sighed and tried to let such beauty work its magic.

"Florrie, that missive from your father—" He broke off.

She wouldn't let her hard-fought contentment wane. "Think nothing of it, Adam. Though it was a blow, I gradually realized it was not unexpected. I was always an afterthought to my father, and he wanted to be rid of me one way or another. You provided a legitimate excuse."

"But you had hoped for . . . contentment in the convent."

He sounded so wary, she almost laughed. "So I told myself. I will find contentment in other ways.

You do not need to worry. I am certain Christina would gladly allow me to live with her. Thank you so much for giving me the opportunity to know her better. She's—"

Suddenly, he grasped her shoulders, and her traitorous body began to surge to life.

"I do not wish to talk about Christina, or the distant future. I want you to know I've reconsidered, and I will not challenge your father to combat."

Her gasp was deep and ragged, and her eyes stung with grateful tears. She wrung her hands together to keep from clutching him. "Oh, Adam what made you change your mind?"

He looked away. "Many things, but my decision is final."

He might be annoyed if she cried, so she kept it inside, humbled by gratitude toward God for allowing her to somehow help Adam.

"I am glad, Adam," she said quietly. "For you see, 'twould have been an easy victory for you. My father is old and frequently ill."

He frowned at her. "How can that be true? Only last spring, I heard word of his victory over that Frenchman named . . ."

His voice died away as she shook her head.

"All his recent 'victories' of the last few years were fabrications on his part. He was too vain to believe that the world should know he was an old man, long past his prime. I didn't tell you this, because I knew you would make the right decision eventually."

He folded his arms across his chest. "You could not be certain of that. Even I was not certain until just this morn, although I'd begun to have my doubts. Are there any other truths you've withheld?"

Solemnly, she said, "You know everything I know."

"Then I will tell you the rest of my decision," he answered. "I must yet face your father, Florrie, even though I have promised not to challenge him."

She bit her lip, her worries returning. "I thought you would simply . . . go home."

"My home is not safe for me or my brothers until I know what to expect from Martindale—or should I call him Becket, your family name?"

She shuddered even as she shook her head. "He still has the title, Adam."

"Very well. But I have to talk to him; I have to see the truth in his eyes. And I will try not to injure him unless it means my life."

Florrie was so overcome with relief and gratitude that she flung her arms around his neck. "Thank you, Adam." All she could give him was her trust, and her belief that he would do the right thing. Would he?

It frightened her, how much she wanted to believe in him and the promise of his words. Her own future was uncertain, and there was a part of her that realized she'd almost longed for the security of the convent, for she would know her place and have a place to belong. She had none of that now, and she should be frightened. For after all, she'd spent her life carefully keeping her distance from people, never needing anyone too much because they always disappointed her.

Hope and trust in Adam had been building within her for many days, and she still had trouble believing her trust would be satisfied. How could she love him without trust? Perhaps she'd never been meant to love at all.

But right now, he was in her arms, and he felt so good, so solid, as if he could defend her to the world. And London was beckoning, with all its uncertainty and changes. Neither one of them might ever be the same after they confronted her father. For she had her own things to say to the man who'd discarded her without a thought.

She felt . . . desperate, as if this might be her last moment alone with Adam. His arms held her tight, their bodies pressed so close together. She could hear his heart picking up speed, felt his desire for her pillowed against her stomach. Lifting her head from his chest, she looked up at him. He was watching her almost warily, as if he did not know what she would do.

She put her hands on either side of his face and pulled him down for a kiss.

The gentle lover of the previous night was suddenly gone, replaced by a man of desperate passion. He slanted his open mouth over hers, drinking her in, tasting every part of her mouth.

He sucked on her tongue, nibbled her lips, then his mouth journeyed on a path down her throat. He bent her back over his arm until he could reach the hollow between her collarbones, where he dipped his tongue. The magic of the passion between them was overwhelming.

He brought her upright, and then his hands were suddenly everywhere, exploring and touching, and she did the same. She loved the feel of his chest, the wide expanse, the firm curves of muscle. He obviously appreciated her chest, too, by the way he lifted her breasts through her garments, and teased her nipples with his thumbs. Every intimate touch made her want to squirm, brought her legs weaker, coming ever closer to where she wouldn't be able to stand anymore.

Then to her shock, he picked her up, facing him, then guided her legs about his waist, forcing her skirt to slide up to her thighs. She gaped at him, while he only gave her a grin full of concentration and intent.

Then her back was against a tree, and his hips between her legs. She understood then, and a whole new wave of comprehension made her sigh with pleasure and clutch him with excitement. His hands were beneath her thighs and backside, cradling her, holding her where he wanted her. His fingertips touched the hot center of her, and she realized he'd been working her skirts ever higher.

"Now, oh please, now," she whispered, holding back a groan that would be too loud.

Adam loved the feel of Florrie in his arms, willing and eager. She didn't stop moving, didn't stop touching him, an equal partner rather than a woman just accepting his passion. His experiences had been few, and had left him unprepared for the innocent, aroused Florrie.

She pulled on his tunic and shirt until they were above his waist, tugged at his laces. It was incredibly erotic to have her trying so desperately to disrobe him. Between the two of them, they pushed aside every garment standing between them and ecstasy.

And it was certainly ecstasy when at last he was deep inside her, as far as he could go, stretching and filling her. She pulled against his tunic front to keep him against her until he began to move, in and out, rotating his body, wanting her to find even more pleasure with each position.

His mouth caught her cry as she reached fulfillment, and they exchanged groans. He wanted to make this last forever, to share every bit of joy that he could, but somewhere in the depths of his lust-crazed mind, he knew his men were waiting.

So he let himself drop over the edge of pleasure, plummet through each wave that shook him, until at last he was breathless against her.

She locked her legs tight about his waist and collapsed against his chest. Into his tunic, she murmured, "I . . . I had no idea . . ."

He laughed hoarsely. "Frankly, neither did I."

She lifted her head and searched his face, but he could not let her see the things inside him that even he didn't understand. So with great reluctance, he pulled from her body, and set her on the ground. Her skirts fell in graceful folds around her, as she swayed back against the tree, watching without shame as he adjusted his clothing.

Hesitating, he asked, "You are . . . well?"

She smiled, slowly, wickedly. "Very well."

It took everything in him not to lose himself in her again.

"We must hurry," he said, taking her hand and tugging her back through the woods. "We can be in London by afternoon on the morrow."

Chapter 22

By sundown that same day, Florrie felt that she might have finally stopped blushing. Facing Robert and Michael that morn, after she and Adam had made love, had been one of the hardest things she'd ever done. Much as the two men had behaved as if nothing had happened, she felt guilty for enjoying herself when the culmination of their trip was approaching.

In the afternoon, she'd seen Adam looking stone-faced, while Robert playfully punched his arm. She was able to read Adam well enough by now to see the embarrassment he was also hiding.

Oh heavens, Robert was teasing him about their relationship. And it was all her fault.

To her surprise, Adam fought back, giving Robert a knock to the shoulder that almost had him sliding from the saddle. The two brothers looked at each other, while Robert laughed and Adam allowed a small smile of triumph to appear.

Though she was not one for envy, there would

have been a time where such sibling playfulness would have made her wistful. Not anymore. She felt confident that she and Christina had reached a new place in their relationship. She was actually looking forward to visiting her . . . when this was all over.

As the day came to a close, and the final night was upon them, all seemed to settle into a serious frame of mind. Now was the time for utmost concentration, for they had League forces to face, her father's men to get through—and another unnamed foe who wanted them stopped, perhaps dead.

To keep all guessing as to their whereabouts, they'd remained well east of the River Lea, which marked the boundary between Essex and Middlesex, the shire surrounding London. They would have encamped in a wooded copse, as usual, but the sky grew dark well before sunset, signaling a storm. The wind picked up, swirling so much dirt that Florrie had to slit her eyes. The horses twitched with nervousness, and she felt like she could no longer see the holes in the road to avoid. It was as if nature was conspiring to keep them from London.

When Robert returned from scouting duty, Adam called above the wind, "We have to stop for the night!"

Florrie's horse resisted, dancing as she gripped the reins. She petted its neck soothingly.

"I've spied a cattle shed in the distance," Adam

continued. "We will cross the fields and hopefully find gates through the hedges."

It seemed that they spent a long time crossing pastureland, opening and closing gates behind them. At last, as the first drops of rain hit, they pulled open the door to the wattle-and-daub-framed structure. Although it was piled with long bundles of hay, there was just enough room for four horses and four people. The was a lantern inside, and they had to leave the door open while Michael tried to light it, first using his flint and steel to start a stalk of hay burning. It was dangerous work, for the wind whipped into the shed, putting out every fire. But at last, the hay smoldered, and he was able to light the candle with it. Once the lantern shield was closed, giving off light, they put out the small fire with water from their skins, then closed the door on the storm.

Outside their shelter, the wind howled its fury and rain began to lash the roof. They could hear thunder in the distance growing ever closer. Florrie began to resign herself to getting little sleep, at least for a while.

The horses huddled together nervously, and the humans did the same. Adam told Robert and Michael that he was no longer going to challenge the marquess to combat.

Michael studied him, while Robert gaped.

"You've changed your mind," Robert said, "just like that?"

"It has been coming on a long time," Adam said slowly. "At last I saw that someone's death was not a good enough answer. So I will confront him and learn the truth."

"And what if he does not wish to give it to you?" Robert asked.

"I will help persuade him," Florrie said with conviction.

Adam glanced at her, but didn't reply. She felt the slight, and told herself that he was simply focused on his plan.

"And how are we to react if Martindale responds with force?" Michael asked.

"We defend ourselves, of course," Adam said. "But I would prefer if few people are injured. If I can find no satisfaction with Martindale's answers, we take our facts to the king."

At that there was stunned silence.

"Surely I can help you find satisfaction speaking with my father," Florrie said.

Adam looked at her gravely. "That will not be possible."

"What do you mean?"

"I do not want you to be there."

She gasped. "But that was the sole reason you took me from my home!"

"'Tis different now that I will not be challenging him."

"But I have a right to confront him, too, after the way he's abandoned me!"

A sudden crash of lightning seemed to shake the shed.

"You are impressive when you're angry," Adam said dryly.

" 'Tis God, saying I am in the right."

"Or the wrong," he countered.

She glared at him, and he returned her gaze with that impassivity that might drive her mad.

With exasperation, Robert said, "Florrie has the right to make her own decision. Just as you have the right, Adam, to change your mind. But you should have consulted me."

Adam frowned.

"I am your brother, with equal to lose."

"Forgive me," Adam said stiffly. "I was thinking about—" He broke off.

Robert waited until another boom had echoed through the night. Lifting his voice, he said, "I know why you changed your mind. And I agree with you. I just prefer to be consulted."

"And so do I!" Florrie agreed.

Robert lifted an eyebrow. "You did not know about his change of heart?"

"Oh, well . . . aye, I did."

Robert shook his head with a sigh, and Adam rolled his eyes.

She continued, "I meant consulted about future plans—like Adam thinking he could tell me I had to stay behind. Wouldn't I have been in more danger alone?"

"I would have asked Michael to watch over—"

"Do not bother," she said, lifting her chin. "After everything I have been through on this journey, I am seeing it through to the end."

Florrie felt Adam's resistance, knew he wanted to protect her, but she could not back down. At last he nodded, just as another flash of lightning shone through the shutters. The thunder and lightning had picked up speed, occurring only moments apart. The horses had grown more and more restive, and Michael went to comfort them. There was a succession of loud booms and flashes, and in the small confines, one horse jerked with fright, catching Michael between it and another. Michael's breath left him in a grunt. Adam and Robert jumped to their feet, and Florrie tried to follow, but Adam pushed her into a corner.

"Stay here," he ordered. "They could seriously harm you."

She nodded, hugging herself.

The three men stood among the horses, holding them tight by their halters, talking to them, but not much could be heard beyond the pounding of thunder and the sizzle of lightning. The roof had begun to leak in several spots, one of which was right where Florrie was. She took a step to the side and shivered.

Adam held her horse as well as his, and with another flash, hers reared wildly, just missing Adam with its flailing hooves. She could not stand aside and watch a tragic accident. Wrapping her arms around her horse's neck, she spoke soothingly, comforting with the tone of her voice as well as her steady hands. Shivering, the animal at last quieted.

They stood with the horses for another hour, until at last the storm began to subside. The thunder moved into the distance, taking with it the worst of the lightning.

Florrie straightened, her hand on her lower back, and smiled at Adam with confidence. "And if you think I'm good with horses, wait until you see how good I can be with my father. You need me. You know nothing about him or how he'll react." She thought again about how crazed her father had acted that night of his illness, when he'd showed her the proof of his illegitimacy. For years, she'd told herself it was the fever that had made him talk about the priest's ghost, but somewhere inside, she couldn't be certain.

Adam gave her a short bow, smiling. "Aye, my lady, you have won my consent. And we have all won our rest. I think the horses will be only too glad to sleep."

Halfway through the morn, Michael guided them through the fens that encroached upon the River Lea. The river had separated where it crossed the low marshland, and there were several bridges, all well maintained being so close to London. Adam, who'd planned to hire guides along the journey if he hadn't had Michael, was glad for his knowledge.

But bridges meant people, and excluding the Thames, this was the main road to London from Essex. So there were far too many people. Now that they had supposedly ruled out Bladesmen or Martindale's men following them, Adam felt uneasy and constantly on guard. Who else knew or cared what they were doing? Could the Crown somehow have gotten wind of Adam's plan? Perhaps King Henry did not care what Martindale had done in the past, as long as he was a loyal supporter now. For the king had never met Adam's parents, and might not consider their deaths as relevant to his reign's uneasy peace.

As soon as they were over the last bridge, Adam debated turning south, away from the main road to London, but there were now so many people, that the crowd proved a defense of its own. Adam decided that they would have to risk the final two leagues of the journey out in the open. They ate their midday meal in a crowded village tavern, and after journeying another hour, they could see the walls of the city in the distance and the spires of towering churches. Adam had never seen anything so massive, and he saw Florrie's mouth sag open when she first realized what she saw.

The road they traveled was soon lined with cottages, thickening as they approached the city. They passed beneath Aldgate, Michael told them, a massive many-storied building arching over the road in between the curtain walls that protected the city at night. A headless body hung from the battlements, and although Adam saw Florrie flinch at the sight, they did not have much time to look up. Traffic slowed to a crawl beneath the gate, and did not improve inside. When they saw an empty stretch of road, muddy from the previous day's rain, they had to aim for it, weaving past horses and carts and coaches. A flock of geese being driven in for slaughter startled many a horse.

Adam, Robert, and Florrie rode side by side, with Michael behind. Almost shouting to be heard above the many sounds of merchants hawking their wares, and animals protesting, Adam said, "Now is when men will be looking for us, though I fear there is not much they can do. Be on your guard."

His eyes were focused everywhere, searching for someone paying too much attention to them. There were timber-framed buildings lining the road, two and three stories high, each story wider than the one below.

Michael had told Adam to head straight into the city along Lombard Street, where they would eventually run into Martindale House, a mansion in an older parish. Just past Trinity Priory, the street widened a bit where Aldgate branched off of Lombard. It was there that a sudden sound from behind made the voices of the crowd rise. People started flowing wildly to each side of the street, pointing behind Adam's party. He turned in the saddle to see a troop of knights galloping straight toward them, ignoring the wild cries of people trying to get out of their way.

There was too much purpose in their movement. Had they been waiting just within the gate, hoping to spot Adam's party?

The panicked crowd surged around them, and Adam had to detour around a coach. Fighting to control his horse, it took every inch of his strength to rejoin his party.

And he could neither find Robert, Michael, nor Florrie. He stood up in his stirrups, trying to see over the mass confusion around him. The horsemen had thundered past, but now they were wheeling around, fighting against the carts and horses and pigs.

Robert expertly guided his horse past two grinning boys running through the street. He pulled up hard next to Adam. "Do you see them?" he shouted.

Adam shook his head. "The coach separated me from all of you."

"The knights forced me off to the right, and I got caught up in a group of women carrying baskets of laundry. Damn, but this city is busy. Do you think Michael is with Florrie?"

He had spoken the question that Adam feared. "I hope so."

"The knights are returning," Robert began. "I will head down the street on the right—"

Adam cut him off. "'Tis too dangerous. You need to stay with me and—"

"Cease, Adam! You cannot protect me for the rest of my life. Just like last night, you're still treating me like a child, from not consulting me about important decisions about Martindale to being too controlling." He lowered his voice as much as he was able. "You do not have to be my father. Just be my brother."

Adam felt something tighten in his throat as he thought of leaving his brother at the mercy of such a city. He'd felt the same way when Paul left them.

But Robert was right. Adam was still trying to make his decisions for him—too keep him safe. But Adam could no longer take on such a responsibility. Florrie was the one who needed him now.

The knights had almost completed their turn and, more haphazardly than their first thunderous approach, were beginning to head for them.

"Let me go to the right before you move," Robert said, controlling his horse as it danced in a circle. "We look enough alike that if they're truly watching for us, they might follow me. Where will you go?"

"To Martindale House. Michael would take her there." He prayed fervently that she still had Michael.

"I'll see you there!" Robert called, giving a wave

as he wheeled his horse about and aimed right for the horsemen.

Adam headed for a side alley. The horsemen seemed surprised by Robert's bold move, and broke ranks before he could hit them full on. In the confusion, many turned to follow Robert, but Adam saw no more.

He had to find Florrie.

Chapter 23

A coach maneuvered sideways in traffic, blocking the road so quickly that Florrie didn't know what to do, causing her horse to rear up. She flung her arms around its neck so that they wouldn't topple over. Then there was a man with a sack on his back, gaping up at her from practically beneath the horse's front hooves. She pulled to the left and somehow missed the man's skull. He shook his fist at her, but he was soon swept away with the panicked crowd.

She couldn't see Adam, Robert, or Michael anywhere. She'd been forced to react to the fleeing of the throng, simply to avoid hitting anyone. Before she knew it, she'd been led from the main street and into a smaller one, where the crowds had fled to safety. The buildings were far closer together here, leaning almost precariously over the street itself, as if a stiff wind could knock them together. A sewer ran down the center of the street, and the smell was so bad she felt nauseated.

And now more men were noticing she was a

lone woman on a fine horse. She could not afford
to wait for Adam to find her, she realized. She was
on her own.

She knew she had to get back on Lombard
Street, but the knights might still be there. Two
men nudged each other and started toward her. As
she galloped right for them, the well-trained horse
didn't break stride as they both fell to the way-
side in surprise. She kept to small alleys, dodging
people and ducking merchants' signs. She passed
a man held captive in the stocks, his back bloodied as he waited out his sentence. London was a
fearsome place, crowded and filthy, with cramped
streets that twisted in upon each other. But she
had lost her pursuers.

At last she was back on a wider, paved road, and
she could see market stalls manned by women as
well as men selling their produce from the countryside. After dismounting, she led her horse near
them, and was able to ask for directions. It took
more than one person's assistance, but at last a
woman wearing a yoke across her shoulders,
milk pails hanging from it, who had sold cheese
directly to Martindale House was able to describe
where it was.

When Florrie reached the mansion, she was confronted by gated walls far above her head, manned
by guards. She wished she were brave enough to
casually ride by and look inside, but the guards
could have been given her description, knowing

her father. She couldn't risk it. So where the walls took a turn down an alley, she dismounted, kept her horse behind her, and watched for someone from her party.

This was certainly a better neighborhood, since no one accosted her. Was it the presence of Martindale guards nearby? She was able to wait for what seemed like at least an hour, watching the shadows lengthen.

"Katherine?" a man's voice called her false name from behind her.

Hardly daring to hope, she turned around and saw Adam riding toward her. Her relieved grin surely matched his, for he dismounted swiftly and swept her into his arms.

"You are safe," he whispered against her ear.

"And you." She leaned away and looked up at him. "When we were separated, I could only hope you would come here."

"Smart thinking," he said with approval.

"Maybe not so smart, if we cannot outwit the guards at the gates."

He waved a hand in dismissal. "You forget whom you are speaking to, my lady. I have not come all this way to allow a few soldiers to stop me."

"Should I simply announce myself? I am the master's daughter."

"I debated that, but we are too many servants removed from your father yet. We do not want to give him enough warning that he can have us dealt with before we reach him. I have been examining the rear entrance. Follow me."

They mounted their horses and rode back along the length of the wall, then turned down the alley. Except for a servant entering the metal garden gate of the mansion across the alley, they were alone. When the woman had hurriedly closed the gate behind her, Florrie looked at Adam.

"Our gate is locked," he said, "but 'tis of little consequence. Come to me quickly."

Confused, she rode as close to him as possible, and was surprised when he pulled her across his lap.

"Stand up," he said. "I'll hold you. You should be able to reach the top of the wall."

Never had her uneven legs been asked to bear her weight so awkwardly. Not wanting to disappoint him, she used one leg to stand up on his thigh, and the other for balance. The top of the wall was chest height.

A lush garden spread out before her, and she could hear the gurgling of a fountain somewhere out of sight. A stable loomed to her left. There could be grooms working within, or gardeners among the flowerbeds.

"What do you see?" he asked tightly.

"A garden, with no one in sight."

"Then you need to straddle the wall and look below, to see what could break your fall."

"Break my fall—!" But she bit her words off, determined not to question him.

"Do you need to be boosted higher?" he asked from below.

"Nay, but I will jump, so be prepared."

She gave a start as she felt his hand on her rump. She pushed off, and with his help, she found herself braced straight-armed on the wall. She swung a leg over to straddle it, then sighed with relief.

Again, he asked, "What do you see?"

She looked below and grimaced, then called softly, "Nothing but a border of flowers below. This will not work, Adam."

To her surprise, he was already standing on his horse, and with a leap, he caught the wall and with powerful muscles pulled himself up to sit on the top. She gaped at him.

He grinned. "I was learning these skills when I had but eight years."

"Such training does have its benefits. But the horses . . . ?" She looked down into the alley below.

"They'll wait."

The animals lowered their heads and looked for something on the ground to nibble. She prayed they wouldn't be stolen.

"And us?" she continued, looking to the garden side. "If I break my leg, I will be useless to you."

"I'll lower you down, so the drop will not be too far. Take my hands quickly."

She didn't have time to feel frightened. It was far

more dangerous to be so exposed on the wall. She took both his hands, let her legs slip over the side, and then she was hanging freely. She watched the narrowing of his eyes, but that was the only strain he showed as he bent over the wall, lowering her as much as he could.

She looked down past her feet to see the flowers not too far below. "Let go!" she called softly. He did, and she hit the soft flowerbed, falling backward onto her rump. She smiled up at him.

Holding on to the wall, Adam lowered himself as far as he could, then released the edge. He landed beside her. He pulled her behind a nearby bench so they could crouch out of sight.

"We do not have much time," Adam said. "Bladesmen might have been watching the alley."

"I saw no one."

He only arched a brow.

"Oh, well, of course, they wouldn't *allow* me to see them."

"To be truthful, I saw no sign of them either, which surprised me, after Timothy's warning. Regardless, we cannot go through the front door, so we'll walk in through the servant's entrance as if we belong there."

"Then I should go first," she said with confidence. "You can follow meekly behind me, as if you're a servant working for me. 'Tis a good thing my sister gave me a new gown. And 'tis only a little damp," she insisted.

He grinned and shook his head. "Much as I

do not like the vulnerability of it, it sounds like a decent plan."

She beamed at him. "I am ready."

His eyes, once focused so intently on the mansion, now turned their intensity on her. "Florrie, this will be dangerous."

" 'Tis my father's house. Should anyone confront us, I will resort to that truth. You will still be my servant."

"I am always your servant," he said.

She saw the softening in his eyes, heard it in his voice, and knew the time was coming when at last she would be able to explore his feelings for her without the fear of coming battle. And she wanted that badly. Asking him no questions, she leaned in and kissed him.

Then she stood up and began to limp across the gravel paths of the garden like the master's daughter, knowing Adam would fall into place behind her. She opened the rear door of the mansion and entered a long corridor. As she passed various doors, she could smell a wide variety of odors from the kitchen and its pantries and the dairy. More than one person passed them in the corridor, and although she received several curious looks, she only nodded regally, as if she belonged—and she did. This was her home, much as she might never have seen it before.

They were almost to the end of the corridor when a man wearing a black doublet emblazoned with the Martindale coat of arms stepped out of a room before them. His expression of surprise was brief. Florrie tried to walk right by him, as she had the others, but he did not move out of her way. He was of middling years, his blond hair lightened with white, and he bore an unmistakable air of authority. Her heart, already pounding with nervousness, threatened to beat out of her chest. She reminded herself that no one could dismiss her; she was a daughter of the household.

"I am Hewet, Lord Martindale's butler. Do you have cause to be here?"

"I am Lady Florence, Lord Martindale's daughter. I have just arrived from the north."

Hewet blinked at her, betraying his surprise. "Lady Florence? Although I have met his lordship's other daughters, I have never met you."

"If you noticed my limp, then you can see that it is difficult for me to travel."

Suddenly, his manner eased, and she was glad he had seen her walking down the corridor.

"I had heard of your infirmity, my lady. Forgive me for questioning you."

"Is my father available?" As if she'd take no for an answer.

"Allow me to lead you to him, my lady. He will be quite pleased."

Her smile felt frozen on her face. Nay, her father would not be pleased at all, but he had brought this on himself. She felt Adam close behind her, could sense his impatience and expectation. He was about to meet the man who'd altered his entire life, caused his family hardship yet allowed Adam to be trained by the most elite of military societies. It was as if her father had helped to create the man who wanted to defeat him.

The corridor led into the great hall, which was nothing like the stone-walled hall of their castle. Wainscoting paneled the walls into intricately carved squares. In the center of those squares were the marquess's coat of arms—rearing dragon on a shield—crossed swords and other displays of armory. Suits of armor were interspersed by elaborate cupboards displaying gold and silver plate. Two guards stood at the double doors against the far wall.

And there was her father, alone but for the soldiers, with his feet propped on a stool before the fire, surrounded by the heraldry of a title he did not deserve—that he had killed for. He seemed to be muttering to himself.

Adam felt a shock of thwarted retribution. Martindale was a frail old man, sunken in his cushioned chair. Time had taken everything away from the warrior, and Adam wished he himself could take the rest.

But there was Florrie standing so proudly before him, her shoulders back, her chin lifted. This was her family's home, and she'd never been allowed to be here before. Though Adam had no parents, he'd never felt an outcast, and had his brothers for companions. Florrie had been alone through her whole life. How could he feel that he'd suffered in comparison to her?

He put his hands on her shoulders in a brief gesture of support, then went to move past her. She put up an arm to stop him.

Hewet, the butler, looked between them in surprise, but then Florrie nodded to him. He cleared his throat and said, "Lord Martindale, may I present your daughter, Lady Florence."

Martindale's head slowly came up. His white hair was thinning over his red scalp. Deep lines marred his face, and his shoulders looked bony rather than strong.

He didn't bother to stand up. "Florence?" he said in a cracked voice. "Impossible. You are mistaken, Hewet. Send the woman away."

He took another sip from his tankard, betraying the shaking of his hand. It seemed strange to Adam that that hand had ever been strong enough to hold a sword. The muttering continued, as if he didn't care who saw.

"Good day, Father," Florrie said calmly.

Martindale's gaze locked onto her, and he seemed to squint. "Come closer."

She did so, and Adam stayed with her, wondering if Martindale would recognize something of his father in him. Timothy had told him there was a resemblance, which Adam had always taken pride in.

But Martindale was looking at Florrie, and his face grew red. "But you were supposed to be . . ."

"Kidnapped?" she countered sweetly. "Aye, and at the beginning I feared for my life. 'Twas truly harrowing. But you did not care about that, or about what kind of man held me. You abandoned me."

"There was nothing I could do," he blustered angrily. "I was taking the chance that if the kidnapper thought you meant nothing to me, he might let you go safely."

Adam cocked his head. For Florrie's sake, he hoped that was the truth.

"Or he might have killed me," Florrie countered coldly.

Adam realized that Florrie saw through Martindale's attempts to make his actions sound desperate but reasonable.

"He would not have killed you," Martindale said. "I counted on the fact that he was Keswick's son."

Adam saw the brief confusion on Florrie's face. He'd never told her of his lineage, not even his surname. He'd been so used to hiding it from the world, that he'd even hidden it from the woman he loved.

"Nay, he did not kill me," Florrie said. "So I brought him to you."

For the first time, Martindale's gaze went past Florrie, as if he'd only thought Adam a servant. Adam wasn't sure if he expected to see hate there, but instead he caught a glimpse of fear and furtiveness, quickly banished. There were old, ugly secrets buried inside the man, and they'd rotted him from within.

After another moment of muttering, almost as if he were talking to himself, Martindale demanded, "Keswick, or one of the brothers?"

"'Tis I, Keswick, who wrote to you," Adam said, standing at Florrie's shoulder.

"You grew into a coward, hurting a woman."

Florrie opened her mouth, but Adam shook his head. "I never deliberately hurt her. But I knew that with an untrustworthy opponent, one needs leverage. I had meant to come here to challenge you over what you did to my parents, but I had already decided that you weren't worth it. And now I see that it would have been pointless. Time and your guilt have damaged you."

Martindale rose to his feet, hands braced on the chair. Then he quickly stood unassisted, as if he didn't want them to see he needed support. "What was done to your parents? I did not understand your missive."

"You know all about the murders," Adam said, pulling the pendant from his neck and holding it up to the torchlight. "I found this near my parents' bodies the night you slew them."

Those old eyes fixed on the emblem of the Martindale crest, and he couldn't seem to look away. "Where did you get that?"

"Where you dropped it in blood."

"You are lying."

"You thought by killing them you would protect your ugly secret, but 'tis a secret no longer."

Martindale's eyes widened in sudden horror. "You cannot speak the words—"

"You are not the legitimate heir of the marquessate. You are a bastard, and somehow my parents discovered it and confronted you. And you killed them."

Rage burned in Martindale's eyes. "You lie!"

A sudden pounding of feet echoed through the hall, and Adam turned to see Claudius Drake, Martindale's heir, running down the grand staircase from the next floor. He brandished a dagger, and he was closer to Martindale than the guards were.

"Bastard!" Drake shouted at Martindale, the dagger upraised.

Adam found himself catching Drake's arm and bending it backward until he dropped the dagger. How could he be defending the one man he'd spent years hating?

Chapter 24

Adam kept himself between Drake and the old man, fighting to hold him still.

"How can you not be the heir?" Drake shouted at Martindale, spittle forming in the corners of his mouth. "I spent my life doing your bidding! I thought I was protecting my inheritance by protecting you! When I read the missive about Florence's kidnapping, *I* sent men to intercept them in Huntingdonshire, and more men to intercept them in London."

Martindale staggered back against the chair and sank into it. Adam exchanged a glance with Florrie, who looked shocked that her sister's husband—her own cousin—could deliberately put her in danger.

"And instead my father and, now, *I* were the real heirs all along?" Drake demanded.

Martindale shook his head, eyes wide and darting back and forth, as if he saw more than the people in front of him.

"My father was the poor cousin to nobility,"

Drake continued, "having to fight as a mercenary to survive, when his life—and mine!—should have been full of wealth and power and ease."

As the words poured out of Drake, the violence seemed to as well, for he'd stopped fighting Adam, who was able to release him. Martindale's mouth opened and shut, as if he should speak, but didn't know what to say.

"Can you control yourself?" Adam asked Drake coolly.

For the first time, Drake seemed to really study him. "I have seen you before. You were the wounded man in Christina's care." And then he looked at Florrie. "Were you there, too?"

"Aye, we were both there," Adam said angrily. "Recovering from what your men did to us."

Drake put his hands on his hips. "You'd kidnapped her. What was I supposed to think?"

"You should have *thought* to tell your men not to harm your cousin. I was wounded saving Florrie from certain death."

Drake paled. "I did not instruct them in that."

"Perhaps not, but you did not hire trustworthy men."

"I did not have the money," he said, his hate-filled glare turning back on Martindale.

"Make no more mistakes like that, Drake. Because your luck is about to change. You'll have your inheritance soon enough, but not if you're in the Tower for murder."

Suddenly, three armed men appeared from

the servant's corridor, and Hewet boldly stepped before them.

"And who are you?" he demanded.

The first man met Adam's gaze over the butler's head and Adam recognized him as a Bladesman.

"We are with Sir Adam," the man said. "We are here to observe."

They went to stand beside Martindale's two guards, leaving Adam to realize that those two men were also Bladesmen. And they'd allowed Adam to speak with Martindale. The League not only wanted to observe, they wanted to judge the truth for themselves.

Yet they hadn't interfered with Adam's intentions. Did they trust him after all?

Through all of this, Martindale never moved from his chair, continuing to mutter to himself. Was he trying to come up with denials or motivations for the things he'd done? Florrie only watched her father. Adam wondered if she was seeing her past—and her future—in a totally new light.

Someone pounded on the front double doors, and the Bladesmen opened them, but stood before them threateningly—and then stepped aside. To Adam's relief, Robert and Michael had found each other, and now rejoined them.

"Did I miss everything?" Robert asked, looking beyond Adam to Martindale. "He doesn't look as if he were ever a great warrior."

"We all age," Adam said softly. "He has not confessed, but he has been accused, and not just by us." He explained what had already happened, including Drake's actions.

Drake stood apart from Florrie, but he kept glancing at her as if he wished to speak, but didn't know what to say. An apology would be a good place for him to start, but Adam didn't know if she would accept it.

"But Martindale didn't confess?" Robert continued.

"We no longer need a confession," said another voice loudly.

Timothy Sheldon and several other men came down the carved staircase from the upper floor. Adam stared at his foster father, not exactly surprised by the intrusion of even more Bladesmen. When the League took an interest, they saw it through until it was finished.

Florrie felt very distant and unreal. She was standing in a home she'd never been allowed to see, watching the disintegration of her father beneath the collapse of a mountain of his terrible lies. So many people had been hurt while he'd helped himself—and his family, she admitted to herself.

And now here was Sir Timothy, already within the mansion, though she hadn't seen him. She turned to Adam, who watched his foster father. There was no triumph in Adam's expression, only solemnity and sadness, for he understood how many people had been hurt—and would be hurt.

"Why is no confession needed?" Adam asked, when Sir Timothy reached them.

"No confession because I did nothing!" her father said shrilly.

The sound of his voice, so out of control, made her shudder with horror and pity. Sir Timothy held up a torn piece of parchment that Florrie recognized too well.

" 'Twas hidden in a coffer in his bedchamber."

As I told Adam, Florrie thought, surprised that she didn't feel more guilty that he'd passed the location on to his foster father.

"Nay," her father cried. "You cannot touch that! *He* will not like it."

Florrie remembered the way he'd raved when he was ill, talking about the priest as if he were still alive. Was that who he meant?

Claudius looked between her father and Sir Timothy. "What is that?"

"Proof that the late marchioness was already two months dead when Martindale was born."

"And he kept it?" Claudius asked in disbelief.

Watching her father, Florrie couldn't be surprised. He was staring at the parchment in fascinated horror, muttering, gesturing, eyes wild. She may have suffered beneath his treatment for many years, and knew that he'd killed people for his own selfish ends, but seeing him reduced to this sickened her.

"We may never know why he kept it," Sir Timothy was saying, "but it will allow me to go to King Henry for permission to grant you the title of marquess of Martindale immediately."

There was no greater punishment for her father, she knew. He might have preferred a quick death to watching everything he'd assumed about his life be destroyed. But Adam's parents were still dead, and nothing could bring them back.

"'Tis cursed," her father suddenly said, watching Sir Timothy, who was perusing the document. "He never let me destroy it."

"Who?" Sir Timothy asked.

"The priest, the one who wrote it."

Sir Timothy cocked his head. "It was written months before your birth. The priest must be long dead."

Her father shook his head, and Florrie found herself holding back tears.

"Nay, since the night I found out the truth, he has never left me," he said, looking to a corner of the great hall as if someone stood there. "Because of what I did . . . the priest tells me that he can never rest in peace. He was full of guilt on his deathbed when he told Keswick the terrible secret, giving him that document and asking him to set things to right."

Florrie held her breath, saw Adam watching intently, knew this was the confession, the truth, he longed for.

"And Keswick confronted you," Sir Timothy said, speaking in a carefully calm voice.

"Before he showed me the proof, I never knew ... anything," her father said, his expression full of an old disbelief. "How could I believe such a terrible thing about my own father? Yet ... I knew he'd wanted sons, and that his wife—the woman I thought for so many years was my mother— had given birth to many stillborns before dying when I was born. But ... Keswick told me that wasn't true. The priest had explained everything, had lived with my father's blackmail his whole life. The marchioness died with another babe, not me, and my father substituted his own child by a concubine. He *was* my father!" he suddenly shouted, as if desperate that they should believe him. But again, he wasn't looking at them, but at the empty corner. Then his wild eyes pleaded with them all. "How could I let such a secret come out? I had daughters who would suffer!"

Florrie flinched, hugging herself, feeling too weary to cry.

"So you killed them both," Adam said coldly, "one a defenseless woman, a young mother."

"But she knew! She was guilty."

Adam stiffened, but didn't move.

"I suffered, too," her father cried. "He cursed me, to make certain I never had sons, so the title would go to Claudius after all. These long years I have listened to his voice condemning me."

"The priest would have stopped haunting you," Sir Timothy said, "if only you'd told the truth. Instead you forced three young boys to grow up orphaned, in hiding because all feared they might suffer the fate of their parents."

"I—I—" He slumped back in his chair, looking dazed, mouth hanging slack.

Sickened, Florrie turned away and found Adam there. He took her in his embrace, and she pressed her face against his chest, glad for the reassuring sound of his heartbeat. It was over. Her father was no longer the marquess—Claudius was. And Matilda would be his marchioness, as she'd always wanted.

But Adam was Florrie's strength. When she saw him stop Claudius from killing her father, a man Adam himself had wanted dead, she knew then that he'd really changed. For her. No one had ever rewarded her trust as he had.

"You do not need to be here anymore, Florrie," he whispered.

She nodded her acceptance, let him lead her toward Hewet, the butler, who was looking a bit confused.

"You need to prepare a bedchamber for Lady Florence," Adam said.

"I am no longer Lady Florence," she said apologetically to Hewet.

"But she is my cousin," Claudius called, "my

sister by marriage. Martindale House gladly welcomes her."

She looked at him for a long moment, and knew that he had spent his life suffering for her father's sins, another innocent warped.

"I ask your forgiveness," he said.

She nodded and turned away. Adam started to accompany her, but she stopped him. "Nay, you need to finish here. Speak to your foster father and the other Bladesmen. Let me know what is decided about my father's fate. But come to me this evening?"

She saw the way his expression eased, and he gave her a faint smile.

Bringing her hand up, he kissed it. "Wait for me, my lady."

"Always," she whispered.

Florrie was surprised by how hungry she was. She ate everything on the tray that was brought to her, then she fell into a deep sleep untroubled by dreams. When she awoke, Adam was sitting in a chair beside the bare hearth, watching her. Several candles had been lit, and the shutters closed against the encroaching night.

She sat up slowly, smiling at him.

He smiled back.

"Is it over, then?" she asked softly.

He nodded. "Your father has been taken to the Tower of London, where he awaits the king's final word. But, my sweet, I fear the end will not be long. Your father said the priest will not permit him to eat."

She bowed her head. "He brought this on himself, regardless of the crime his father committed. He must accept the consequences." With a deep breath, she met Adam's gaze again, and gave him a small smile. "What of you, Adam? You are free of the need for justice at last."

He sighed. "I cannot say it made me feel good. But 'tis done, and at last my brothers and I are free to live the lives we'd been denied." He rose and came to the bed to sit and take her in his arms. "Florrie, I have become the man I am today because of you. Anger was ruining my life, and I didn't even realize it. I thought I was being so calm and logical. And the anger wasn't just toward your father. 'Twas also directed at the League of the Blade, for forcing me into a life that every other Bladesman was given the chance to choose. I know they were protecting me, and I owe them my life, but they made me *give* them my life. Do you understand?"

She nodded, caressing his cheek, smoothing the frown from his brow.

"But they do good works, Florrie, and so many people benefit. I . . . like helping people. Even though you may think my childhood difficult, 'twas peaceful and productive, and I felt honored by the work. Aye, I wasn't given a choice, and that was wrong, but how many children are offered such a thing? You were not, and yet you flourished to become the woman I so admire. So if you do not mind, I will stay a Bladesman, and serve my yearly mission for them."

"I am glad you've come to peace with the role they've played in your life," she said, "but why should I mind what your choice is?"

"Because if you consent to marry me, as my wife, your opinion would count equally with mine. My life can only be complete if you allow me to share it with you."

She covered her trembling mouth, feeling happy tears swim in her eyes.

"I love you, Florrie," he said gently, "but I would live alone if you thought to marry me only to bring peace between our families."

"Nay," she whispered, her face lifted to his, "'tis my turn to be selfish. I love you, Adam. I have spent my life making things easier on everyone else, and was too ready to accept what they thought of me. But not this time. I am not going to the convent, or becoming a nursemaid to any of my sisters' children. I want to be your wife, whether in a cozy little manor or an inn, as you do your work for the League."

He laughed aloud then, kissing her soundly before saying, "Would you mind being a countess and living in a castle, where I swear the spirits of my parents would be so glad to see love and laughter?"

"A countess," she breathed, shocked and almost too stunned to understand him. "Keswick . . . ?"

"The earldom. My family surname is Hilliard. Forgive me for not telling you, but I've spent my life hiding from people, and now at last I've found someone to share everything with."

Tears spilled down her cheeks, and she dashed them away happily. "After all my belief that legends couldn't come true, a Bladesman really did come to rescue me and change my life."

He kissed her tenderly. "I think you have it backwards. You rescued me."

Next month, don't miss these exciting new love stories only from Avon Books

Forbidden Nights With a Vampire by Kerrelyn Sparks

Vanda Barkowski is a vampire with a hot temper, and now her employees at the nightclub she owns have filed complaints, sentencing her to anger management class. Worse, Phil Jones has agreed to be her sponsor, but can she resist her attraction to this forbidden mortal?

A Scotsman in Love by Karen Ranney

Margaret Dalrousie is a talented artist who lets no man interfere with her gift. But she has dark memories that haunt her, and she has not painted a portrait in ages. Yet she soon discovers that there is nothing so dangerous—or tempting—as a Scotsman in love.

The Angel and the Highlander by Donna Fletcher

After Alyce Bunnock's father tried to marry her off, she fled, taking shelter at Everagis Abbey and disguising herself as a nun. But when Lachlan Sinclare arrives to return her to her family, Alyce fears for her freedom—yet the sight of him weakens her with desire.

Night Song by Beverly Jenkins

Cara Lee Henson knows no soldier can be trusted to stay in one place—and that includes handsome Sergeant Chase Jefferson of the Tenth Cavalry. Dallying with the dashing man in blue could cost the independent Kansas schoolteacher her job and reputation, but Chase has a lesson of his own to teach her.

Unforgettable, enthralling love stories,
sparkling with passion and adventure
from Romance's bestselling authors

At Avon Books, we know your passion for romance—once you finish one of our novels, you find yourself wanting more.

May we tempt you with . . .

- **Excerpts** from our upcoming releases.

- Entertaining **extras**, including authors' personal photo albums and book lists.

- Behind-the-scenes **scoop** on your favorite characters and series.

- **Sweepstakes** for the chance to win free books, romantic getaways, and other fun prizes.

- Writing **tips** from our authors and editors.

- **Blog** with our authors and find out why they love to write romance.

- **Exclusive content** that's not contained within the pages of our novels.

Join us at
www.avonbooks.com

An Imprint of HarperCollins*Publishers*

Available wherever books are sold or please call 1-800-331-3761 to order.

FTH 0708

On a barren hill overlooking a vast expanse of sand, a lonesome hanging tree stood barren and defiant. From a distance, it looked like a hand rising up from a grave. At its foot, a handful of survivors both living and dead stood before a small hole in the sand. There were a dozen such holes that had been recently dug and filled, over a quarter-mile spread with no pattern to link them. But this one was the last.

Jake's severed head stared up at them from the bottom of the hole, mutely pleading with tearful, flyblown eyes. He looked so scared it was almost heartbreaking, till you remembered who he was, and what he'd done.

There was no fucking way on earth that Evangeline was going to kneel before this grave. Not even to piss in it. And she'd seen more than enough of his snivel-ing, now that he was down, to last her the rest of her days.

The good news was, he'd finally learned how to say basic phrases like *I'm sorry*, and *I love you*, and *please*.

The bad news was, that didn't quite qualify as redemp-tion, no matter how many times you wrapped your ugly mouth around the words.

So she stood back, holding the shovel, and waited for Esther to do whatever she had to do.

But Esther had Eddie beside her, and even dead, he still played the heart to her head.

Give him to God, Eddie said to her with his soundless, throatless, bloodied lips. *There is no one more lost than him. Or more needing of God's healing grace.*

And though she could barely bring herself to look at his mutilations, it was impossible to argue with that. One thing was for certain: his love was true.

So she knelt before the grave, and said the first prayer she'd learned in childhood: not from her parents, but from a fellow student and friend who'd actually be-lieved in God and the angels.

"Our Father," she said, "who art in heaven, hallowed be thy name. Thy kingdom come, thy will be done—" She choked. "On earth, as it is in heaven."

Jake stared up at her—at Eddie beside her—and though he did not pray along, he did begin to cry. And that was also something.

"Give us this day our daily bread. And forgive us our trespasses—" Taking deep, hitching breaths. "As we forgive those who trespass against us.

"And lead us not into temptation, but deliver us from evil.

"Amen," she concluded.

"Amen," said the rest.

Then they filled in the hole, and Jake was gone. Another secret for the desert to hold. Whatever else he might have to discuss would be done in the dark, through a mouthful of dirt, with the demons who shared his tomb with him.

Alone together. Forever and ever.

In an intimate, infinite hell.

Up above, it was magic hour: that brief slice of sunrise when the sky seems to glow like a jewel from within. The most beautiful, multicolored moment of the day, replicated only once again, at dusk.

Evangeline wanted a cigarette. Jasper handed her one. Christian gave her a light. He had all the lighters now.

"Hey, you guys," she murmured as Jasper nuzzled her wild red hair.

"Hey, yourself," they said as one. Happily united once again.

"Oh, that's nice . . ."

The leading edge of the sun emerged from behind the purple mountains at the far end of the valley. The soft violet light of predawn turned to gold, lifting their gazes, as well as their hearts. And making them smile.

Not everything was broken.

Together, they soaked in the dawn for a long peaceful moment, while the desert awakened all around them to a life that only looked like death.

Sharing a little glimpse of heaven.

In the brave new world that had just begun.

And Jasper thought about his body. How heavy, how useless it seemed to him now. He thought about Jake, lumbering around in a place that had clearly outlived him. What was the fucking point in that?

Then he thought about the little Bible girl, and why it was that she alone had not come back in the flesh.

He contemplated Evangeline's description of her death. How she'd lifted her arms, as if to fly.

When it's time to go, you go, he thought.

Blowing life a little kiss.

And just like that, he went.

L. H. MAYNARD & M. P. N. SIMS

At an old manor house on a remote Scottish island, six managers of a large corporation arrive for a week-long stay. Within days they will all suffer horrifying deaths and their bodies will never be found. The government assigns the case to Department 18, the special unit created to investigate the supernatural and the paranormal. However this is no mere haunted house. The evil on this island goes back centuries, but its unholy plots and schemes are hardly things of the past. In fact, while the members of Department 18 race to unravel the island's secrets, the forces of darkness are gathering . . . and preparing to attack.

BLACK
CATHEDRAL

ISBN 13: 978-0-8439-6199-7

To order a book or to request a catalog call:
1-800-481-9191

This book is also available at your local bookstore, or you can check out our Web site **www.dorchesterpub.com** where you can look up your favorite authors, read excerpts, or glance at our discussion forum to see what people have to say about your favorite books.

BRIAN KEENE

They came to the lush, deserted island to compete on a popular reality TV show. Each one hoped to be the last to leave. Now they're just hoping to stay alive. It seems the island isn't deserted after all. Contestants and crew members are disappearing, but they aren't being eliminated by the game. They're being taken by the monstrous half-human creatures that live in the jungle. The men will be slaughtered. The women will be kept alive as captives. Night is falling, the creatures are coming, and rescue is so far away. . . .

CASTAWAYS

ISBN 13: 978-0-8439-6089-1

To order a book or to request a catalog call:

1-800-481-9191

This book is also available at your local bookstore, or you can check out our Web site **www.dorchesterpub.com** where you can look up your favorite authors, read excerpts, or glance at our discussion forum to see what people have to say about your favorite books.

BRYAN SMITH

SMITH

Beautiful. Sexy. Inhuman. Jake McAllister knows that his brother Trey's new girlfriend is a bad influence, but he doesn't know what Myra's really after—Trey's soul. Trey is just one of her new playthings, a pawn in her centuries-long game. One by one, Myra has seduced and enslaved the young men of the town. The women have joined her cult as eager priestesses, lured by promises of sex and power. But Myra's unholy plan is almost complete. Can one man hope to battle such seductive evil? Will he be able to resist the...

SOULTAKER

ISBN 13: 978-0-8439-6193-5

To order a book or to request a catalog call:

1-800-481-9191

This book is also available at your local bookstore, or you can check out our Web site www.dorchesterpub.com where you can look up your favorite authors, read excerpts, or glance at our discussion forum to see what people have to say about your favorite books.

RICHARD LAYMON

For two families, it was supposed to be a relaxing camping trip in the California mountains. They thought it would be fun to get away from everything for a while. But they're not alone. The woods are also home to two terrifying residents who don't take kindly to strangers—an old hag with unholy powers, and her hulking son, a half-wild brute with uncontrollable, violent urges. The campers still need to get away—but now their lives depend on it!

DARK MOUNTAIN

ISBN 13: 978-0-8439-6138-6

GORD ROLLO

AUTHOR OF THE JIGSAW MAN

The small town of Dunville is no stranger to fear. Evil has stalked its dark streets once before. These days, no one in the town likes to talk about it much. Some folks deny it ever happened...

But four boyhood friends are about to discover the truth, though no one will believe them. Their parents think they've been listening to too many scary stories. But what the boys have released from an icy well is no legend, and it will soon terrify Dunville to its very core. Unspeakable horror is running free...and the nightmares of the past are about to begin again.

CRIMSON

ISBN 13: 978-0-8439-6195-9

WRATH JAMES WHITE

Could serial killers be victims of a communicable disease? Fifteen years ago, Joseph Miles was attacked by a serial child murderer. He was the only one of the madman's victims to survive. Now he himself is slowly turning into a killer. He can feel the urges, the burning needs, getting harder and harder to resist. Can anything stop him—or cure him—before he kills the only woman he's ever loved? Or before he infects someone else?

SUCCULENT PREY

ISBN 13: 978-0-8439-6164-5

To order a book or to request a catalog call:
1-800-481-9191

UNCUT VERSION!
IN PAPERBACK FOR THE FIRST TIME!

THE
PINES

Deep within the desolate Pine Barrens, a series of macabre murders draws ever nearer to an isolated farmhouse where a woman struggles to raise her disturbed son. The boy has a psychic connection to something in the dark forest, something unseen... and evil.

The old-timers in the region know the truth of the legendary creature that stalks these woods. And they know the savagery it's capable of.

ROBERT
DUNBAR

ISBN 13: 978-0-8439-6165-2

To order a book or to request a catalog call:
1-800-481-9191

This book is also available at your local bookstore, or you can check out our Web site www.dorchesterpub.com where you can look up your favorite authors, read excerpts, or glance at our discussion forum to see what people have to say about your favorite books.

☐ **YES!**

Sign me up for the Leisure Horror Book Club and send my FREE BOOKS! If I choose to stay in the club, I will pay only $8.50* each month, a savings of $7.48!

NAME: _____

ADDRESS: _____

TELEPHONE: _____

EMAIL: _____

☐ I want to pay by credit card.

☐ VISA   ☐ MasterCard   ☐ DISCOVER

ACCOUNT #: _____

EXPIRATION DATE: _____

SIGNATURE: _____

Mail this page along with $2.00 shipping and handling to:

Leisure Horror Book Club
PO Box 6640
Wayne, PA 19087

Or fax (must include credit card information) to:
610-995-9274

You can also sign up online at **www.dorchesterpub.com**.

GET FREE BOOKS!

You can have the best fiction delivered to your door for less than what you'd pay in a bookstore or online. Sign up for one of our book clubs today, and we'll send you *FREE* BOOKS* just for trying it out... with no obligation to buy, ever!

As a member of the Leisure Horror Book Club, you'll receive books by authors such as **RICHARD LAYMON, JACK KETCHUM, JOHN SKIPP, BRIAN KEENE** and many more.

As a book club member you also receive the following special benefits:

- **30% off all orders!**
- **Exclusive access to special discounts!**
- **Convenient home delivery and 10 days to return any books you don't want to keep.**

Visit www.dorchesterpub.com or call 1-800-481-9191

There is no minimum number of books to buy, and you may cancel membership at any time.

*Please include $2.00 for shipping and handling.